SINGLE COMBAT

As the dust began to clear, Dreaming Wolf saw he was in grave danger.

From the shallows of Horse Creek rode a handful of bare-chested warriors. From the black and yellow paint worn on their faces, Dreaming Wolf identified them as Crows. He turned to face them with his stringless bow, knowing an unhorsed man stood little chance against a mounted Crow.

"Chien!" the Crow leader called. "Son of dogs!"

The others laughed and waved their bows. Then their leader charged.

Dreaming Wolf waited, a great calm filling him. At the final instant, he leaped to one side and jabbed the Crow's pony with the stringless bow. The horse turned suddenly, throwing its rider to the ground. Dreaming Wolf pounced on his enemy, drew his knife, and plunged its blade into the Crow's vitals.

"Ayyyy!" Dreaming Wolf howled as he cut the dead Crow's forelock and held it up for the others to see. "Come, find your deaths!"

THE MEDICINE TRAIL
DREAMING WOLF

G. CLIFTON WISLER

ZEBRA BOOKS
KENSINGTON PUBLISHING CORP.

One

The rising sun sprinkled the snow-clad hills with glittering light. Its warmth would come later. Dreaming Wolf felt only the numbing cold of winter, for each night the freezing moon hung low over the shoulders of *Noahvose,* the sacred heart of the world, and the People knew only its icy touch. As he stood ankle-deep in powdery snow, watching Sun bathe the earth in its amber light, the reassuring words of his uncle flooded his memory.

"Even the bitterest day has its end," Younger Wolf had said. "Nothing lasts long. Only the earth and the mountains."

It was the death song uttered by a warrior when his moment came to climb Hanging Road and join the great mystery beyond. Now Younger Wolf had begun the long walk, and his nephew wondered if the bitter taste of death would leave as certainly as winter would pass.

"It's time we made our prayer," Stone Wolf whispered as he touched his son's bare shoulder.

"Yes, *Ne' hyo,*" Dreaming Wolf replied. Each

morning, they walked to the crest of the ridge overlooking the camp of the *Hev a tan iu,* the Rope Men, and greeted the sun with the old prayer.

"Man Above, give our feet the difficult path to walk," Stone Wolf spoke reverently, as he raised a pipe skyward.

"Help us to keep the old ways," Dreaming Wolf added.

"Make us mindful of our obligations," Little Dancer, Dreaming Wolf's young cousin, said solemnly. "Give us the hard things to accomplish, and the heart to try to do them."

"Yes," Stone Wolf agreed, gripping his nephew's shoulders.

The three of them stood before the sun, shivering as an icy wind tore at their naked flesh. It was the proper way to make the morning prayers, bare as the day they had first greeted the light. A warming fire sometimes drove off the worst of the cold, but that morning even the good oak and willow logs were little help.

Stone Wolf performed the pipe ritual, and the three of them huddled close as they smoked and prayed. Then they dressed themselves and returned to the camp.

"Was there ever such a freezing time, Uncle?" Little Dancer asked Stone Wolf when they entered the sacred Arrow Lodge together. "Even now I don't feel my toes."

"Put them nearer to the fire," Stone Wolf suggested. "Once, before Man Above presented the medicine bow to the People, we all walked the

6

earth bare and helpless. Then winter was a welcomed time, for many of the great flesh-eating creatures began their long sleep. For a time, the People were free from great peril."

"I don't remember those days," the Dancer grumbled. "That was even before your grandfather's time."

"Yes, long ago," Stone Wolf agreed. "We once feared Bear and Wolf. Later it was the Chippewa and the Pawnee."

"The Rees. And Crows. They killed my father."

"Yes," Stone Wolf said, sighing.

"His was a remembered death," Dreaming Wolf noted. "We miss his voice in the Fox council."

"And elsewhere," Stone Wolf observed. "Now the dangers which stalk the People are the gravest ever. Too many of our great men are gone."

"Stone Wolf is still with us," Dreaming Wolf boasted. "You keep the Arrows, *Ne' hyo*. They will protect us."

"No, they're too often ignored," Stone Wolf muttered. "And I'm growing old. Soon it will be time to pass on my burdens. You two must practice the medicine cures and assist in the sacred ceremonies. *Mahuts* have long been safeguarded by our family. The welfare of the People may depend on you."

The boys nodded, but Dreaming Wolf prayed his father would remain many years. Even a young man of fifteen winters could not hope to learn all the cures and ceremonies. As for Little Dancer, he was scarcely twelve.

"I was young when Man Above called me to walk the medicine trail," Stone Wolf had often told them. "A man doesn't choose the path his feet will find. No, a man's destiny is always a puzzle to him. The Great Mystery is beyond understanding. He can only hope to walk the world in harmony and keep the old ways. If he does so, he may come to find peace in the end."

That was beyond Dreaming Wolf's comprehension, though. He had only walked man's road a short time. Nevertheless, he had known pain and sorrow enough for ten lifetimes. Stone Wolf's dreams warned of danger or promised success. His son saw only terror. He remembered mostly death and sickness.

"Later, you'll see more," Stone Wolf had promised. "You can't hope to understand everything now. Be patient."

"Sometimes I wish you had chosen some other boy to learn the medicine cures," Dreaming Wolf had confessed. "I envy the boys who ride with their brothers to steal Crow ponies or hunt elk and deer. Warrior's road is simpler."

"It wasn't for your uncle," Stone Wolf had scolded. "Ours is a difficult task, but the welfare of the People rests on our shoulders. You say I should select another boy? I have invited others to Arrow Lodge to learn the cures, but where are they now? Talking Stick was one, and see him now. He knows mostly hate for the *wihio*, the pale people, and he leads the young men into many dangers. He speaks of dreams, but when has he performed the correct ceremonies? He ignores the old ways. It's necessary you and Little Dancer walk with me, help safeguard *Mahuts,* the sacred Arrows. Their medicine is the great hope of the *Tsis tsis tas.*"

"I know," Dreaming Wolf had admitted.

Now, sitting beside the fire, he glanced up at the medicine bundle dangling overhead. He knew Stone Wolf had been right. Keeping the Arrows was crucial to the survival of the People. The burdens were weighty, though. Were his own slim shoulders capable of bearing them?

"The skies will be clear of clouds today," Stone Wolf predicted. "Later, a warming sun will hang high overhead."

"Yes, it's certain to be a good day, *Ne' hyo,*" Dreaming Wolf agreed.

"The young men will hunt deer," Little Dancer said, sliding over beside his cousin. "Ah, Uncle, we haven't had fresh meat in a long time."

"No," Stone Wolf lamented. "Our camp knows need of it, too. Perhaps it would be a good thing if Dreaming Wolf strung his bow and shot a deer."

"We have charms to make," Dreaming Wolf said, grinning at his cousin's ill-concealed excitement.

"And a cure to make for Fox Tail," Stone Wolf added.

"Hoop Woman will help you," Little Dancer pointed out. "It's a woman you need to help Fox Tail's child be born."

"It is, *Ne' hyo,*" Dreaming Wolf said, grinning. "Young men should be hunting."

"Yes, it's the day for it," Stone Wolf said, matching his son's smile. "Perform the proper prayers, though, and don't wander far from our camp. We have too many enemies in these hills now."

"We'll hunt the thickets near the frozen pond," Dreaming Wolf promised. "We won't be away long."

"Remember, make the old prayers, *Naha',*" Stone Wolf urged. "And share the kill."

"I know what's to be done, *Ne' hyo,*" Dreaming Wolf said, clasping his father's hands. "I'm no child in need of a breast."

"Nor too old to be cautioned," Stone Wolf insisted.

"I'll do what's required, *Ne' hyo.* I'll keep the Dancer safe as well. We'll bring back a deer to fill the bellies of the helpless ones."

"We will," Little Dancer vowed, rising solemnly. Once outside Arrow Lodge, the younger cousin whooped and jumped with excitement.

"Quiet yourself!" Dreaming Wolf scolded as he collected his bow and a quiver of arrows. "We're not riding out to count coup on the Crows. We only mean to hunt deer. Hunters go forth solemnly, with reluctance, for killing any creature disturbs the harmony of the world. We must make the proper prayers so that we don't cause offense."

"We'll ask deer's forgiveness," Little Dancer whispered.

"Even as the first boy to aim a bow was commanded to do," Dreaming Wolf explained. "In keeping the old ways, we help restore the ancient power to the People."

10

"Will it be enough to keep our enemies away?" the boy asked.

"Who can know?" Dreaming Wolf replied. "I don't have the far-seeing eyes like my father."

"You will," the Dancer declared confidently. "I hear the spirits visiting your dreams. You, too, will be a man of power."

"Perhaps," Dreaming Wolf admitted. In his heart, he hoped it would be otherwise. He'd witnessed the torment and frustration his father had endured. The medicine trail was plagued by high cliffs and deep rivers. How much simpler his life would be if he rode the war trail as his brothers did!

Stone Wolf had spoken the truth, though. A man never did the choosing. And so Dreaming Wolf led his cousin out of the camp and into the rocky hills beyond. He paused upon reaching a small clearing sheltered on one side by a rock wall. He and Little Dancer scraped away the snow from a small circle of earth and built a modest fire. The Dancer split several twigs, exposing the dry hearts of the wood, and Dreaming Wolf supplied a handful of dry kindling. He struck flints until a spark ignited the kindling. Then, as yellow flame licked the damp twigs and churned blackish smoke skyward, he drew out a pipe.

Solemnly, Dreaming Wolf made tobacco offerings to earth, sky, and the four directions. Then, after puffing twice so that the tobacco leaves glowed brightly in the red earth ball of the pipe, he passed it to his cousin. Little Dancer accepted the pipe and touched his lips to the stem. The boy drew out only a bit of smoke and exhaled rapidly, for he wasn't yet accustomed to the bitter taste of *kinnikinnik*. *Wihio* tobacco was richer and more easily tolerated, but few traders came to the *Tsis tsis tas* winter camps even when there was peace between the peoples.

"It's best a hunter's prayer is made in the old way, with our own smoke," Dreaming Wolf said as he took the pipe back into his hands. *"Kinnikinnik* burns your lungs, but Man Above welcomes its smoke."

"Yes," Little Dancer said, coughing.

Dreaming Wolf smoked again, then began his prayer. He began with an old hunter's song, summoning the spirits of the woods to his council. He spoke to rock and tree and hill. Finally, he gazed out into the thickets near the frozen pond.

"Brother Deer, you bring the People many good things. Help us. We are cold and naked. The little ones stare at their mothers with hungry eyes. Ayyyy! Long have we suffered. Give us your children to fill the emptiness in our bellies. Give us their coats to keep away the icy fingers of the wind. Spare us, that we may walk this land in harmony with you, as our fathers and yours once did."

"See how we carry only bows," Little Dancer said, touching the soft doeskin quiver that rested beside his hip. "Our arrows carry stone points."

"We will take only what's needed," Dreaming Wolf promised. "Our hearts are heavy as we undertake this hunt, for we desire no creature's death.

12

Even so, we ask the life of our brother, so that we may draw strength from his flesh."

"Ayyyy!" the Dancer howled. "We two walk the sacred path. Grant us the true aim, Brother Deer."

"Hear our prayer," Dreaming Wolf concluded.

They smoked and considered their task as the fire warmed their toes and the sun rose high overhead. Then Dreaming Wolf emptied the pipe and restored it to its red cloth cover. After extinguishing the fire, he took up his bow and slung his arrow quiver over his left shoulder.

"Take your bow, Cousin," the Wolf instructed. "Follow me."

Little Dancer rose and took up his weapons. The two boys then quietly wove their way through the thicket, shaking off the sting of the knee-deep snow. Soon they reached the frozen pond. Dreaming Wolf worked his way around the pond until he located a stand of cottonwoods. There the wind blew into their faces, and both their shape and scent would be hidden from an approaching deer.

"This is how your father taught me," Dreaming Wolf explained as he strung his bow. "It was he who crafted this bow."

"I remember," Little Dancer said, breathing deeply. "That was after his arm was severed. It gave him life, the crafting of that bow."

"Yes," Dreaming Wolf agreed. "When he presented that bow, he said the gift was mine. But it wasn't. Each time I carry this bow, I recall the wisdom of the man who made it. Each notch admonishes me to keep to the sacred path."

"It's a good bow," Little Dancer observed. "A man who carries a good bow is sure to win a brave name."

"True, Cousin. I owe him that, too. He was the one who gave me my name."

"Now he's gone," the Dancer lamented. "I'll walk man's road soon, and there will be no father to give me a name. No one will craft a bow for me."

"Ah, that's no proper task for a father," Dreaming Wolf argued.

"It's an uncle's task," Little Dancer agreed.

"Or a cousin's. I don't hold the medicine power of Younger Wolf, or even my own father's skill. But I know wood, and I've watched them both make bows and craft arrows. It's for me to do."

"I would welcome such a bow," Little Dancer said, eyeing his small bow with its bird arrows. "This is no weapon for hunting deer."

"No, a man must have something better."

A sound in the distant brush silenced them then, and they huddled in the shadows of the cottonwoods. Soon three deer emerged from the thicket and cautiously approached the pond. Another might have fired as the first came within feet of the cottonwoods, but Dreaming Wolf held back. His patience was rewarded when the other animals followed.

"Brother Deer, give up your life," Dreaming Wolf prayed quietly as he notched an arrow. A great peace seemed to settle over the land, and a young buck stepped toward the cottonwoods. The

14

Wolf held his aim a moment, then loosed an arrow. It struck the buck's chest, and the flint point drove deep into the vitals and tore into the animal's heart.

"Here," Dreaming Wolf said, passing the powerful bow into his cousin's smaller hands. Little Dancer had watched enviously, knowing his short bow lacked the power to drop a full-grown deer. The younger boy notched an arrow and turned toward a second buck. He fired an instant later, and the second animal, too, fell.

"Ayyyy!" Dreaming Wolf shouted as the third animal raced away. "Brother Deer, you've given us your children to make us strong!"

"Ayyyy!" Little Dancer cried, waving the bow skyward. "It's a great gift you've given us!"

The boys then approached the slain creatures with awe and respect. Dreaming Wolf made the throat cuts, and the cousins hung the carcasses on the bare branches of a cottonwood so that the blood would drain. Next they cut away the hides and butchered the meat.

They were half the afternoon dressing the deer and making a drag to carry the meat back to the camp. Once there, they passed among the lodges, offering a shoulder or a section of ribs to one family or another. First and foremost they went to the lodges with little ones.

"My husband is Far-flying Hawk," Speckled Egg Woman announced proudly. "He's sick. That's why our kettle is empty. He would never accept meat offered by boys in need of it themselves."

15

"Ah, we're skinny," Little Dancer said, laughing. "It's true. But we hoped Far-flying Hawk's woman might honor us by accepting food for her small daughters. And to hurry the Hawk to health. We're young and need good men to lead us."

"Honor us by taking these ribs," Dreaming Wolf implored. "He's been generous, hasn't he? What boy in all our camp has not enjoyed a ride on one of his ponies?"

"That's true," Speckled Egg Woman admitted. "I'll take these ribs and cook them up. Far-flying Hawk and his daughters will grow strong from them. But when he's well, he will want to give you horses."

"If he has too many," Dreaming Wolf said, nodding. "My cousin and I would be honored if he gave them in our name."

"To boys in need of them," Speckled Egg Woman whispered. Her eyes brightened as she understood. The giving of horses to those in need would stand her husband in high regard. To make the giveaway in the name of two half-grown boys would bring all of them praise.

The cousins resumed their walk through the camp. As they cut off slices of venison roasts for one family after another, people gathered to watch. Few had horses enough to match Far-flying Hawk's offer, and some greedily pleaded for more than a fair share. Little Dancer frowned, but Dreaming Wolf responded generously.

"Ah, look at these two!" Dancing Lance exclaimed. "Younger Wolf's blood is in them! Here are sons of the People!"

"Ayyyy!" others howled.

In the end, Dreaming Wolf brought only scraps to Hoop Woman's kettle, and Little Dancer appeared with empty hands.

"You gave away the hides?" Stone Wolf asked. "You're in need of clothing yourselves."

"Others needed them more," Little Dancer explained. "We can hunt again tomorrow."

"What can I say to them?" Stone Wolf asked.

"Nothing," Hoop Woman answered. "They remind us of the old days, when no able man ate when a child was hungry."

"The chiefs may see and follow your example," Stone Wolf observed.

"No, too many sit in the council who consider only their own dark hearts," Hoop Woman grumbled. "I weep for the defenseless ones. Who will feed them when our sons starve?"

"We'll hunt again tomorrow," Little Dancer pledged. "Dreaming Wolf is making me a man's bow. Soon winter will pass, and we'll hunt Bull Buffalo."

Hoop Woman drew her son to her side. She tried to feign a hopeful expression. Despair clouded her face, though.

Two

Dreaming Wolf and Little Dancer hunted the next day and the day after that, but their efforts met with little success. Dreaming Wolf shot two rabbits, and the Dancer managed to kill a third. The deer that had passed winter in the nearby thickets had found safer ponds from which to drink, though.

"I don't mind for myself," Dreaming Wolf remarked to his young cousin. "I understand how hunger makes a man strong. It's only the suffering of the little ones I can't bear."

"Yes," Little Dancer agreed. "I'm bothered by the emptiness in the old people's eyes, too. Even your father seems weary."

Dreaming Wolf nodded. Stone Wolf often remarked he'd seen too much. When he set out with the boys to make the morning prayers, the Arrow-keeper stumbled along as if carrying a boulder on his back.

"He's grown old," Little Dancer said, sighing.

"It's not the years that torment him," Dreaming

18

Wolf argued. "His burden is obligation. He keeps *Mahuts,* and he blames himself for the difficult times facing the People."

"It's not his fault," the Dancer complained. "He warns of danger again and again. Who listens?"

"Your father did," Dreaming Wolf said, remembering. "But now he's gone. It seems sometimes that all the good men are dead."

"Too many ignore the sacred path."

"And those who don't die young," Dreaming Wolf lamented.

The sun rose and fell many times after those words were shared, but nothing in the *Hev a tan iu* camp changed. Hunters rarely brought in fresh meat, and what had been set by to stave off winter starvation had long since been consumed. Old people, reading the hunger in their grandchildren's eyes, set off by night and found peace in snowdrifts. Dreaming Wolf discovered old Sky Watcher standing frozen on a ledge overlooking the frozen river. The old man's face was painted an unearthly blue-white by frost.

"Soon the children will begin to die," Hoop Woman said, gazing with concern at her two daughters, Red Hoop and Little Hoop. They had seen eleven and ten summers, but although they were only a hand shorter than their brother, they lacked Little Dancer's confident stride. They'd always been frail, and Little Hoop suffered from fevers.

19

"It's time the council met," Hoop Woman grumbled. "Don't the chiefs see we're all of us dying?"

"They know," Dreaming Wolf remarked. "They just don't care."

"Perhaps we should let the women decide," Stone Wolf said, glancing up from the fire. "Maybe my son should wear a chief's bonnet and say what's best for all."

"Ne' hyo, someone should act," Dreaming Wolf argued.

"The chiefs will soon gather, and a decision can be made," the Arrow-keeper told them. "These men who we've chosen to lead deserve our patience and respect. We must wait for them to tell us what's to be done."

"If we wait another moon, there may be no *Tsis tsis tas* here to follow a chief," Dreaming Wolf said, eyeing his hungry little cousins. "People are starving. Even your Arrow medicine can't bring life back into a child's empty eyes. *Ne' hyo,* speak to them. Say what everyone knows. The People are dying."

"I'll consult *Mahuts,*" Stone Wolf pledged. "I'll smoke and pray. Perhaps a dream will come. Man Above will not ignore us."

"Man Above never has," Dreaming Wolf insisted. "It's the fault of the men who lead us. If they hadn't been so hungry to raid the *wihio* last summer, we would have meat enough to last us through winter."

"Naha', your voice carries anger," Stone Wolf scolded. "You must cast it from your heart. A man

20

can never know harmony when he tastes such bitter words. Make yourself one with the sacred world. Remember the old ways. Only then will your bow know the true aim. Only then can your feet find the sacred path."

"You're right, *Ne' hyo*," Dreaming Wolf said, lowering his gaze respectfully. But in his heart, the young man knew he, too, spoke the truth. If the head men didn't act soon, the *Hev a tan iu* would be no more. Perhaps all the *Tsis tsis tas* would die. Could such a thing be possible?

"Tomorrow we'll find a deer," Little Dancer whispered hopefully.

"We'll save a shoulder for Hoop Woman's pot," Dreaming Wolf promised. "Then your sisters can forget their hunger."

"Yes," the younger boy said, smiling.

"Ne' hyo, perhaps afterward we three can climb *Noahvose* and invite a dream," Dreaming Wolf said, turning toward Stone Wolf. "We can starve ourselves. Bleed so as to invite a dream."

"Haven't you suffered enough already?" Stone Wolf asked, his hands trembling as he gazed deeply into the boys' eyes. "Ayyyy! It's for me to seek the dream. Maybe then the council will meet, and *Mahuts* can lead the People from this terrible time."

"Yes, Uncle," Little Dancer declared. "Everyone knows you have the far-seeing eyes. They'll listen."

Dreaming Wolf turned to his father. Stone Wolf's face betrayed doubts. A terrible chill gripped Dreaming Wolf's heart, and he shuddered.

If the chiefs ignored Stone Wolf's medicine, if they turned from the power of *Mahuts,* there would be no tomorrow. That wasn't possible! No one was that foolish.

No great journey or extended fasting was required to bring a dream to Stone Wolf. That very night, the old man's sleep was troubled. Dreaming Wolf awoke to find Hoop Woman sitting beside his father, administering a cool cloth to the Arrow-keeper's tormented brow.

"Nah nih?" Little Dancer asked when he noticed Dreaming Wolf gazing with concern toward his father. "Cousin, what's happened?"

"It's always like this when a dream comes," Dreaming Wolf explained. "First the fever. Later the knowledge."

"I know," the Dancer said, nodding solemnly. "But I've never heard him cry out before."

If Little Dancer's observation wasn't enough, Stone Wolf screamed a muddle of old *Tsis tsis tas* phrases.

"I don't know these words," Little Dancer said, frowning. "I haven't heard them. Do you know what they mean, *Nah nih?"*

"Yes, I do," Dreaming Wolf confessed. "It's part of an old healing prayer. *Ne' hyo* used it to fight the *wihio* spotted sickness."

"It's powerful medicine, then," the Dancer observed.

"Ne' hyo thought so," Dreaming Wolf answered.

He didn't add that it had made no difference. The sickness had swept through the *Hev a tan iu* lodges unabated. Even strong words lacked the power to turn the deadly sickness from the People.

"You must try to find some rest," Hoop Woman told the boys. "Stone Wolf will be weak. You must find good meat to restore his power."

"How can a man sleep when his father's in pain?" Dreaming Wolf asked.

"He prays to find the strength," she replied. "There's nothing to be done I can't do. He's walking the clouds. Man Above will keep him safe."

Dreaming Wolf thought it likely, but although he closed his eyes and burrowed into the nest of buffalo hides that made up his winter bed, he found little rest. And no peace. Stone Wolf continued to cry out, and the haunting echo of those cries troubled his son.

When dawn arrived, Dreaming Wolf and Little Dancer made the morning prayers alone. Stone Wolf remained inside Arrow Lodge, smoking a pipe and singing ancient chants. The boys shot a small buck and brought the carcass to the camp. Even after allotting good pieces to the helpless ones, there was good rib meat and a shoulder roast to revive Stone Wolf's strength.

"You made the appropriate prayers?" Stone Wolf asked. "You took only what you needed?"

"Only that," Dreaming Wolf assured his father. "Hoop Woman will cook it up, and we'll know no hunger this night."

"That's good," the Arrow-keeper judged. "Now, sit with me. I have words to share."

"About the dream?" Little Dancer asked.

"You know of it, then," the old man said, sighing. "Did I cry out much?"

"Not so often, *Ne' hyo,*" Dreaming Wolf declared. "What did you see?"

"Too much," Stone Wolf answered.

"The bad days aren't at an end then?" Little Dancer asked.

"No," Stone Wolf lamented. "And harder paths lie ahead. Go, *Naha',* and find Talking Stick."

"Him?" Dreaming Wolf cried. "When has he ever had time for me? Better I should speak with his brother or another of the chiefs."

"It must be Talking Stick," Stone Wolf explained. "His voice is always loudest when the council meets. I must know his intentions."

"I can tell you that," Little Dancer grumbled. "He intends to hunt the *wihio* wagon people. He would kill them all."

"His eyes are dark with hate," Dreaming Wolf agreed.

"Then he must know of my dream," Stone Wolf insisted. "The council must gather. Tell them!"

"Yes, *Ne' hyo,*" Dreaming Wolf promised.

Dreaming Wolf hurried through the camp, summoning the chiefs to the council fire.

"Why should we meet now?" many asked.

"The ground remains frozen," others complained. "Better meet later, when it's time to organize the hunt."

24

In the end, though, they all came. Others, too, circled the blazing council fire. Crazy Dogs, Elks, and Foxes came. Many heard how Man Above had visited Stone Wolf's dreams. They wanted to know what wisdom their medicine man would bring them.

Iron Wolf and Goes Ahead, Stone's Wolf's elder sons, came from the young men's lodge to escort their father to the council. Stone Wolf sat close to the embers, for the night air was cold, and the aches of too many old wounds made themselves felt on such nights. Dreaming Wolf and Little Dancer were there as well, keeping watch over the Arrow-keeper's shield.

It was a night to remember, Dreaming Wolf told himself. The chiefs were there in their finest clothes. Whirlwind sat stern-faced on the far side of the fire. He carried a coup stick decorated with twenty eagle feathers—each marking a brave deed. The war bonnet of his father, old Wood Snake, rested on his head. Although he had seen but thirty snows, he was looked upon as the principal chief of the Fox Warriors.

Thunder Coat and Talking Stick, brothers who had once ridden with the Foxes, stood higher with the Crazy Dogs now. Thunder Coat's whitening hair and lined face brought him great respect. The rash actions and hot words which often brought him in conflict with the older men drew followers from the young men. The Elks and Crazy Dogs, who were hot to raid *wihio* wagons and trading posts, shouted his name loudest.

25

Dreaming Wolf, like many among the *Hev a tan iu,* considered Thunder Coat a poor chief. Rarely did he share the horses or possessions taken on a raid with the helpless ones, and his constant raiding drew men away from the buffalo hunt that was vital to the People's survival. Worse, Thunder Coat invited his younger brother, Talking Stick, to sit beside him in the council.

"It's said an owl flew into his lodge the day he was born," Iron Wolf had once told Dreaming Wolf. "There's an omen that should have been heeded. Only death will come of that one."

"You're too harsh," Stone Wolf had complained. "When he was a boy, he fought bravely to defend our camp. Then he was called White Horn. I hoped he might walk the medicine trail."

"Ne' hyo, he stayed only long enough to learn the medicine prayers," Iron Wolf had grumbled. "He hung from the pole in the New Earth Lodge as a young man, too, gaining power through his suffering. But when has he ever turned that power to the good of his people?"

"He knows only hatred," Goes Ahead had added.

Stone Wolf had raised his hand to silence his sons. He would never hear such angry words, for they disturbed the harmony of the camp. Then, too, he recalled a boy who had been an eager student, a cheerful companion. The man who sat beside Thunder Coat, wearing a bright cloth shirt studded with *wihio* silver coins, was a fiery-eyed stranger.

26

It was Talking Stick who rose first to speak.

"My brother calls us to council," the Stick explained. "It's good to see so many faces gathered on this cold night. Ayyyy! We're *Hev a tan iu*. What band among all the *Tsis tsis tas* is our equal?"

"Yes," the warriors murmured. "Well spoken."

"Good words won't feed the hungry children," Dancing Lance observed. "You say Thunder Coat calls us to council. I heard it was Stone Wolf who had words to share."

"Yes," others added. "Let the Arrow-keeper speak."

"His time will come," Thunder Coat insisted. "First my brother will talk."

"Talking Stick will talk," Dancing Lance muttered. "Was ever a man better named? He would talk until even the rocks rolled away and hid."

Some of the Foxes laughed. The Elks and Crazy Dogs glared.

"Talk, Brother," Thunder Coat said, passing an eagle feather to the Stick.

"I have few words," Talking Stick began. It was a lie. Instead he spoke a long time, recounting the many raids he and his brother had led. He reminded the warriors of the many shared dangers and numerous triumphs.

"Speak louder!" Whirlwind urged. "Many who rode with you are far away. They've climbed Hanging Road and are on the other side."

"Yes," Dancing Lance agreed.

"When has Talking Stick been second to strike at

27

the enemy?" young Lame Elk cried. "He leads every raid."

"Yes, he rides hard when the enemy are little girls and half-grown boys," Whirlwind agreed. "But when the men come, and the fighting is hardest, Talking Stick rides away, leaving others to drive the lance into the earth and make a suicide stand."

All eyes turned to the empty place beside Stone Wolf once occupied by Younger Wolf, his brother. Even now, the brave heart stand made by the scarred old warrior was recounted in the young men's lodge.

Stone Wolf, feeling the weight of those many eyes, rose. He held no feather in his hand, but all grew silent.

"Is this a council?" the old man asked. "To hear so many angry voices! We are *Tsis tsis tas*. Not Pawnee. Not Crows. I've heard Snake women talk less. And more pleasantly, too," he added. Many laughed, and the Arrow-keeper continued.

"Brothers, the People are suffering," Stone Wolf said, waving his arms at the encampment. "Children weep, for their bellies are empty. Women have no meat for their kettles. Where are the hunters? It's for us, the men, to provide for the helpless ones."

"Game is scarce," Talking Stick argued.

"It's winter," Stone Wolf noted. "Deer and buffalo are hard to find. It's always been this way. We must hunt in summer."

"Yes," many murmured.

"I have invited a dream," Stone Wolf explained.

28

"I've consulted *Mahuts*. The Arrows know of our calamities. Man Above sees all. Both counsel caution. I've seen White Buffalo Cow nearby. She'll provide for us. But we must make the proper prayers. And we must not shorten the hunt again."

"Summer's the season the *wihio* wagons come," Talking Stick interrupted. "We can't shoot arrows into buffalo and sweep our enemy from this country at the same time."

"What does it matter if you kill a hundred, ten times a hundred of these pale people?" Stone Wolf asked. "The *Tsis tsis tas* will be no more."

"Old woman's stories," Talking Stick insisted. "We'll ride the *wihio* ponies. We'll eat his beef cows and bake his flour into bread. His rifles will make us feared among all the peoples who ride this country!"

"Ayyyy!" the young Crazy Dogs howled.

"No!" Stone Wolf argued. "Where's the honor in fighting these people? It's only killing. It disrupts the harmony of our world, and it brings us only pain. You say we'll grow strong, but where is this strength? Last summer you raided many times, but see how the People are starving!"

"Old fool, sit down!" Talking Stick shouted. "You speak of old medicine. Once you had power, but now you would have us hunt with stone-pointed arrows. You'd have us dance and pray while game escapes us. Your time's past. You should climb *Noahvose* and give up *Mahuts*. When have the Arrows lent their power to our raids?"

"Have you forgotten how the Pawnees took the

Arrows?" Iron Wolf exclaimed. "Who was it restored them to us? My father!"

"His dreams hold power!" Goes Ahead added. "When has Stone Wolf ever led the People astray?"

"Silence these pups!" Talking Stick urged. "They have no voice here."

"No voice?" Iron Wolf cried. "Is truth not to be heard in the council of the *Hev a tan iu?*"

"You're no chief," Thunder Coat declared. "There are Foxes here. They can speak."

"And have!" Whirlwind shouted. "But you have no ears to hear the truth."

"He's right," Dancing Lance agreed.

The Elks and Crazy Dogs hooted their displeasure, and soon the council broke into two bands of angry warriors.

"Enough!" Stone Wolf shouted, but his words were lost in the tumult. Sadly, with leaden feet, he motioned to Dreaming Wolf. The young man lifted his father's shield, and Little Dancer took up the medicine bags. Iron Wolf and Goes Ahead escorted them back to the Arrow Lodge.

"I'm sorry, *Ne' hyo,*" Dreaming Wolf said, as they stood beside the sacred lodge and glanced back at the council.

"I saw it all," Stone Wolf told them. "And more."

"You screamed in your sleep, Uncle," Little Dancer said, frowning. "Will any of us live to see another winter?"

"Some will," Stone Wolf answered. "But when *Mahuts* are no longer respected, when wise words

30

are ignored, hard days are certain to follow."

"Harder days than the ones we've already seen?" Dreaming Wolf asked.

"Ah, what's hunger?" Stone Wolf asked. "Cold? These are difficulties given to a people so that they may taste the sweetness that follows. What's coming is darkness. Slow, tormented death. We'll come to regard these difficult days with fond recollection."

Dreaming Wolf searched his father's eyes and read only truth there. How was it possible the day had come when *Mahuts* should be ignored? What would become of the People when Stone Wolf, too, was gone. All the good, wise old men would then be gone. And the People. . . . Dreaming Wolf grew cold just thinking of it—colder than he'd imagined possible.

Three

Often during those difficult days that followed, Dreaming Wolf thought the choking white robe of snowy winter would never lift from the sacred hills and free the People from their icy torment. Too often, hunters returned from difficult journeys with nothing but hunger to reward their efforts. Old people continued to walk off into the snowdrifts. Children closed their eyes on the distant sun and began the long walk up Hanging Road.

"They're the fortunate ones," Little Dancer remarked more than once. "For them the struggle is over."

Dreaming Wolf wished he could be certain. Too often he helped place the stiff, frozen little corpses upon scaffolds or on ledges carved by ice over the ages in the sacred hills. The faces always appeared so lonely . . . abandoned.

"Our sons should have hunted Bull Buffalo together," he whispered sometimes. "Wait for me on the other side, little friend. We'll all of us join you soon."

Summer did come, though, and the warming glow of the sun drove off the worst of the People's despair. As snows melted and the grasses and trees greened, new hope flickered. There were deer to hunt in the thickets, and soon Bull Buffalo would flood the valleys along Shell River.

"It's a good day to be alive!" Iron Wolf shouted when he returned to camp with two slain elk. "Ayyyy! We'll be hungry no longer!"

It was only a few days afterward when the criers spread word it was time to move the camp. Dreaming Wolf gladly helped his father break down the Arrow Lodge. He welcomed the chance to set off onto the plains again and to escape the memories of winter hardships. Even though his arms and legs ached with the required effort, he began making a travois from the lodge poles and buffalo hide covering.

"Perhaps we'll visit our *wihio* cousins at the Shell River Fort," Little Dancer suggested as he packed medicines in doeskin pouches.

"Perhaps," Dreaming Wolf answered. "We'll certainly find game to hunt."

"Rivers to swim," the Dancer added. "Crow ponies to steal."

"Ne' hyo will keep us busy," Dreaming Wolf said, scowling. "We won't be allowed to join a raiding party until the New Life Lodge is made and the buffalo hunt had been completed."

"That won't be so long a time," Little Dancer insisted.

"You're too young to ride with horse stealers."

"I could hold your pony," the younger boy said

hopefully. "We've hunted deer together. You know I can be trusted with a task."

"Then go and help my brothers gather our horses," Dreaming Wolf said, trying to gaze sternly at his cousin. The Dancer grinned, though, and Dreaming Wolf found himself laughing.

"I'll go," Little Dancer said finally. "But not because you ordered me."

"No?"

"Because I, too, wish to leave this sad place. Ayyyy! Soon we'll ride Shell River once more."

Dreaming Wolf nodded. It was a warming thought.

The *Hev a tan iu* passed those first moons of summer making their way westward along Shell River. From there they swept northward into the Big Horns before turning south once more. As the Green Grass Moon of midsummer appeared overhead, Stone Wolf smoked by his fire and whispered the ancient prayers. Afterward, he summoned the chiefs and instructed them to send riders to the distant *Tsis tsis tas* camps.

"Soon it will be time to renew the world," the Arrow-keeper told them. "We must gather the many bands and prepare for the New Life Lodge ceremonies."

"Yes, it's time," Thunder Coat agreed. "My brother and I will sponsor the earth renewal this year."

"It's appropriate," Talking Stick added. "We two

34

who lead the People should provide for their prosperity."

Dreaming Wolf heard those words. He readily agreed. After all, no one else had the property necessary to make the required giveaways. Thunder Coat and Talking Stick would have to do it.

"Perhaps they will return to the sacred path," Little Dancer said hopefully. "They can't be blind to the suffering endured by the People last winter."

"They only wish to gain the power an earthmaker acquires," Dreaming Wolf observed. "They understand nothing."

"You can't be certain," the Dancer objected. "They're chiefs. They've seen many hard fights. Maybe they know better than you what should be done."

"Perhaps," Dreaming Wolf replied. "I only know they ignore *Ne' hyo's* warnings. And I remember they left your father to die alone when they struck the Rees. Others returned to stand with him, but those who should have, the chiefs, rode away."

"They're brave men," Little Dancer argued. "I've heard their many coups recounted in the hunting camps."

That was true. Thunder Coat was a fierce fighter, and even as a boy Talking Stick had fought bravely. There was a difference between courage and devotion, though. A brave man was sometimes a foolish one. He didn't always value the lives of his companions, either. In his heart, Dreaming Wolf knew some men would always ride away and leave others to die.

35

Iron Wolf and Goes Ahead were among the young men who rode off to collect the scattered *Tsis tsis tas* bands, for the entire tribe gathered for the earth renewal. Some bands were as far away as Swift Fox River—far south past the Pawnee country—or up north along Elk River, where the Lakotas wintered. It was no simple matter to bring everyone together.

Dreaming Wolf had little time to consider the difficulties facing the riders, though. The New Life Lodge ceremony was complicated, and many preparations were necessary. In addition, he often joined the other young men to hunt deer and elk, so there were hides to work and meat to distribute to the helpless ones. Stone Wolf required his help collecting medicine herbs and treating the sick.

"It's for you to do," the Arrow-keeper told Dreaming Wolf when Whirlwind summoned them to the lodge where his small son, Cut Ear, lay suffering. "Soon the People must rely on you to make the medicine cures."

Dreaming Wolf gazed sadly at his father, then cradled the feverish boy's head and examined his clammy chest.

"Yes, I know what's to be done," Dreaming Wolf explained.

"He won't die?" Whirlwind's wife, Singing Bell Woman, asked.

"Man Above decides such things," Dreaming Wolf answered. "I will speak the appropriate prayers and make medicine. The boy's small, but his heart is strong. He should live to ride with his father to the buffalo hunt."

As Dreaming Wolf sang, he shook his medicine rattle. Then he prepared a tonic to ease the boy's suffering and revive his spirit. Although he'd watched Stone Wolf do it a hundred times, Dreaming Wolf performed each task with great care. And not a little nervousness. For all the boasts he made among his young friends, he was not yet fully grown. He had walked sixteen summers upon the earth, but age alone did not make a man.

"Naha', you did well," Stone Wolf told him afterward. "It's good. Whirlwind stands tall in the eyes of the *Hev a tan iu.* He'll speak of your power to others, and all will know you as a medicine man."

"Ne' hyo, this is what you wanted," Dreaming Wolf said, studying his father's sad eyes. "What troubles you?"

"I see the road ahead," Stone Wolf explained. "Your path won't be an easy one."

"It's the struggle which makes a man strong."

"When it doesn't kill him. You'll have help, though. Little Dancer will walk at your side. As you prove yourself, others will eagerly follow your steps."

"Those days are far ahead, though," Dreaming Wolf declared. "It's for me to follow my father now."

"Yes, for now," Stone Wolf agreed. "But soon you must erect your own lodge. Walk your own path."

"Soon, *Ne' hyo?*"

"Very soon," the Arrow-keeper said, grasping his son's shoulders with firm, gnarled hands. "I would have it otherwise, but no man decides what will be. All he can ask is a steep climb and the heart to continue."

"You've climbed well, *Ne' hyo.*"

"Yes, and the trail's been difficult. It should be easy in the beginning. For you, it hasn't been."

"Maybe it will grow easier."

"No, my dreams say the darkest times loom ahead. But we will talk of that another day. There's work to be done, and who else can do it? Come."

Dreaming Wolf nodded, and his father managed a faint smile. It didn't entirely conceal the gloom behind it, but there were too many cures to perform and countless preparations to undertake before the earth renewal began. Dreaming Wolf devoted himself to the tasks at hand and trusted the future to his father's dreams.

When the scattered bands assembled in the sacred hills to remake the earth, the chiefs met to discuss the future. Even though the counting sticks would be collected afterward, all with eyes could see the toll winter had taken on the People. Too many old friends were gone. Among the chiefs, new faces sat in the council of forty-four. Scarred warriors of forty summers like Thunder Coat were tribal elders now. The soldier societies often appeared to be little more than bands of boys playing games.

"See what the *Tsis tsis tas* have become!" Stone Wolf cried, as he repeated his admonitions to the chiefs. "See to the welfare of the helpless ones. Devote yourself to the old ways. Renew the earth. Make the proper prayers, and hunt Bull Buffalo as our fathers and their fathers once did."

"And what of the *wihio,* old man?" Talking Stick asked. "Are we to allow the wagon people to ruin our country, kill our game, foul the rivers, and spread their spotted sickness in our camps?"

"We should kill them all," Thunder Coat suggested.

"You let your anger rule your tongue," Stone Wolf argued. "If there was a way to stop the *wihio* flood, I would lead you against them myself. But they can no more be halted than can the summer rain or the winter snow. They're here, and we must learn to let them pass like a wind, unheeded. If our young men die fighting them, who will hunt? Another starving winter may find us gone, our names a memory like the Mandan ghosts on Fat River."

"Yes," many of the older men agreed. "We must hunt first."

"The *wihio* don't pass over us like a wind," Talking Stick argued. "No, they build their log lodges, carve roads through our sacred country, and give pieces of our country to the Pawnees and the Crows, our old enemies. There can be no living with them."

"If you continue your war on them, there will be

39

no living at all for many of us," Dancing Lance declared. "Let's speak no more of war here. This is a time of renewal, of rebirth. Let's perform the old ceremonies and speak the ancient prayers."

"Then we'll hunt," Two Moons, chief of the Windpipes, insisted.

"Then, if you still have the heart to raid the *wihio,* carry a pipe among the camps," Dancing Lance instructed. "But for now, let's have only peace. Such disharmony disturbs the power of *Mahuts* and spoils our hunting."

"He's right," Stone Wolf said, gazing sternly at the faces of the chiefs. "Now is a day for feasting. Tomorrow many undergo great suffering. Later, when *Mahuts* have led us to Bull Buffalo and filled our bellies, there will be time to talk of these other matters."

Talking Stick rose to argue, but Thunder Coat silenced his brother with a wave.

"It will be as you say," Thunder Coat insisted. "Later, after the hunting is finished, my brother and I will carry a pipe around the camps. Now we must sponsor the New Life Lodge. With the new power we gain, we'll stand tall. Ayyyy! We'll be men to lead the warriors then."

"And where will you be, old man?" Talking Stick said, gazing with fiery eyes at Stone Wolf.

"Ne' hyo, has he heard nothing?" Dreaming Wolf whispered to his father afterward.

"He hears only his own heart," Stone Wolf lamented. "Only that."

In the days to follow, Dreaming Wolf had few chances to reflect on Talking Stick's anger. The young man was busy helping his father with the ceremonies. Later, as the People danced and celebrated, he drifted off with his brothers to Two Moons's camp. Among the maidens waiting outside their fathers' lodges were the three daughters of Gray Eyes. Iron Wolf wasted no time inviting the oldest, Running Doe, to join him under his blanket. The middle girl, Two Springs, eagerly joined Goes Ahead. The youngest, a girl of fifteen summers named Singing Doe, took Dreaming Wolf's trembling fingers.

"Shall we walk to the river?" she whispered.

"Yes," Dreaming Wolf agreed. His voice broke as he spoke, and he felt bubbles of cold sweat forming on his brow.

"I think soon your brothers will have wives," Singing Doe whispered, as she slid her slender shoulder inside the Wolf's arm. "It will be good to have them in our family. My father's grown old, and there's never fresh meat."

"Iron Wolf and Goes Ahead are always among the first to strike Bull Buffalo," Dreaming Wolf boasted. "Your sisters won't be hungry."

"Stone Wolf will miss them."

"Ah, but they are mostly off with the other young men now. Little Dancer and I provide for *Ne' hyo* and Hoop Woman."

"Soon you, too, may take a woman, though."

Dreaming Wolf felt a surge of blood rushing to

his face. He turned away from her eyes to hide his embarrassment.

"Him?" a voice called from the reeds along the river.

"He's barely weaned," a second called.

Dreaming Wolf turned and faced a cackling band of his age-mates. Their jests struck him like hot iron, and he charged them with furious eyes. No longer laughing, they dashed off into the shallows—all save Raven's Wing, who stumbled and was battered considerably before his companions pried Dreaming Wolf from his back.

"Just weaned?" Dreaming Wolf shouted. "Does anyone else want to test me?"

"It was only a prank," Otter Foot insisted.

"Only that," Raven's Wing said, wiping a smear of blood from his chin.

Dreaming Wolf steadied himself. His anger ebbed, and he returned to Singing Doe.

"You don't have to be so serious," she whispered. "I gave their words no value."

"Yes," he said, sighing. *"Ne' hyo* will be angry, too. I must try to maintain the harmony of the world."

"Always?" she asked, grinning.

"Always," he answered. "I won't walk warrior's road as my brothers do. I'm to walk the medicine trail. If I'm worthy, the day may come soon when I will lift my father's burden and keep *Mahuts.*"

"You're very young to accept such an obligation," Singing Doe observed. "Don't you fear it?"

"Young?" he asked. "I'm small, perhaps, but I

don't know that I've ever been young. Difficult times have molded me. So *Ne' hyo* has always told me. I won a man's name, after all, when my age-mates were content to hold their fathers' ponies. I have dreams that tell of the steep path I must climb, but my medicine will guide me. I'll prove capable of lifting my burden."

"You will," she told him confidently. "I see it in your eyes."

Dreaming Wolf smiled at her. He wished he could be as sure.

"It would be a wonderful thing if three brothers took sisters for their wives," Singing Doe said. "It would weave our families together tightly. Such a strong bond would endure even the greatest hardships, don't you think?"

"Perhaps," Dreaming Wolf confessed. "I doubt your father would find me suitable as a husband, though."

"You're weaned," she said, smiling.

"But no man of many horses. No, I have a son's obligations to meet now."

"Maybe," she noted. "I'm young myself. There's time for you to raid the Crow pony herd."

He found himself laughing, not so much at her suggestion as at the notion it put into his head. Later, when he sat with her at the marriage feast of his brothers, he had already swept it from his mind.

"Our camp seems oddly quiet," Dreaming Wolf told his father that night when they took to their blankets.

43

"I feel the silence, too, *Naha'*," Stone Wolf confessed. "My sons have gone to ride with Two Moons. We've forded a river."

"Now you are the oldest son," Little Dancer said, nudging Dreaming Wolf.

"I'll miss them," Dreaming Wolf said, shuddering. "Especially in the Fox council."

"True," Stone Wolf agreed. "But life is a circle, *Naha'*. You'll see them again. And perhaps they will not be alone. Nephews can be a good thing, after all."

Little Dancer grinned as Stone Wolf's eyes brightened at the notion. Dreaming Wolf only felt the weight of a growing burden. He could think of nothing that eased it.

Four

Dreaming Wolf welcomed the buffalo hunt for the opportunity it afforded him to join his age-mates in the hunters' camps. He was especially grateful for the chance to race his pony across the grassy plain unfettered by the burdens of responsibility. For once, he was just another young Fox Warrior, charging after Bull Buffalo, notching a stone-tipped arrow and preparing to strike down the great thunder beast.

Even as he sat beside his father, stoking the fire and readying tobacco for the sacred pipe, Dreaming Wolf sensed this hunt would be a remembered time. His dreams had been full of Bull Buffalo, of wild riding and great adventure. There had been danger, too, for often he felt the hot breath of the hairy monsters close on his neck. But he also had a vision of the Fox council in which he stood before Whirlwind and Dancing Lance, an equal in their eyes.

Before the hunt could begin, though, Stone Wolf had to perform the many ancient prayers and ceremonies. The Arrow-keeper had brought out the two sacred Buffalo Arrows, and appropriate sacrifices had to be made to invoke their favors. Afterward, the young men gathered and danced, pairing off in mock combat, with first one and then another imitating the actions of Bull Buffalo.

Dreaming Wolf found himself matched with River Fork, the son of Hairy Mane. The Fork was taller and heavier, and Dreaming Wolf had a difficult time when the two wrestled beside Shell River. That night, as the council fire blazed high, it was River Fork who was outmatched. His movements were like a wounded bull, and Dreaming Wolf had little trouble touching his lance to the Fork's bare ribs. River Fork was far too clumsy afoot to return his age-mate's jabs.

"You've found yourself in pursuit of an antelope!" Dancing Lance remarked, as a perspiring River Fork dropped to his knees, defeated.

"Yes," young Raven's Wing added. "It's good you'll have a swift horse to carry you on the hunt."

"And a slower enemy," Whirlwind observed.

As he helped River Fork to the outer rim of the council, Dreaming Wolf almost felt sympathy for the larger youth.

"For one who passes his days in a medicine lodge, you have deer's feet," River Fork grumbled.

"Remember that when you consider ambushing me on the river walk," Dreaming Wolf replied. "A man must not be hindered when courting."

"A man?" River Fork asked, grinning. "You may be quick, but man's road remains far away."

"I should have struck your tongue instead of your ribs," Dreaming Wolf declared.

"Perhaps," the Fork admitted. "Go back to the dancing now. See how the little boys are eager to test themselves. Even you'll be Bull Buffalo to them."

"And what will you be?" the Wolf countered. "An old cow with hobbled feet? Rest yourself. It won't be a friend you'll chase tomorrow."

River Fork replied with a few well-chosen insults, but they were not mean-spirited, and Dreaming Wolf only laughed. He danced through the smaller boys, occasionally tapping one of them rudely on the backside. Finally, he faced Little Dancer.

The boy's eyes burned with an intensity that muted the council fire, and his movements were well-practiced. He deftly dodged his cousin's lance and even managed to tap Dreaming Wolf's flanks once.

"Nah nih, tomorrow I'll ride with you," he declared.

"You can go and hold the ponies," Dreaming Wolf answered. "I will ride ahead with the scouts, and you'll be welcome in our camp. But when it comes time to turn the herd, you must stay back. It's no place for a boy."

"When was I ever a boy?" the Dancer cried. "From the day my father fell, I've walked man's road. You've seen me mornings at the river. My legs are long, and I'm a match for any boy of thirteen summers. You gave me a hunter's bow. Would

47

you keep me with the children?"

"No," Dreaming Wolf said, sighing. "It's time you hunted Bull Buffalo. But to turn the herd . . ."

"Requires a crazy man," Little Dancer said, repeating Stone Wolf's words. The Arrow-keeper had not been pleased to hear his youngest son would be among those charging the herd.

"You should wait. There will be many summers."

"Will there?" Little Dancer asked. "Who can say? My dreams call for me to ride at your side, *Nah nih*. Should I ignore them?"

"We'll ride together, but the charge must be left to me and the older ones. There will be danger enough when the hunting begins."

"I can join you, then?"

"I expect it," Dreaming Wolf said, motioning his cousin aside. "I have watched you at the river, *See' was' sin mit*," he added, using the word normally reserved only for a younger boy born of the same mother. "My father and I recognize the signs of your manhood. We celebrate them. We also know the obligations you and I will one day take upon our shoulders. The People will need you. Don't hurry to a foolish death."

"Only if Man Above chooses it so," the Dancer answered. "I haven't seen death in my dream, *Nah nih*. Only danger."

"There's always danger when we ride to hunt Bull Buffalo," Dreaming Wolf said, laughing as he tapped his cousin's shoulder with a lance. "It's that knowledge which tests a man. What honor could we win without it?"

"Yes," the Dancer agreed. "But when you charge Bull Buffalo, remember it's there, waiting." There was a renewed intensity in Little Dancer's eyes, and Dreaming Wolf noted it as he gripped his cousin's hands.

"I will," Dreaming Wolf promised.

"Be only a little cautious," Little Dancer whispered. "I'll be close by."

"Yes, you will," the Wolf replied, grinning. "Why should I worry at all?"

Even if he had concerns, Dreaming Wolf had no time to ponder them. The following morning, Dancing Lance led the young Foxes out in search of Bull Buffalo. As they rode out of the camp, Dreaming Wolf noticed like bands of Crazy Dogs and Elks mounting ponies. One party of Bowstrings was already disappearing from view to the north.

"Which direction will we go?" Raven's Wing asked.

"West," Dancing Lance answered. "Always west."

"And perhaps north a bit," Dreaming Wolf suggested. "There's always good grass along the creeks there, and Bull Buffalo has a fine memory."

Dancing Lance nodded. After a time, the Fox scouts split into smaller parties, and Dreaming Wolf found himself following his brother, Goes Ahead. Goes Ahead had twice been the first to strike Bull Buffalo, and Dreaming Wolf considered it likely to happen again this year.

"What's an old married man like me doing leading the way?" Goes Ahead asked that evening when the small parties reassembled to make their camp. "It's for a young man to do?"

"Yes, everyone can see your hair whitening already," Otter Foot said, laughing.

"I'll lead," River Fork volunteered.

"You have trouble finding your own toes," Otter Foot argued. "No, it's for a man with far-seeing eyes."

"Nah nih can do it," Little Dancer suggested.

"Yes," Goes Ahead agreed, slapping his brother's back. "Dream well tonight, *See' was' sin mit.* Tomorrow you'll lead us to the herd."

"Ayyyy!" the others howled. "It will be a good day. The Foxes will find Bull Buffalo, and all the People will honor us!"

Dreaming Wolf felt the weight of their gaze on his chest, and he sighed. He wasn't like Stone Wolf, after all. The Arrow-keeper could smoke and pray, and a vision would follow. Dreaming Wolf saw things, but they came unexpectedly, and often a haze accompanied them which defied understanding.

It was no different that night. As he thrashed about under the heavy buffalo hides, Dreaming Wolf saw White Buffalo Cow thundering across a dark cloud.

"Come, little one, and strike well," she called. "Feed the helpless ones. Put an end to the People's hunger."

She vanished into the cloud, then, and a world of dust choked the world. A hoof here and a horn there was all that could be seen. Then Dreaming Wolf saw himself riding in their midst, alone, naked, with only the pointed end of a stringless bow with which to defend himself.

"Foolish boy," a huge bull shouted as it emerged from the haze, pawing the earth and preparing to charge. "Look how you have invited your death!"

Dreaming Wolf saw nothing more, for a small hand stirred him to consciousness. Shivering from an icy chill and soaked in cold sweat, the Wolf gazed up into the concerned eyes of his young cousin, Little Dancer.

"It's only a dream, *Nah nih,*" the Dancer declared, sitting at his cousin's side.

"An interrupted dream," Dreaming Wolf said, sighing. "I saw only part of what will happen."

"I was worried, *Nah nih.*"

"I know, but you should have left me to suffer. The dream was intended as a warning, I think."

"Yes," Little Dancer agreed. "You must be careful. I've dreamed myself."

"So, tell me what you've seen," the Wolf said, wiping his brow and steadying his nerves.

"Bull Buffalo on Horse Creek," Little Dancer explained. "Near the fort where our *wihio* cousins trade."

"Two days' hard riding," Dreaming Wolf observed. "And the danger? Are there *wihio* nearby?"

"No, others," the Dancer said. "Like us, but different. Maybe Rees. Or Crows."

51

"Crows ride the northern country," Dreaming Wolf assured his young cousin. "And Rees? Your father punished them badly. They won't trouble us there, either. They would have to ride through all the Lakotas to reach us."

"I haven't dreamed often," Little Dancer lamented. "And I don't know the other peoples as you do. I could be mistaken. Perhaps it was only a party of Bowstrings."

"Tell me the rest."

"You led the young men," Little Dancer said, closing his eyes and fighting to recall every detail. "Ayyyy! You and the others screamed as you struck the herd and set the animals in motion. One after another, you charged the lead bull and turned him. Around and around the buffalo raced. Finally, you turned them toward the waiting hunters. But even as you let others chase the herd, your horse stumbled and fell, leaving you alone. That was when the enemy came."

"And the rest?" Dreaming Wolf asked anxiously.

"That's all I saw," the Dancer answered.

"I saw much the same," Dreaming Wolf muttered, pondering his own vision. "It's a great thing, turning Bull Buffalo."

"And the danger?"

"We saw no death, *See' was' sin mit*. Don't worry. When the herd is turned, I will be cautious. I have my bow, after all, and many good arrows."

"There are many Foxes here, too," Little Dancer declared.

"Nothing to fear."

"Nothing."

But concern remained in both cousins' eyes.

Dreaming Wolf shared the dreams with the other scouts, and Dancing Lance yielded his place at the head of the band to Iron Wolf and Goes Ahead. The brothers flanked Dreaming Wolf as they rode west and north, hurrying toward Horse Creek so as to be the first to find Bull Buffalo. Two days they rode hard. Two nights they rested wearily. The third morning they splashed across the creek and made their way along a low ridge. Below, as promised, lay a thousand grazing buffalo.

"It's as you saw," Goes Ahead remarked to his younger brother.

"As Little Dancer saw," Dreaming Wolf insisted. "Now, we'll speak the medicine prayers and smoke."

"Then we'll turn the herd toward the other hunters," Dancing Lance added. "Ayyyy! They'll all know the Foxes are the bravest!"

Others waved lances and gestured at the herd, but no one spoke. Bull Buffalo was close by, and there remained prayers to speak before driving the herd.

The Fox chiefs oversaw the ceremonies, but Dreaming Wolf said the prayers himself. His companions recognized the power of his medicine, and he warmed at the realization that he was now regarded as an important man. When all the preparations had been completed, the men selected to turn the herd mounted fresh ponies and started down the ridge.

"Now's the day we've long waited for," Dreaming Wolf sang as he turned his horse toward the lead bull. "Ayyyy! We're Foxes! Ours are the difficult things to do!"

Others echoed the song as they galloped alongside, waving bows and blankets. The buffalo heard them coming and began stirring. Soon clouds of dust rose to choke the sun, and the riders coughed in agony as their eyes burned and their lungs ached. Gradually, they closed in on the lead bulls and turned them into Horse Creek. On and on the herd surged, plunging into the creek and storming out on the far side. Now the other scouts joined the pursuit. Soon other hunters would appear, too, and the killing would begin.

"Ayyyy!" a hundred voices shouted as one.

Dreaming Wolf forgot all caution as he raced through the lead bulls, touching first one and then another with the tip of his bow. He was first to count coup, and it would be a remembered summer, the one when Dreaming Wolf turned the herd. Suddenly, his horse bucked him high in the air. One hoof had found a gopher hole, and the animal reared up in agony as bone and tendon snapped.

"Hoooah!" Dreaming Wolf pleaded as he struggled to remain atop the lame creature. The pony screamed its pain, though, and flung its rider earthward.

Dreaming Wolf struck the earth hard. For a moment, the air was driven from his lungs and he fought desperately to breathe. Hundreds of buffalo rumbled past. Miraculously their pounding hooves missed his limp arms and legs.

It was only after the last of them had passed that he managed to sit up. His bow remained in his right hand, but the string was torn and twisted — useless. It didn't matter. The arrows in his quiver were snapped like so many river reeds.

Dreaming Wolf rose slowly to his feet. His left hip ached where it had struck the ground, but he was otherwise unhurt. As the dust began to clear, though, he saw he was nevertheless in grave danger. From the shallows of Horse Creek rode a handful of bare-chested warriors. From the black and yellow paint worn on their faces and the strange markings on their ponies, Dreaming Wolf identified them as Crows.

"Cousin, I'll never again question your dreams," he whispered. "Or my own." He turned to face them with his stringless bow, knowing, even armed, that an unhorsed man stood little chance against a mounted Crow.

"Chien!" the Crow leader called. "Son of dogs!"

The others laughed and waved their bows. Then their leader charged. Dreaming Wolf waited, a great calm filling him. Then, at the final instant, he leaped to one side, avoided a killing lance, and jabbed the Crow's pony with the stringless bow. The horse cried out in surprise and turned suddenly, throwing its rider to the ground. Dreaming Wolf pounced on his enemy, drew a knife, and drove its blade into the Crow's vitals.

"Ayyyy!" Dreaming Wolf howled as he cut the dead Crow's forelock and held it up for the others to see. "Come, find your deaths!"

Setting aside his bow and taking up the Crow's lance, Dreaming Wolf prepared for the next charge. It never came. Instead, a solitary rider splashed across Horse Creek and raced to the Wolf's side.

"Nah nih, I'm here!" Little Dancer shouted as he drew his pony to an abrupt halt.

"My rescuer," Dreaming Wolf observed as he climbed up behind his young cousin. The Crows screamed angrily as they started to charge, but surprise had won vital seconds. The Dancer had his horse turned and across the creek before the Crows could draw to within striking distance. And on the far side, Iron Wolf and Goes Ahead were forming Fox Warriors in a line.

"Chien!" the Crows taunted. "Dogs!"

Dreaming Wolf waved their leader's scalp defiantly and challenged them to come and retrieve it. The Crows turned away instead.

"Ayyyy! You've counted coup on the Crows!" Otter Foot cried.

"Yes," Dreaming Wolf declared. "But I would have met my death there among the old enemy if my cousin had not rescued me."

"Ayyyy!" the other screamed, slapping the Dancer's slender shoulders and cheering his brave heart deed.

"You are your father's son," Dreaming Wolf observed. "How many times did my uncle save the helpless?"

"Many," Goes Ahead quickly agreed.

"His memory honors you," Dreaming Wolf declared.

"As you walked at his side," the Dancer declared, "I'll walk at yours."

"Yes, it should be that way, little brother," Dreaming Wolf said as he gripped Little Dancer's shoulders. "This is a remembered thing."

"Your coup," the Dancer whispered.

"My rescue," Dreaming Wolf insisted. "Our bond."

Five

The presence of Crows on Horse Creek caused much alarm, but the death of their leader disheartened the others, and a party of scouts who rode out to investigate returned with news the Crows had ridden off northward.

"We should chase them," Talking Stick declared. "We should punish them."

"They were only a few," Whirlwind argued. "Dreaming Wolf has killed their chief already. We have Bull Buffalo to hunt."

"Would you ignore this raid?" the Stick cried.

"Raid?" Dancing Lance asked. "Boys mostly. Our own young ones ran them. They're far from here already, and I won't honor them by considering them men to fight."

"Don't forget the obligations shared by us chiefs," Whirlwind added. "The hunt was ignored last year. The People suffered. It must not happen again."

The other chiefs muttered their agreement, and

for once even Talking Stick's hot words drew no followers.

As for Dreaming Wolf and Little Dancer, they found no time to consider their escape from the Crows—or anything else. With buffalo to hunt, the young warriors were far too busy. Even before the sun stood high in the sky, messengers had ridden off to summon the other hunters. As for the Foxes, they split into smaller bands and began the hunt that same afternoon.

Dreaming Wolf and seven other young men followed Dancing Lance toward the restless herd. Little Dancer came along. His eager eyes contrasted with Dancing Lance's stern, wary gaze.

"We'll bring fresh meat to our camp, *Nah nih*," the Dancer boasted as he galloped alongside his cousin.

"Your sisters will have warm coats," Dreaming Wolf replied. "And our names will be spoken when the Foxes gather in council."

"Ayyyy!" Little Dancer cried. "That's a fine thought."

Dreaming Wolf agreed. Soon he had other matters to consider, though. The buffalo were turning back toward Horse Creek. Dancing Lance raised himself up and waved his lance.

"Bull Buffalo awaits us, brothers!" he shouted. "Strike hard! Make the killing swift and the torment brief!"

"Ayyyy!" the young Foxes screamed as they charged the herd. Horses whined and surged onward. Hunters notched arrows and prepared to send their stone points deep into the hearts of their chosen animals.

Dreaming Wolf selected a large bull to his left and swung his horse over so that he could make a quick kill. The spotted pony raced alongside, and Dreaming Wolf aimed his arrow low, just inside the right shoulder. When his fingers released the deadly projectile, its stone point tore through muscle and struck hard and deep. Blood bubbled on the dying bull's lips, and it fell heavily.

Little Dancer required two shots to drop a large cow, for the animal turned an instant before the Dancer fired his first arrow. The second shot struck below the hump and punctured a lung. The cow managed only a few paces before death robbed its strength.

It was much the same along the flanks of the herd. First the Foxes and later the other soldier bands struck down bulls and cows. By nightfall, an odor of death clung to the plain. Women arrived and began butchering the carcasses, and smoking racks were erected.

"We've done well," Dancing Lance told his weary companions as the hunters took to their beds. Already they'd eaten thick steaks and roasted humps. Nearby, the thickest hides were spread out on frames to be stretched for shield-making. Exhausted ponies grazed on the tall grass near Horse Creek.

Yes, we've all of us done well, Dreaming Wolf thought as he gazed at Little Dancer, fast asleep beside him. *And tomorrow we'll do it all again.*

For three days, the Foxes hunted Bull Buffalo on Horse Creek. Only when the chiefs decided the People had all the meat they could currently smoke were the young men called in. The soldier societies then met in council to celebrate their successes and honor young men who had proven themselves.

Dreaming Wolf led his father and young cousin to the Fox Warrior council. Iron Wolf and Goes Ahead were there already, seated with the other Foxes from Two Moons's band.

"It seems strange, seeing them there, apart from us," Little Dancer observed.

"It's natural a man should join his wife's band," Stone Wolf declared. "They remained with me longer than many of our young men. I'm glad they follow a good, wise man."

There were, after all, plenty of fools a man might follow. Already, with the hunting scarcely finished, Talking Stick was said to be carrying a pipe through the camps. Whether he was urging a belated raid on the Crows or renewing his war on the *wihio,* Dreaming Wolf didn't know.

"It's clear what value our chief places on his People," one old woman had already observed. Thunder Coat was insisting that meat already dried be set aside for the war party. Those who remained behind to finish the smoking would have to provide for themselves.

So it was that Dreaming Wolf sat in the Fox council with a growing bitterness filling his heart. No chief had recognized the Fox Warriors for locating the herd. In past summers, a man who first counted coup on Bull Buffalo would have been honored with a feast. Other bands praised men who killed two or three bulls, but Talking Stick and Thunder Coat spoke only to their young Elk and Crazy Dog followers.

"A man doesn't hunt for the praise he may hear," Stone Wolf had said that very afternoon. "If you struck down six bulls, it was to feed the helpless ones. Man Above knew your purpose, and he gave you the true aim."

"Was it *Heammawihio,* then, who struck down the Crow?" Dreaming Wolf asked. "Who sent Little Dancer to rescue me?"

"You seek answers," the Arrow-keeper said, laughing. "Who can know? The Great Mystery decides all things. It can be no accident you dreamed of the danger, though. Consider that."

There was truth in those words, and Dreaming Wolf heeded them. And yet the bitterness remained.

The council began with the smoking of a pipe, and only after it had made its way around the circle did the first old man rise to recount a coup. Another and then another followed, and for a time the younger men stared in dismay at the blazing fire. At the last council many of these same stories had been shared. When would a young man be recognized?

Finally, Otter Foot rose.

"Brothers, I was among the Foxes who first sighted Bull Buffalo," he explained.

"Ayyyy!" the others howled. "We're Foxes. It's

for us to do the difficult things."

"Ah," Otter Foot said, grinning. "It was no difficult task. Our brother, Little Dancer, saw it all in a dream. He told us Bull Buffalo was waiting at Horse Creek, and it's there we found him."

"Ayyyy!" the men shouted, gazing at Little Dancer. "He's a Fox."

"I can't claim to be the first to strike Bull Buffalo," Otter Foot continued. "No, my pony was too slow. Dreaming Wolf was first."

"Yes," Iron Wolf said, rising even as Otter Foot sat. "My brother was first to strike Bull Buffalo. See these good horses? I give them away in honor of my brave brother and his hard fight."

"Hear now how he fought the Crows," Goes Ahead said as he led horses to two poor young men whose fathers had died during the hard winter. Each took a pony in Dreaming Wolf's name, and the men called for the young warrior to stand.

"Speak of it," Goes Ahead urged. "Recount your coup."

Dreaming Wolf gazed at the faces of his companions, and the bitterness flowed out of him. It seemed that the harmony of the world was restored in that single instant. And as he recalled the slaying of the Crow chief, boys edged closer to the fire and old men relived their own hard fights. Dreaming Wolf spoke modestly, speaking eerily of how the Crow's horse seemed to turn, allowing the Wolf to escape the killing blow. Dreaming Wolf told them all of the dream and the calm that filled him even though he had but a stringless bow to fight with.

"A stringless bow," the boys murmured. "Doesn't a Fox carry such a weapon?"

The others stirred, and Dreaming Wolf smiled.

"Yes," he confessed. "I was reminded of the day Sweet Medicine originated the Fox Warriors, giving them a stringless bow as their symbol. 'Brave up,' I told myself. I was a Fox."

The others took in every word of the struggle, but Dreaming Wolf made little of the Crow chief's killing. He saved his words for the rescue.

"Once another sat in this council and was praised for his many brave heart deeds," Dreaming Wolf told the others. "My uncle wore few ornaments, and he never took trophies from the dead. He considered the highest honor a man might earn was the saving of his companions."

"Yes," the others said, remembering Younger Wolf's many rescues.

"Now my cousin, his son, sits beside me. Little Dancer, he's called, but I say it to all of you, he's no small man in heart. When the other Crows looked down upon me, a man alone, with but a knife and a stringless bow as weapons, they numbered me already among the dead. Then, from Horse Creek, came *See' was' sin mit,* this little brother of mine, riding as if Thunderbird had taken a pony upon his wings. While the Crows looked on helplessly, Little Dancer drew me upon his horse, and we escaped Crow death."

"Yes, I saw it," Iron Wolf said, giving his own descriptive account of the rescue, adding the cousins' defiant taunts at the perplexed Crows.

Others rose and spoke of it as well, and finally Whirlwind himself summoned Little Dancer to his side.

"It was a brave deed, this rescue," the Fox chief said, taking an eagle feather from his bonnet and tying it in the boy's hair. "What you've done will long be remembered here, in this council. We recognize you, little brother, as a man of dreams. As you grow tall, yours will be an honored path."

After Little Dancer returned to his place, men rose to recount their exploits in the hunting. Two older boys were presented to the Foxes and given names, for they were deemed worthy to walk man's road. Then a drummer struck up a tempo, and the Foxes danced to celebrate the successful hunt.

"You won great honor," Dreaming Wolf told his young cousin when they sat together afterward beside the creek. "Whirlwind is slow to praise."

"He gave me a feather," Little Dancer grumbled. "I thought perhaps I might win a name."

"Your father gave you the one you carry now. It's a good name."

"For a child. A man should carry a warrior's name."

"There's time for that."

"Is there? Who can say? Haven't I stood as tall as the boys whose fathers honored them this night? It's only because my father's dead that I'm ignored."

"Your father survives in Stone Wolf, in Iron Wolf, Goes Ahead, and in me. A name requires great consideration, *See' was' sin mit*. Stone Wolf

65

will know when the moment is right, and then he will honor you."

"I *am* younger than those others."

"Much younger," Dreaming Wolf assured him. "Other brave deeds remain to be done, too. By both of us. Whirlwind marked you as a man to notice. The naming won't be long delayed."

"I wish I could be certain of it."

"When was I ever wrong?" Dreaming Wolf asked, laughing. "Now come with me. There must be some good pieces of meat yet to be eaten. Let's find one."

They set off hungrily, and Dreaming Wolf hoped the hurt would pass. He would speak to his father of a name, and perhaps the next time the Foxes gathered in council, Little Dancer would receive the name he hungered for. It was little enough payment for a life.

Even as Dreaming Wolf and Little Dancer stood with Stone Wolf, making the dawn prayers that next morning, the great camp of the *Tsis tsis tas* was breaking up into its many bands. Some would remain near Horse Creek, adding to their supply of dried meat and working the hides into robes they could trade at Fort John or use to repair lodges. Talking Stick and Thunder Coat were collecting warriors for a raid on the Crow camps in the Big Horn country.

"Where will Stone Wolf go?" Little Dancer whispered when the prayers were finished.

"To Horse Creek for our morning swim," the Arrow-keeper replied.

"And afterward?" Dreaming Wolf asked.

"I'll speak with some of the chiefs," Stone Wolf explained. "If Dancing Lance means to join Thunder Coat, then I must ask *Mahuts* what to do."

"And if Dancing Lance means to break apart, to walk his own road?" Dreaming Wolf asked.

"I would welcome his company," Stone Wolf replied. "He would surely invite the helpless ones to come with him, and my power should be with them."

"Many believe in Talking Stick's dreams," Dreaming Wolf said, frowning. "They will consider the Arrows' place is with our war chief."

"Once, when *Mahuts* received respect, they would have ridden beside a war party," Stone Wolf admitted. "But this man asks no advice. He heeds no warning. He will ride to his death one day. Before that day arrives, he will lead many others to their deaths."

"You don't warn them of it, *Ne' hyo*," Dreaming Wolf pointed out.

"If I did, who would hear the words?" the Arrow-keeper asked. "No one. A man would speak to better purpose on a mountaintop, with only wind and thunder to hear him."

Dreaming Wolf thought it a sad pronouncement. It was also absolutely true.

Dreaming Wolf accompanied his father and

67

cousin to the river for the morning swim. After washing the summer sweat and morning weariness from his body, he raced Otter Foot and Raven's Wing to the far bank and back. Then he wrestled Bent Arrow for a time. It was later, after helping repack Arrow Lodge and his family's belongings, that he returned to the creek to gaze at two departing bands.

He was tossing rocks into the water when Singing Doe appeared.

"I thought you might have left already," she said, sitting beside him on a large boulder.

"Soon," he told her.

"With Talking Stick?" she asked.

"No, not with him," Dreaming Wolf said, laughing. "He quarrels with my father."

"You would be welcome among the Windpipes," she suggested. "Two Moon's a good man to follow."

"I believe that. He stands tall in the Fox council."

"Your brothers ride with him now."

"My father will go with Dancing Lance, though," Dreaming Wolf explained. "He relies on my assistance. I must follow him."

"Even the Windpipes speak well of Stone Wolf. If he rides with Dancing Lance, so will the helpless ones. Too many of the young men will follow Thunder Coat and Talking Stick, though."

"They offer a chance to fight," Dreaming Wolf explained. "To win honor and recognition."

"It's all foolishness," Singing Doe declared. "My

sisters say if women decided things, there would be no starving. It's the men who cause all the trouble."

"And what do you think?" he asked, grinning.

"That they're probably right," she answered. "But so long as there are Crows and Pawnees, we'll know war. They can never forgive the many raids we've made on them, and we can never forget the good men they've killed. My grandfather once spoke of the world before the *wihio* came, when we knew harmony. It was a better time."

"Yes, but it's gone," Dreaming Wolf declared. "There's no going back to those times. We must walk our path today, not in the world of old men's dreams and recollections."

"I thought perhaps that if you rode to war, you would return with many horses. You'll be taller soon. My father might welcome your horses. We could find our path together."

"It's a warming thought," he said, gazing past the river at the distant plain beyond. "I have an aging father, though, and small cousins to look after."

"That's for Man Above to do," she declared. "They'll be women themselves soon, and their husbands will provide for their needs. They have a brother, too."

"He's young. I'm obligated to help him along man's road."

"We all make our own path, Dreaming Wolf. He may resent your shadow."

"Perhaps, but we have a bond, we two."

"There will be more summers, I suppose."

"Many," he assured her.

"You won't forget the foolish girl who sat with you on Horse Creek?"

"Have I known the favors of so many that I could?" he asked. "Whenever horses are nearby, I'll raid a few. Then, when the moment is right, I'll have several for your father."

"Five at least."

"As many as that?" Dreaming Wolf asked, laughing.

"At least," she insisted, feigning insult. Then she laughed and hugged his side. "You won't forget me?"

"No," he promised.

She left smiling, and a warmth flowed through him for an instant. Singing Doe would soon be off in the north country, though, for Iron Wolf had said Two Moons meant to pass the summer in the Big Horns. There were many fine young men there, both among the *Tsis tsis tas* and the Lakota bands who camped nearby. What chance did that leave a young man?

Six

Dancing Lance led his fragment of the *Hev a tan iu* south to Shell River. There, in the rugged chalk hills east of Horse Creek, they made camp. Hunters rode out each morning to bring in fresh meat while women worked buffalo and antelope hides. From time to time, a small party of men rode down to Fort John and traded hides with the Freneaus. On one such occasion, they returned with two yellow-haired young men.

"Wihio!" a girl shouted, and immediately young men raced to find their bows and prepare a defense. Dancing Lance quieted them with a wave of his hand and a laugh.

"These are our friends," the chief declared. "Yellow Rope and White-haired Frog."

Dreaming Wolf heard only the mention of his *wihio* cousins' names. Setting aside the arrows he was fletching, he rushed out to greet Louis and Tom Freneau. In truth, he hardly recognized them. Louis, now tall and broad-shouldered at twenty-one, had clipped his amber hair short in the white

71

man's fashion, and a nest of curly whiskers occupied his upper lip. Young Tom, at eighteen, was only a finger shorter. His face was as hairy as that of any *wihio* beaver man emerging from a winter in the Big Horns. If not for the shining blue of his eyes, the Wolf would never had known Tom.

Louis was the first to notice Dreaming Wolf. He slid off his horse, detached a bundle from his saddle, and started toward Arrow Lodge, grinning and gesturing.

"Cousin, you've grown tall!" Louis declared, speaking the words flawlessly in the *Tsis tsis tas* tongue.

"Not so tall as you, Yellow Rope," Dreaming Wolf answered. "I'm disappointed to see you have become a hairy face. Ah, there's no disguising you as *Tsis tsis tas* now."

"And me?" Tom asked, holding his *Tsis tsis tas* cousin in two bearlike paws.

"A grizzly bear perhaps," Dreaming Wolf said as he managed to shake himself free. "Never a *Tsis tsis tas*."

"This can't be the little one we called a frog," Stone Wolf observed as he joined the visitors.

"Uncle, we've been too long absent from your fire," Louis said, presenting his bundle. "My brother and I welcome you to Shell River. Please accept these gifts."

Stone Wolf opened the cloth parcel and discovered a splendid beaded shirt.

"You honor me," Stone Wolf told the young white men. "Your father is well?"

"Papa is dead," Louis explained, frowning.

"Ah?" Stone Wolf asked. "When?"

"Winter's a hard time," Tom explained. "He was walking beside the river and fell. When we found him, he was nearly frozen. I don't believe he suffered much. He just drifted off in a deep sleep."

"He was a good man," Stone Wolf observed. "A friend to the People. I trusted his voice above that of all other *wihio*."

"We'll try to prove as worthy of your trust, Uncle," Louis pledged. "Dancing Lance and others have come to trade, bringing fine hides. We have good long-firing rifles to offer you."

"I will not hunt with *wihio* guns," Stone Wolf insisted.

"Told you," Tom said, laughing. "He would have brought you rifles, but if all the world changed, Stone Wolf would remain a rock. Unmoved."

"My power flows from the old ways," Stone Wolf told them.

"And my cousins'?" Louis asked.

"We follow *Ne' hyo's* path," Dreaming Wolf explained.

"Many will want your rifles, though," Stone Wolf said sadly. "You will find good trading among our band."

"Yes," Louis agreed. "But you are few in number. Winter was hard for you, too."

"All seasons are hard for a hunted people," Dreaming Wolf declared. "Pawnee and Crow, Ree and Snake, all would kill us. And among all our tormentors, the *wihio* stand foremost."

73

"Some do," Louis admitted. "Wagon people, mostly. They don't know one tribe from another, and their heads are full of stories. They're afraid, so they shoot down anybody. Still, we all know how some of your people feel. Even at Fort John, the word 'Cheyenne' is spoken fearfully."

"This is Talking Stick's doing," Dreaming Wolf muttered.

"Yes, we talk of him often," Louis said, frowning. "He leaves his mark on Shell River. For that one, it's never enough to kill. No, he burns and mutilates so nobody who happens by can forget."

"His road isn't ours," Stone Wolf declared.

"You've broken with him, then," Tom observed. "I'm glad. We came to warn you that soldiers have come to Shell River. They would welcome a chance to fight Talking Stick."

"They may have it," Dreaming Wolf said, scowling. "If so, many will die."

"There will be another time to speak of that," Stone Wolf said, waving off the words. "This is a time to celebrate the visit of our *wihio* family. We'll eat and smoke. We have much news to share."

"Iron Wolf?" Louis asked. "Goes Ahead?"

"They ride with the Windpipes," Dreaming Wolf whispered. "They've taken wives."

"Yes, that's news," Tom said, grinning. "Tell us all about it."

As the sun crept across the noon sky, the cousins sat around a small fire while Hoop Woman served roasted hump meat and corn cakes. Dreaming Wolf had presented the visitors with buffalo hides

74

in return for the beaded shirt presented his father. It was Stone Wolf who told of the hard winter and the splitting of the *Hev a tan iu*.

"Too many have died," the Arrow-keeper lamented. "But they are nothing to the sea of death I see coming."

"There are those who erect their lodges at Fort John now," Louis observed. "Lakotas mostly. Some Crows. *Tsis tsis tas*. Arapaho. There's no fighting among them. We employ some as hunters to bring fresh meat to the fort. Others take trade goods to the distant bands. It's not·the old, free life we all miss, but it's far from a bad path to walk."

"Not for a *wihio*," Dreaming Wolf agreed. "But to walk that road, a *Tsis tsis tas* would lose himself."

"Maybe not," Tom argued. "Why not come and stay with us for a time? Find out."

"Ne' hyo needs us," Dreaming Wolf objected. "I'm no trader."

"How would you know?" Louis asked. "Stay for a time. Get to know us. Even if you find it difficult, you'll learn much of the *wihio* way. Once before, you camped at the fort, learning our words and our ways. Even as Tom and I rode with you and learned to speak your words and honor your ways."

"We have meat enough to last until the yellowing of the leaves," Stone Wolf announced. "It would be a good thing for you to go with them, *Naha'*, learning what you can."

"Ne' hyo?" Dreaming Wolf asked, searching his father's eyes for understanding.

"I, too, will go," Little Dancer declared. "It will be easier if there are two of us."

"He's right," Tom agreed. "A solitary man would feel alone, and there are quick-tempered whites who would taunt you, certain of winning a fight."

"It's a hard path you would lead me to, *Nah nih*," Dreaming Wolf told the visitors.

"It won't be so difficult as you imagine," Tom declared. "We'll swim and fish the river. Hunt. Race ponies. It will be a long-remembered time."

"Go," Stone Wolf urged.

"Some will question our going, *Ne' hyo*," Dreaming Wolf suggested. "It won't be a thing Talking Stick and Thunder Coat will easily swallow. They're not alone, *Ne' hyo*."

"There's no mending the broken bond between them and ourselves," Stone Wolf muttered. "My heart tells me this is a good thing to do. Go, *Naha'*, and learn from your cousins. We may yet come to understand the *wihio*."

The Freneau brothers remained in the *Hev a tan iu* camp that night. Next morning, accompanied by Dreaming Wolf and Little Dancer, they returned to Fort John.

Dreaming Wolf felt the strangeness of the place immediately. He'd visited the *wihio* trading post before, but much had changed. As Yellow Rope had said, there were lodges of many tribes spread

76

along Horse Creek near where it emptied into Shell River, but the people dressed in *wihio* fashion. If not for their hairless faces and bronze flesh, they might have been whites themselves.

Only when the people were collected in family groups did the familiar harmonious tongues of the plains fill Dreaming Wolf's ears. Otherwise everyone spoke in the odd, methodical speech of the *wihio*.

That wasn't all, either. Few made the traditional prayers, and even the families of *Tsis tsis tas* cooked food from the strange *wihio* tins and baked bread in iron ovens.

"I hunger for buffalo steaks and fry bread," Little Dancer complained when Louis's sister Mary handed them platters of tinned beans and hog meat.

"We should not have come," Dreaming Wolf confessed later as they rolled out buffalo hides on the hard wooden floor of a storeroom. "Who can sleep here, with no stars to see and no crickets to hear?"

Dreaming Wolf felt cut off from the world he knew, from all he understood. And in spite of the warmth he felt for his cousins and the effort they made to help him comprehend the odd *wihio* ways, he remained a stranger.

As the first *wihio* wagon bands arrived at Fort John, Dreaming Wolf found the newcomers' angry stares directed at himself and his young cousin.

"I feel the burning spears of their hate," Little Dancer remarked after a small *wihio* boy had thrown a rock at him. "What have we done to earn such bad hearts?"

"It's the *wihio* craziness," Dreaming Wolf suggested. "They have bad hearts for all who are different. Because our skin is the color of Earth Mother, they would kill us."

Later, Louis explained there was more to it. "These people were raided on Shell River," he explained as he passed an arrow into Dreaming Wolf's hands. "See this? Look at the markings."

"Hev a tan iu," Dreaming Wolf observed. It was easily recognized. The arrow bore the band's traditional markings, as well as Crazy Dog notches.

"Talking Stick has returned from the north," Little Dancer grumbled. "Many will die this summer."

"Some already have," Louis explained. "Come, there's someone you should meet."

Louis led his *Tsis tsis tas* cousins out to the river. There, not far from where the Lakotas had their camp, Tom Freneau stood beside a willowy *wihio* boy of fourteen.

"Isaiah Williams," Louis said, swallowing hard. "My cousins, Dreaming Wolf and Little Dancer."

Isaiah slipped behind Tom, perhaps hoping Tom's bulk might afford some protection, but Tom merely stepped aside.

"No need to hide from these two," Tom assured his young companion. "They'll do you no harm."

Dreaming Wolf managed a grin, but Isaiah was frozen. His pale skin and odd dress contrasted with the beaded buckskins of the others. The Wolf marked the newcomer as a wagon boy, but there was none of the usual boastful manner. Instead, Isaiah's eyes held pain. They attested to suffering of a kind Dreaming Wolf knew all too well.

"His mother died at the forks of Shell River," Tom explained. "Raiders killed his father two days ago."

"Murderers," Isaiah muttered. "Just like you."

"I was here," Dreaming Wolf told the boy in the *wihio* tongue. "My cousin, too. Tell me of the raiders."

"Horrible!" Isaiah said, hiding his face in his hands.

"The leader," Little Dancer said, swallowing hard. "How did he appear?"

"His face was painted blood red," Isaiah said, shuddering. "He waved a painted lance. Mr. Riley rode out to meet with them, waving his hand real friendly. The devils shot him down, stripped him naked, and cut him into pieces. Everyone saw it. We knew they meant to do the same to us. Some of the men formed a line, and the others got the wagons movin' on to the fort. Pa stayed. The Indians killed 'em all. When we went back this mornin' to find 'em, I couldn't even tell which one was which. That's how bad they were cut up."

"This is a sad time," Dreaming Wolf said, gripping the tormented boy's wrists. "Come, we'll make prayers. They'll ease your pain."

"No, nothin's ever goin' to do that," the boy insisted.

"My father, too, is dead," Little Dancer said. "Maybe one of your uncles will take you."

"I've got nobody," Isaiah said, sinking to his knees.

"You'll get past it," Tom assured the boy. "We've all of us lost somebody. The pain passes."

"What would you know? You've got a brother. Uncle. Cousins. I'm alone. The other people on the wagon train don't want me. Oh, they were quick to split up the flour and biscuits, and Grandpa Burnett's already loadin' my wagon with his gear. Nobody's invited me along, though."

"Gave him fifty dollars to get back home," Tom explained. "Nobody there to go back to, though."

"Among our people, a boy alone would be taken in by someone," Dreaming Wolf grumbled. "Can these others have stone hearts?"

"They've got their own troubles," Louis declared. "Too many little ones already."

"He'll stay here, with us," Tom announced. "We'll make a trader of him. Charles is back at Ash Hollow, moving supplies. We can use another man."

"I'd work hard," Isaiah promised. "I minded a store back in Indiana. Pa owned it for a time. Till he got the itchy foot and wanted to head west."

Dreaming Wolf turned to Tom, confused, and the younger Freneau explained itchy feet so the *Tsis tsis tas* could comprehend.

"Figure there's room in the storeroom for another?" Louis asked. Dreaming Wolf nodded, and Little Dancer helped Isaiah stand. The Dancer and Tom then led the wagon boy to the fort. Louis and Dreaming Wolf remained at the river.

"Some things I'll never understand," the Wolf said as he gazed past the river at the distant Medicine Bow country.

"Itchy feet?" Louis asked, laughing.

"*Wihio* ways," Dreaming Wolf said soberly. "I think sometimes all *wihio* are cut off from each other. From Earth Mother, too. From Man Above. They are all crazy men, wandering the land, taking and killing and never seeing the harmony they might find by stepping lightly, seeing, and listening."

"You're mostly right, Cousin."

"This boy. He belongs to no band. No one will help him up man's road. How can it be? Are the wagon *wihio* different, or are all of your people so alone?"

"I suppose in some ways we are. My mother's family was close. She used to share stories of her grandparents, of old days. But now everyone's in a hurry to start over. They only want to forget what came before."

"Many *Tsis tsis tas,* too, would forget the old ways. They ignore the ancient prayers, forsake the ceremonies. They don't understand that all we are flows from those who came before."

"I envy you, Wolf. You always know who you are, what you are. Mostly, I'm confused. All *wihio* are, I guess."

"I could teach you the *Tsis tsis tas* path, the medicine trail."

"No, it's too late for that," Louis said, frowning. "My own people would consider me a renegade, and yours . . . well, there are too many Talking Sticks."

"There's much that separates us, *Nah nih*," Dreaming Wolf agreed. "But our bond is not one of blood. It is stronger, forged in the heart. No matter what dark days find us, we'll always be brothers."

"Or cousins at the least," Louis said, grinning.

"Yes, that," Dreaming Wolf agreed.

They turned to walk back to the fort, then. As they walked, Dreaming Wolf searched his experience for some understanding. He had none. Perhaps if he stayed a bit longer, it would come. He hoped so.

Seven

Isaiah Williams slept fitfully in one corner of the Freneau storeroom, a twisting, thrashing spasm of tormented flesh. Often he cried out in the night, and sometimes Dreaming Wolf would awake to find the boy curled in a ball beside the window, clutching a knife and shivering with fright.

"He's even crazy for a *wihio*," Little Dancer declared.

"No, only lost," Dreaming Wolf argued. "When your father climbed Hanging Road, your sisters' dreams were troubled in much the same way."

"I was bothered myself," the Dancer confessed.

"We must help restore the harmony of this *wihio's* world."

"How?"

"I don't know," Dreaming Wolf admitted. "But the hurt in his eyes calls me to do it. A medicine man should have the power to heal, after all."

But Isaiah was a puzzle. He rarely spoke, and he was happiest when left alone to sweep the floor or stack tins and flour sacks on shelves.

"Perhaps he should be left to find his own way," Dreaming Wolf suggested to Louis.

"No, solitude won't heal the hurt," Louis said, frowning. "We should take him to the river with us in the morning. And when we ride out to hunt antelope, he must come along."

"You haven't seen him in the mornings," Little Dancer argued. "If we rouse him, he takes his knife and waves it about. It's possible to be badly injured."

"Take the knife away first," Louis suggested.

"No, he'll only think we're attacking him," Tom argued. "I'll wake him. He'll come along with me. The morning calm and the cool of the river will help. It's about as peaceful as life gets out here."

The others nodded their agreement, and next morning Tom slipped silently into the storeroom and roused his young friend. Isaiah leaped up, brandishing the knife, but he calmed when Tom motioned to the sleeping *Tsis tsis tas* across the room.

"Calm yourself," Tom advised. "I have to wake them, too. We're going down to the river to wash and greet the morning."

Dreaming Wolf feigned sleep, but he had trouble hiding his delight when Isaiah objected to the invitation.

"I'm not goin' down there with those murderers!" the boy cried. "They kilt my pa! They're sure to scalp me if I give 'em half a chance."

"They mean you only kindness," Tom scolded. "We've been patient, my friend, but this talk has to end. You must either become our brother or find another trail to walk. Now, which will it be?"

Isaiah hung his head, grabbed his trousers, and began dressing. Tom then crossed the room and roused his cousins. Neither was asleep, but both made a show of waking slowly.

"You're coming to share the morning prayers?" Little Dancer said when Isaiah followed them outside.

"It's good," Dreaming Wolf said when Isaiah nodded. "You can learn our ways. And we, perhaps, can learn from you."

Isaiah stared blankly, but he hurried along with them to the river. Once there, the five young men gathered in a circle. Dreaming Wolf built a small fire and performed the pipe ritual. When Isaiah's turn came, the boy puffed on the pipe like an old man, surprising his companions.

"I know all about pipes," he explained. "Pa taught me when I was twelve."

Dreaming Wolf had great difficulty restoring the sober nature of the ritual. Then he made the morning prayer.

"Man Above, thank you for this new day. Ayyyy! We'll try to walk the sacred path. Give us

85

the struggles to make us strong, and the heart to do what is necessary."

Louis and Tom joined Little Dancer in repeating the oft-spoken *Tsis tsis tas* prayer. Afterward, Louis translated the words for Isaiah.

"It's not so different from one of Ma's favorite prayers," the boy said, smiling faintly as he closed his eyes. "Father, bless this bright new day you've given us. Watch over us as we try to live as you've taught us. Amen."

"Amen," Louis and Tom whispered.

"There aren't as many differences as you might suppose," Tom observed.

"Guess not," Isaiah admitted.

Later, as they swam in the cool waters of Shell River, Isaiah seemed to brighten. He raced Little Dancer to the far bank.

"You beat me fair," Isaiah declared as he spit a mouthful of water back into the river. "I best practice up. Nobody bested me swimmin' back home."

"It's easier," the Dancer noted, "when you don't drink the river along the way."

Isaiah actually grinned then, and the two raced back across the river.

"I never knew anyone with skin so pale," Tom observed when they finally crawled out of the river. "You need sun, Isaiah."

"Call me Ike," the boy answered as he pulled on his overalls. "I get the whiteness from Ma. Milky white, Pa used to call her."

"The sun will tan you proper," Louis declared. "And the plains will work some of the soft off."

"I won't turn Indian, will I?" Isaiah cried.

"Not unless you start plucking your chin hairs," Tom said, rubbing his beard. "You'll be a hairy face like me before long, I suspect."

"A terrible thing," Dreaming Wolf said, moaning. "No proper girl would walk the river with a man whose face resembles Bull Buffalo's hindquarters!"

"Don't know I'd want a beard," Isaiah said, scratching his chin. "Pa had a mustache, though. Ladies considered it handsome. I might grow myself one by and by."

"Sure, by and by," Tom said, laughing.

Thereafter, Little Ike, as he was known, joined in the morning swims each day. Often he rode out to hunt with the four cousins as well. He remained ill at ease among the Lakota lodges outside the fort, but gradually he came to accept Dreaming Wolf and Little Dancer as friends, if not actual brothers.

"Your ways are strange," Ike remarked one morning at the river. "But I admit there's sense to some of 'em. And I guess once I'm grown tall, I'd consider you welcome in my cabin."

"As you will be in our camp," Dreaming Wolf replied.

It was later that summer, as the cherries were

ripening in the hills to the north, when the five young men rode out to hunt antelope on Horse Creek. They had barely lost view of Fort John when the whine of wagon wheels warned of an approaching band of *wihio* travelers.

"There's no end of them," Dreaming Wolf muttered as he pulled his horse aside so that Louis might lead the way. No point in alarming the wagon people. Even dressed in buckskins, the yellow-haired Louis wasn't going to be mistaken for a *Tsis tsis tas*.

"Hah!" Louis shouted as he approached the lead wagon. "Hello, friends."

Instead of the usual friendly reply, a trio of men walked out, rifles in hand, to challenge the unexpected riders.

"I'm Louis Freneau," Louis explained as he reined in his horse and dismounted. "You surely met my brother Charlie out at Ash Hollow. He's set up a trading post there. My brother Tom here and I run the store at Fort John with our sister Mary."

"That right?" a thick-waisted mountain of a man asked. "You need Injuns to do that, do you?"

"My cousins," Louis said, growing cautious. "Dreaming Wolf. Little Dancer. That shaggy-haired fellow on the left's Ike Williams."

"I wouldn't judge any of you old enough to run a trading post," the burly man declared. "What do you want?"

88

"Just being friendly, mister," Tom explained. "We don't any of us get much news from the east, and I thought you might share any you had."

"Got no news," the big man grumbled. "Nor time to waste, either. Now get clear of our trail!"

"Friendly, huh?" Tom asked Dreaming Wolf. The Wolf merely grunted.

"What'd he say?" the wagon captain yelled. "He insult us?"

Before Tom could answer, the giant pulled out a whip and cracked it. The split ends cut the air and lashed Dreaming Wolf's left cheek. His eye went blind for an instant as fingers of pain tore at his flesh.

"Ayyyy!" Little Dancer screamed as he reached for his bow. Tom managed to prevent the thirteen-year-old from avenging the wrong.

"You had no call to do that!" Little Ike shouted as he nudged his horse forward in order to block the captain's companions from discharging their rifles. "Are you crazy?"

"Get clear of 'em, boy!" the captain demanded.

Louis then produced a pistol and fired a single shot just short of the captain's right foot.

"Drop the guns!" Tom added, leveling his own rifle at the wagon men.

"There's a hundred of us," the captain said as he gazed angrily at the young horsemen.

"Be ninety-seven soon enough," Louis answered

as he turned to examine the Wolf's bleeding face.

"Shoot them," Dreaming Wolf urged.

"You're not dead," Louis said, forcing the Wolf's hand away. "Ear's cut some, and you'll have a fine scar on the cheek. Not even much blood, though."

"You can't mean to ignore this!" Little Dancer objected.

"So what should we do?" Louis asked. "Kill a whole party because some fool lashed you."

"Honor demands I punish this man," Dreaming Wolf declared.

"Then we'll punish him," Ike said, taking Dreaming Wolf's hand in his own. "You wouldn't want to hurt little kids, would you? Look there! Must be a hundred of 'em."

Dreaming Wolf followed the young *wihio's* pointing fingers along the line of wagons. He counted few men. Even boys as young as ten were leading wagons, and many women clutched little children to their skirts.

"No," Dreaming Wolf agreed. "It must be something else."

"Let's go," Tom urged, and Louis climbed atop his horse and led the party off into the low hills past the wagon trail. Even as they rode, Dreaming Wolf felt the sting of the *wihio* whip. And when they made a camp of sorts near a small spring, he gazed back at the narrow line of canvas wagon covers snaking their way across the horizon.

Little Dancer treated the gashes with an herb paste and sang a healing prayer. Even as he worked, Dreaming Wolf planned his revenge. That afternoon, after shooting an antelope, the young hunters returned to Fort John. Later, as night fell, Dreaming Wolf slipped silently through the *wihio* wagon camp, searching out the captain's wagon.

It wasn't hard escaping detection. The men were gathered around a fire, emptying whiskey jugs Louis had been only too happy to sell them. Dreaming Wolf first located the whip and carried it to the river. He buried it in the sandy bottom.

"No one will ever again taste its sting," the Wolf vowed.

Next, with Louis, Tom, and Ike, Dreaming Wolf and Little Dancer managed to cut the hobbles of the saddle horses and run them off onto the plain. Only as the horses raced through the wagon camp, knocking over chests and trampling blankets, did the men rise to investigate.

"Our horses!" the wagon captain cried. "Injuns went and stole our horses!"

Actually, the ponies were but a short distance away, grazing beside Shell River. Dreaming Wolf didn't want or need any bent-backed *wihio* mounts. He enjoyed the sight of the drunk wagon captain stumbling around in the dark, half-naked, cursing everyone but the one at fault—himself.

Later that night, lying in the storeroom under

the comforting buffalo hide, Dreaming Wolf tried to allow his anger to ebb. Honor had demanded justice, and the wagon captain had suffered. But the horses would return, and the man would buy another whip. Was there any forgetting a scar?

"You're thinking we should have cut the man," Little Dancer whispered as he slid close to his cousin. "We could kill him, but it wouldn't change your pain."

"He's right," Ike said, dragging his blankets over for the first time. "You taught me that. I had to put the hurt behind me. I did. Now it's your turn, Wolf. *Nah nih.*" For the first time Ike spoke the *Tsis tsis tas* word for older brother or cousin.

"Yes," Dreaming Wolf agreed. "We must find this pale one a better name, *See' was' sin mit.* He'll make a proper *Tsis tsis tas* if we get him a little darker and put some pounds on."

"Too skinny, huh?" Ike asked. "Back home they used to call me Runt Pig, but I figured to outgrow that. You take some time figurin' out a name. I wouldn't want people callin' me any kind of frog."

Dreaming Wolf smiled. Tom Freneau was forever complaining about his name, and in truth his size produced no similarity to a frog of any sort.

"I'll invite a dream," the Wolf said. "Perhaps I'll see something."

The running off of the saddle ponies should

have marked the finish to the burly wagon captain's intrusion on that otherwise peaceful summer. It proved otherwise. Early that next morning, as Louis led the way back to Fort John following the morning swim, rifle shots punctured the air.

"Stop!" Mary Freneau shouted. "Stop, you fools! They're friendly!"

Another shot and another pierced the quiet. Louis raced toward the fort while Dreaming Wolf and Little Dancer turned toward the encircled wagons. Not a hundred paces past the last wagon milled the saddle ponies. Between the wagons and horses, three dark shapes sprawled on the earth.

"What's happened?" Little Ike cried as he raced to keep pace with his *Tsis tsis tas* companions. Tom Freneau was running, too—toward a line of rifle-wielding wagon men.

"Stop!" Tom pleaded.

Now the fort's occupants spilled outside. Blacksmiths and traders stumbled onto the grassy plain, refusing to believe their eyes. Already a pair of Crow boys were racing toward the horses, screaming and tearing at their hair.

"We got 'em!" the wagon captain boasted. "Thievin' skunks! Thought they could return our horses and collect a reward, I'll wager!"

Now Dreaming Wolf began to make sense of it. Before him, bleeding out their lives, lay three young Crows. Perhaps they'd gone hunting and found the ponies. Too civilized to carry the ponies off to some distant camp, they'd returned them to Fort John instead. And their reward? Rifle balls and curses.

"Yah-ayyyy!" the other Crows screamed. One boy drew out a knife and cut away a finger joint. A woman slashed at her hair.

"Dear Lord," Ike said, dropping to his knees beside a slim-waisted boy no older than himself.

"I bought a buffalo hide off that boy the night your horses were run off, mister!" Mary Freneau screamed at the wagon captain.

"There'll be bad blood come of this," Louis declared.

"Didn't you see them waving?" the blacksmith shouted. "They're just boys aimin' to do you a favor."

"They have kinfolk nearby," the smith added. "Mister, they'll be mourning those boys three days. You best pray you can make some real traveling time 'tween then and now. Else you'll have plenty o' buryin' to do."

The hateful looks of the Crows who came out to view the corpses attested to the truth of those words, and wagon people began packing their wagons and hitching their mules.

"This is our doing," Tom Freneau observed as he knelt beside Dreaming Wolf and crossed himself.

"Our doing?" Dream Wolf asked. "Yes, we ran the horses. But did we aim the rifles? Did

94

we stir the hatred in their hearts? No, this they did themselves."

"We aren't blameless," Louis argued as he motioned his companions back toward the fort. "My fingers burn with the blood that's touched them."

"No point blamin' anybody," Ike said, sighing. "Those boys are dead. Seems that's mostly what's waitin' out here for everybody."

"It wasn't always so," Dreaming Wolf asserted. "Once a man approached another with friendship. Now there's only anger."

"Did you see the bodies?" Little Dancer whispered. "My people have fought the Crows many times, and I feel no love of them. These *wihio* wagon people didn't shoot to defend themselves or their horses. Many bullets marked each body. This was hatred. Is my cousin the one who kindled such rage in these crazy ones' hearts?"

"It's madness," Dreaming Wolf declared. "Blind *wihio* madness. It chokes the skies and washes the earth with blood."

"We must stop it," Ike said, gazing intently at his companions.

Dreaming Wolf managed a faint smile, and Louis nodded. None of them had much hope that the coming flood could be contained, though.

Eight

Better days followed the killing of the Crows.
For a time, peace lingered on Shell River. The *wihio* wagon bands passed unhindered westward,
and the parties of *Tsis tsis tas,* Lakota, and Arapaho who came to Fort John to trade for rifles and
ammunition maintained an informal truce with
the similar bodies of Crows, Rees, and Pawnees
who came to do likewise.

Dreaming Wolf grew to speak the *wihio* language and understand many of their strange customs. Little Dancer, who was most often off riding
with Ike Williams, was an even abler interpreter.

"Those two are like brothers," Louis Freneau observed.

"Yes, they've made the best sort of exchange,"
Dreaming Wolf noted. "Each has traded his
tongue and the understanding of his people to the
other."

Summer's passing brought Dreaming Wolf to a
fork in the road of sorts. Mary Freneau had gone
east to help her brother Charles operate the trad-

ing post at Ash Hollow, and, more than ever, Louis and Tom needed their *Tsis tsis tas* cousins. Soon the autumn buffalo hunt would begin, though, and Stone Wolf would require help making the medicine prayers and performing the ceremonies. Moreover, someone would need to provide meat for the long winter.

"You should stay, *Nah nih,*" Little Dancer said when they spoke of the hunt. "I can kill bulls enough to clothe my sisters, and there will be plenty of meat for *Nah' koa* to smoke. I thought I might invite Hairy Chin to come along."

Hairy Chin, as Ike Williams had come to be known, was eager to see the *Hev a tan iu* camp. Often he'd spoken longingly of hunting Bull Buffalo.

"Many bands will gather for the hunt," Dreaming Wolf reminded his cousin. "Talking Stick wouldn't welcome a *wihio.* It could prove dangerous for our friend."

"I hoped to adopt him into our family. He has none of his own, *Nah nih.*"

"I know, and it's a good idea. But I worry about Talking Stick."

"Hairy Chin would be reminded of his father's death, too," Little Dancer noted. "Yes, it's foolish to consider it."

"We'll both return to Arrow Lodge," Dreaming Wolf declared. "Hairy Chin Ike can help our cousins here at Fort John."

"It's best," the Dancer agreed. "We'll tell them tomorrow, when we go to make the dawn prayers."

Dreaming Wolf nodded his agreement. That much, at least, was decided.

It came as no surprise to the Freneaus that their *Tsis tsis tas* cousins had chosen to return to their people.

"I envy you," Louis told them. "Hunting buffalo. Riding the far country. The life of a trader pales beside such adventures."

"It's your *wihio* madness that keeps you here," Dreaming Wolf observed.

"And when the freezing time comes?" Tom asked.

"Ah, the world turns, doesn't it?" the Wolf asked. "These have been good days, Yellow Rope. Maybe when you next come to our camp, we can give Hairy Chin a proper name."

"And me?" Tom asked.

"Ah, you're a frog no longer, *Nah nih*," Dreaming Wolf admitted. "My dream hasn't come yet, but there is time. Soon, perhaps."

"Until that day, then," Tom said, extending his hand. Dreaming Wolf gripped the arm, then embraced Ike. Finally, Louis stepped over and the Wolf clasped his elder friend.

Little Dancer, too, made his farewells. Then, after sharing a final feast of venison steaks, the two young *Tsis tsis tas* packed their ponies and rode off northward.

They were three days locating the *Hev a tan iu* encampment well to the north. Actually, it was not the Rope Men Dreaming Wolf tracked but Bull Buffalo. He knew the *Tsis tsis tas* wouldn't be far from the herd, for Stone Wolf's vision remained strong. Three days of riding through the dung-strewn hills wasn't the most pleasant of journeys, but when they met Otter Foot and Raven's Wing on a ridge overlooking the grazing buffalo, Dreaming Wolf knew the effort had been worthwhile.

"You've been too long gone from the Fox council," Otter Foot complained as he turned his horse toward the newcomers.

"Much has happened," Raven's Wing added. "The southern bands are hunting on their own. Many of our people are on Elk River, hunting with the Lakotas. Our numbers are few, and we have enemies nearby."

"Enemies?" Dreaming Wolf asked anxiously.

"Crows," Otter Foot explained. "It's no great threat, though. Talking Stick and Thunder Coat are here. Already they carry the pipe among the soldier societies. We'll sweep the Crows from this country!"

"Has Talking Stick learned nothing?" Dreaming Wolf asked. "How many starved last year when the men turned away from the hunting to steal horses and kill *wihio* wagon people?"

"It's decided," Raven's Wing declared. "First we raid the Crows. Bull Buffalo will wait."

"My father has agreed to this?" Dreaming Wolf asked.

"No one listens to that old man," Raven's Wing

muttered. "He speaks of shooting buffalo with stone-tipped arrows when a rifle is much better. He's too often lost in the recollections of the grandfathers. It's Talking Stick who speaks to us. When you ride into our camp, count the scalps he has taken. Twenty. Maybe more. The Stick's dreams hold power, and his bulletproof medicine is strong."

"That's why we have buried so many good men after his raids," Dreaming Wolf grumbled.

"No one dies now that he has captured the power of thunder," Otter Foot boasted. "Come with us and strike the Crows. See for yourself."

"I returned to hunt Bull Buffalo," Dreaming Wolf insisted. "Little Dancer and I must ensure the welfare of our families first. Then we can speak of raiding Crows."

"A warrior should fight!" Raven's Wing argued.

"It's a fine thing for you to speak of fighting," Dreaming Wolf countered. "My cousin and I have fought the Crows. Wasn't it Dreaming Wolf who killed their chief? Don't trouble my ears with your hollow boasts. Save them for someone with the time to listen."

Dreaming Wolf then nudged his horse into a trot, and he rode on, leaving Otter Foot and Raven's Wing to watch the herd.

When the Wolf and Little Dancer reached the *Hev a tan iu* camp circle, they found Stone Wolf sitting alone beside a dying fire. The Arrow-keeper appeared older, a man overburdened too long and bent from the strain.

"Ne' hyo, we've returned!" Dreaming Wolf called.

"Uncle!" the Dancer cried.

"I'm happy to see you both," Stone Wolf said, rising slowly. "But what's happened to your face, *Naha'?* The scar's too faint to have been caused by a lance point."

"A *wihio* used his whip," Dreaming Wolf explained sourly.

"Is that what brought you back to us?" Stone Wolf asked.

"We came to hunt," Dreaming Wolf explained. "There are few preparations, though."

"None," Stone Wolf told them. "It might have been better if you had remained with your cousins. There is no harmony here. The required ceremonies are ignored. The hunt has been postponed."

"So, it's true," Dreaming Wolf muttered. "Talking Stick means to raid the Crows."

"Yes, he'll find his glory, even if the helpless ones starve," Stone Wolf said, frowning.

"You must warn the chiefs," Dreaming Wolf declared. "They'll listen."

"No, it's Talking Stick and Thunder Coat who decide."

"And Dancing Lance? Two Moons?"

"Too few follow the Lance," Stone Wolf explained. "Two Moons hunts Elk River with his Lakota relations."

"There's no hope of turning them from this folly?" Dreaming Wolf cried.

"No, *Naha',*" the Arrow-keeper said, sitting.

101

"I've seen it in many dreams. A two-headed eagle has plucked *Mahuts* from my hands. Even as it soars overhead, though, death is on the wind. It will come quietly, in the night, sweeping the helpless ones away."

"We will stop it!" Dreaming Wolf vowed.

"It's not possible, *Naha',*" Stone Wolf told his son. "I can't even save myself from this dark time."

"We must be able to do something," Little Dancer argued.

"I have no medicine to stop it," Stone Wolf said, plunging his face into his hands. "I only see what is coming. I don't know how to stop it!"

In the troubled days that followed, Dreaming Wolf fought to find hope in the eager faces of his young friends. Little Dancer glowed in the company of Hoop Woman and the girls. Their admiring eyes rarely left their nimble brother.

"When you ride to strike the enemy, *Nah nih,* I'll be at your side," the Dancer declared.

"I haven't decided to go, *See' was' sin mit,*" Dreaming Wolf explained. "To join a man who insults my father . . ."

"You're a man of the People," Little Dancer insisted. "What choice can there be?"

Dreaming Wolf nodded. It often surprised him that for one still young, Little Dancer so quickly grasped the heart of a thing.

That very night, Talking Stick and Thunder

Coat visited the councils of the soldier societies. Already the Crazy Dogs were making medicine and painting themselves. The Elks were certain to follow. There were only a few Bowstrings in the camp, and they pledged to remain behind and guard the camp.

Only the Foxes remained silent.

"Foxes, hear me!" Talking Stick shouted when he appeared before the council fire, pipe in hand. "Soon I go to strike a hard blow at our old enemy. Once I myself sat with you in the council, a boy marked by eight wounds who was welcomed as a warrior. Look here," the Stick said, baring his chest so that the glow from the fire illuminated the old scars."

"Ayyyy!" the young men shouted. "Here's a brave heart."

Thunder Coat recounted three of his brother's coups, and some of the older men nodded as they recalled the events.

"I ask you, Foxes, who will ride with me against the Crows?" Talking Stick asked when Thunder Coat concluded.

"I will!" Otter Foot cried.

"I will!" Raven's Wing added.

Another and another of the young men reached longingly for the pipe. Their elders soon followed.

"I knew my brothers would not disappoint me," Talking Stick said as he offered the younger ones medicine charms. "Always the Foxes have been first to strike the enemy."

"And last to leave," Dancing Lance said, stepping out from the others. "I, too, remember Talking Stick's raids. Too often the young and helpless have been left behind when the enemy pursues. I ask you now, brother, will you accept a Fox lance? Will you promise to stand even if the others flee?"

"I will take the lance," Thunder Coat said, stepping in front of his brother. "If it's our hearts you mean to test, you will find us worthy."

"Then I will carry the other lance myself," Dancing Lance vowed.

"Ayyyy!" the Foxes howled. "It's for us to do the difficult things." One after another promised to stand with their chief if the fight turned against the *Tsis tsis tas.*

"Have no fear, brothers," Talking Stick assured them. "I've dreamed of many Crows with clipped wings. We'll steal their ponies and drive them from this country."

Dreaming Wolf had never placed much value in boasts, and so he and Stone Wolf devoted themselves to making strong medicine to protect the young warriors. Talking Stick, too, made medicine, and the thunderbolts and hailstones he painted were much valued by the *Hev a tan iu* boys. Bull buffalo horn powder was painted on many a face, too.

"You may be safe," Dreaming Wolf told Otter Foot. "The Crows will mistake your face for the moon."

Some of the brightly painted young men could be seen even on a moonless night.

"We'll blind the enemy!" Raven's Wing boasted.

"If he doesn't kill you first," Dreaming Wolf argued. "An elk charm would lend you protection and not expose you to the arrows of the enemy!"

There was no dissuading the others, but Dreaming Wolf himself dressed modestly, as Younger Wolf had taught him. There were many good rifles in the camp, and Talking Stick offered one to Dreaming Wolf.

"Your father and I argue, but I remember his many kindnesses when I was a boy," the Stick explained. "I would arm his son."

"I carry the bow my uncle crafted for me of red willow," Dreaming Wolf replied. "I have crafted the arrows myself, in the old fashion. Each is balanced and will hold the true aim. They have always served me well. My medicine, as my father's, flows from the old ways."

Talking Stick himself disdained such talk. The old prayers were ignored. Instead, Talking Stick made his own invocation of the spirits. He rode from the camp on a pale horse, wearing a great bonnet of many eagle feathers. Dreaming Wolf thought it foolhardy, but he recognized the courage of a man who would mark himself as a chief to friend and foe alike.

"No one has ever questioned his heart," Stone Wolf told his son as he bade him farewell. "Too often a brave man is easily killed. Sometimes needlessly. Watch yourself and your cousin. Strike hard, but be wary. It won't be as easy a thing as Talking Stick expects."

Dreaming Wolf knew that. His own dreams had spoken of a confused battle, and he'd seen many slain eagles among the helpless crows. He didn't understand, but he sensed peril. The air itself seemed to smell of danger, and he kept Little Dancer a pace behind as he rode north.

The *Tsis tsis tas* found the Crows camped on both sides of a steep embankment. Their lodges were shielded by thick woods, and there was no getting at the camp. Instead, Talking Stick sent the Elks and Crazy Dogs to run off the horses. He and Thunder Coat remained with the Foxes to meet the Crows.

Mounted, the Crows were the equal of any fighters on earth. Afoot, they were a poor match for their *Tsis tsis tas* enemies. Nevertheless, they formed bands and charged, shooting arrows or flinging light lances at horse and rider.

Those men with shields fended off arrows and even lances. Younger men with only pounded horn powder for protection felt the sting of Crow arrows or the throbbing pain brought by a lance thrust. Bent Arrow was unhorsed and a Crow managed to cut a piece of his hair before Otter Foot and Dreaming Wolf rescued him. River Fork, too, had a horse killed. Although slow afoot, his powerful shoulders allowed him to uproot a sapling and use it to drive back one Crow charge single-handed.

Soon the fighting became confused. Men paired

off and fought each other hand-to-hand. Dancing Lance killed three men that way, and Dreaming Wolf clubbed one man senseless.

"I'm first!" he shouted as he counted a coup on the stunned Crow.

"I'm second!" Little Dancer screamed as he touched his bow to the Crow's shoulder.

It was difficult to note all the coups counted on both sides, nor did Dreaming Wolf discover who drove a lance through the senseless Crow's side and carved the forelock from his scalp. More serious matters awaited the Foxes' attention. A line of Crows had driven the Crazy Dogs from a nearby hill and recaptured many ponies. Now mounted, they charged the Fox line with a shriek.

"Here's the enemy!" Dancing Lance cried, but at that moment a Crow arrow pierced his horse's side, and the animal fell.

"We're Foxes!" Dreaming Wolf shouted. "Ours is the difficult task!" With a wave of his bow, he charged the Crow line alone. Others soon fell in behind, and the force of the Crow charge was broken. With some of the horses recovered, and many on both sides stumbling helplessly in the faint morning light, the lines drew apart. Some on both sides shouted taunts, and a few paired off in final clashes. The battle was over, though, and Dreaming Wolf busied himself seeing his friends mounted.

"You did well, Wolf," Dancing Lance declared when he rode by on a fresh mount. "Ayyyy! Yours was a brave charge."

"You would have made it," Dreaming Wolf noted, "but for your slain pony. As for me, what choice did I have? *See' was sin mit* was behind me, and I would rather charge a hundred Crows than have him to face."

"Yes, the Dancer did well," Otter Foot agreed. "When others turned to flee, there he stood like a rock."

"Ayyyy!" Dancing Lance howled. "It's good to have another brave heart among us."

"Have I won a name, then?" the Dancer asked.

"We'll honor you when we meet to recount our coups," Dreaming Wolf promised.

So it was that when the Foxes gathered in council three nights hence, Dreaming Wolf gave away three good ponies in honor of his cousin. As for the naming, it was for Stone Wolf to do.

"Brothers, greet Stone Lance," the Arrow-keeper cried.

"Yes, it's a brave heart name," the other boys whispered enviously.

"You're pleased with it?" Dreaming Wolf asked afterward when the two cousins sat together outside Arrow Lodge.

"Yes," the young man answered. "I'll be worthy of it."

"You always have been," Dreaming Wolf assured him.

Nine

Talking Stick and Thunder Coat were much praised for the success of their raid in spite of the fact that a party of Crows took back half the stolen ponies. Many young men had counted coups, and others had won brave names. Three *Tsis tsis tas* had been killed, and their deaths were honored properly, with much mourning. Afterward, Stone Wolf began the preparations for the autumn buffalo hunt.

As Dreaming Wolf and others had feared, the great herd had scattered, and only the greatest effort of the hunting parties brought in meat and hides. Worse, many good men were battered and bruised in the Crow fighting and couldn't join in the hunt.

"There will be hunger among us again, *Ne' hyo,*" Dreaming Wolf told his father. "Already the first winter breezes chill the night. Won't anyone learn?"

"We'll feed the helpless ones, *Nah nih,*" Stone Lance vowed.

"You and I alone, *See' was' sin mit?*" Dreaming Wolf cried.

"There are men enough to ride with us," the Lance boasted. "We may be small, some of us, but our arrows and killing lances will find their marks."

"Yes," Dreaming Wolf agreed.

And so the young men rode out each dawn in search of Bull Buffalo. They rode until their ponies could carry them no longer, and they hunted until their fingers lacked the strength to draw back their bowstrings. Each day, they dragged a few carcasses into camp, and another family was saved from a starving winter.

While chiefs such as Whirlwind and Dancing Lance oversaw the hunting, Talking Stick and Thunder Coat rode off with a party of Crazy Dogs toward Shell River.

"His dreams tell him to strike hard at the *wihio* wagon people," Otter Foot explained as he packed a horse and prepared to follow. "They must be driven from our hunting grounds."

"And what would Talking Stick know of hunting?" Dreaming Wolf asked his friend. "When has he followed Bull Buffalo? No, he prefers hunting the helpless ones."

"*Wihio.*"

"Crow. *Wihio.* It's all the same, Otter Foot. They won't feed your small brother and sister when the Hard Face Moon comes."

Otter Foot only sighed. In a contest of words, what good was truth? Talking Stick painted a world of glory, and his dreams attracted followers in the manner pollen drew bees. When word came that the Stick had captured many good rifles and struck down many *wihio* intruders, others flocked to his band.

"Ne' hyo, are we wrong?" Dreaming Wolf asked. "Do Talking Stick's dreams hold power after all? Is his medicine strong?"

"Is that what your heart tells you, *Naha'?"* Stone Wolf asked. Dreaming Wolf could only sigh.

As the Plum Moon stood high overhead, the encampments finally dispersed. Dancing Lance's band turned south toward Shell River, for the scouts had spied Bull Buffalo there, and there was hope of a final hunt. Instead of Bull Buffalo, Dreaming Wolf, Stone Lance, and Bent Arrow came upon a long stream of *wihio* wagons.

"Come, we can ride down and trade with them," Bent Arrow suggested. "I have no lead for my rifle."

Dreaming Wolf fingered the scar on his cheek and burned with anger.

"No, they're best avoided," the Wolf advised. "So near Fort John, they will be in need of everything. Look how slowly they move! It would be safer to approach a lame bear."

"This way," Stone Lance suggested, and the three young riders turned away.

Later, however, they struck another wagon trail. These *wihio* appeared lost, for they turned north into the hills and away from the old, rutted road.

111

"Can they be blind?" Bent Arrow asked, laughing.

"Who knows what a *wihio* may do?" Stone Lance replied. Before he could add a humorous suggestion, he spied three riders approaching from the west. Swallowing the words, he pointed to the horsemen.

"Wihio," Bent Arrow observed, nervously easing his rifle from its buckskin sheath.

"You won't need that," Dreaming Wolf argued, nudging his pony toward the approaching whites. "I know them."

As they came closer, Stone Lance, too, rode out to greet them. Neither cousin had expected to see Louis and Tom Freneau on Shell River.

"Hairy Chin!" the Lance called as he recognized Ike Williams as the third rider.

"Yah!" young Williams shouted as he kicked his horse into a gallop. "Dancer!"

For a few brief moments, the cousins swapped jests and shared news. Dreaming Wolf introduced Bent Arrow, then nodded to Stone Lance.

"So one of us has found a proper name," Tom grumbled.

"Nah nih, what brings you so far from the fort?" Stone Lance asked.

Ike gazed anxiously at Bent Arrow and explained, in English, "There's been trouble. Some wagons were attacked a few days ago. Everyone's nervous."

"They're shooting at anybody!" Louis added.

"Then we hear three wagons dropped back from this band. We came to find them."

"They're lost," Tom explained.

Dreaming Wolf translated the words for Bent Arrow.

"Will you help us find them?" Ike asked. "Get 'em on to the fort before there's trouble."

"What has this to do with us?" the Wolf asked. "Or you?"

"We were asked," Louis explained. "These people are farmers. I don't believe they have a proper saddle mount among them. They can't be far. Who could lose the trail, after all?"

"They aren't far," Stone Lance said, pointing to the diverging trail. "We'll help you."

"No," Dreaming Wolf objected. Bent Arrow, hearing the request, shouted angrily and turned to ride away.

"*Wihio* killed his uncle," Dreaming Wolf explained. "I have no love of these wagon people."

"I was one myself," Ike argued. "I'm bound to help."

"Can the scar be so deep you would turn away from the helpless, Cousin?" Louis asked.

"It isn't far," Stone Lance said, sniffing the air. "I can smell *wihio*."

"Me or them?" Ike asked, trying to lighten the mood.

"Lead the way, *See' was' sin mit*," Dreaming Wolf said, waving Bent Arrow along. Still lame from his Crow wounds, the Arrow wasn't walking well, but he would have no difficulty riding back

113

to the camp alone. Frowning, he turned and rode off to do just that.

"Long ago, your father spoke to my father of a dream he had," Louis said as they followed the ruts recently carved by wagon wheels in the prairie. "He saw two men bridging a raging river."

"I know," Dreaming Wolf said, frowning. For a long time, Stone Wolf had believed he and Marcel Freneau would be the ones to draw their peoples together and bridge the gap that separated them. Now Marcel was dead, and Stone Wolf's influence had ebbed.

"Perhaps it's for us to do," Louis suggested.

"Perhaps," Dreaming Wolf answered. To himself he thought the differences too great, the pain and anger too fierce. Men like Talking Stick could never forget or forgive. The Stick's father was cut down by *wihio* near Shell River where Charles Freneau now operated a trading post. Ash Hollow, the *wihio* called the place. Talking Stick had put his father and a young brother likewise killed on scaffolds in the cottonwoods there. *Wihio* had torn down the burial platforms and scattered the bones of the dead.

"Look, up there," Ike called out, and Dreaming Wolf noted three wagons formed in a crude half-circle on a nearby hill. Already, Ike and Tom Freneau were galloping toward a small party of frightened *wihio*. Louis approached more slowly with his *Tsis tsis tas* cousins.

"Indians!" a small, yellow-haired woman screamed, clutching a small child in each arm.

114

"They're friends," Tom explained as he dismounted. "What's the trouble here?"

A pair of riflemen emerged from behind the wagons, and Tom exchanged a few brief remarks with the men. Afterward they showed him the left rear wheel of the second wagon. Its spokes were little more than wood splinters. Clearly it wouldn't bear up under a load.

"We sent a man to get help," the taller of the men explained as he set his rifle aside. "Guess he made it. You came along."

"We were looking for you, but we weren't sent," Louis told the travelers.

"Amos!" a large woman cried. "My Amos!"

"No, Sudie. Might be he got lost," a second woman suggested.

Dreaming Wolf thought it unlikely, not with a clear trail to Shell River.

"We won't find him here," Tom declared.

"Can you help us fix our wagon?" the woman named Sudie asked.

"I'm no wheelwright, ma'am," Louis replied. "Those other wheels don't look a lot better, either. There's been trouble hereabouts, and the best thing to do's get all of you along to Fort John. Could be while the rest of your party rests and stocks up with supplies, somebody could come back and get this wagon."

"Don't lie to me, young man," Sudie said, gazing at him with stone cold eyes. "You don't expect Amos is safe, and you know once we abandon our wagon, there'll be no turnin' back to get it."

"That's right," Louis admitted. "Your man could still turn up, though. Even if he doesn't, you have the little ones to consider."

"We'll pack your things in the other wagons," the tall man announced. With two extra mules on each wagon, it shouldn't overburden the animals. It's like these fellows say. Best we rejoin the others."

"And do you plan to carry our things all the way to Oregon, John Harper?" Sudie asked. "Or should we start the long walk back to Illinois now?"

"There's time to consider all that later," Harper insisted. "Just now we got other concerns."

Dreaming Wolf followed Harper's eyes north to where a dust swirl marked the approach of riders. They weren't likely to be *wihio*.

"Easy, Ballard," Harper urged as his companion raised his rifle. "We got these Indians with us. They'll treat with their friends."

"Is that right?" Ballard asked.

"Let's hitch up the mules," Ike said, starting for the animals. "Dreaming Wolf might be more persuasive if we were with the others."

Whoever the horsemen were, they came no closer than a distant ridge. Not even a scout rode out to investigate the derelict wagons.

"Wouldn't be Talking Stick," Stone Lance said, speaking in the *Tsis tsis tas* tongue so he wouldn't alarm the *wihio*. "He would enjoy an easy triumph."

116

"If they're our people, they'll know about the wagons," Dreaming Wolf argued.

"How?" the Lance asked.

"Bent Arrow will tell them. Or maybe they've captured the man who went for help. No matter. Talking Stick would have more interest in the main band. Strays might be easy, but they rarely provide the best horses. Supplies, either."

Stone Lance nodded his agreement. Both were glad when the two surviving wagons set off southward toward the main trail. Sudie remained behind but an instant. Dreaming Wolf realized why when flames began licking at the wagon's canvas cover. Better to burn the wagon than let another find purpose for it! *Wihio* madness!

Pulled by three teams of mules, the wagons rumbled along with surprising speed. By nightfall, they were in sight of the main band, encamped as they were half a day's ride from Fort John.

"You need us no longer," Dreaming Wolf said, leading his horse from the wagon road. *"See' was' sin mit* and I should resume our hunting."

"Don't go just yet," Ike pleaded. "Camp with us tonight. Maybe tomorrow we can all hunt together."

"It's too far to ride back to camp," Stone Lance observed. "It would be good to share our cousins' company."

"I won't sleep in a *wihio* wagon camp!" Dreaming Wolf insisted.

"No need," Louis replied. "I know of a good place nearby. The water from the spring's sweet,

117

and it's not so far from the river that we can't share our morning swim."

"Then it's decided," Ike said, grinning. "I wouldn't mind a wash tonight, matter of fact. Too much dust on this fool rutted road."

"Yes," Dreaming Wolf muttered as he gazed at the deep ruts cut by the rims of hundreds of wagon wheels. "Too much dust. Too many *wihio!*"

When the stray wagons rolled to a stop outside the circle of their company, shouts of relief rose skyward. Friends opened a gap to allow the wagons to join the defensive formation while women rushed out to embrace their wayward comrades. Girls gathered to whisper tales of the adventure while boys ran off to the river to enjoy a twilight swim.

"See there," Ike declared, pulling off his shirt even before jumping down from the saddle. "Not all *wihio* are crazy. Those boys got the right idea."

"First we should see to the horses," Dreaming Wolf argued.

"We'll leave 'em to have a drink and chew some grass," Tom said, abandoning his mount and starting toward the river. "Better to tend 'em when we're camped out at the spring."

Dreaming Wolf thought to ride on, but first Louis and then Stone Lance abandoned him. The river's cool waters were just too tempting. Finally, the Wolf climbed down and walked to the bank himself. With a sigh of surrender, he stripped and plunged into the water. An icy chill ran through him. Shell River was freezing! But soon the pranks of the wagon boys and the laughter of his cousins warmed him. It was a relief to wash the weariness away, and as he raced young Ike to the far bank, he thought of the old stories of how Corn Hair Freneau first came among the People.

That, of course, was Louis's grandfather, or perhaps the grandfather's father. It was hard to remember everything. In those days there had been suspicion, yes, but beyond that *wihio* and *Tsis tsis tas* had formed bonds of honor and understanding.

Now? Mostly there was killing. Anger.

When the sun at last died in the far hills, the *wihio* climbed out of the river and hurried to dress themselves. They were a strange sort, those boys. Pale as moonlight, many of them, and too skinny to face the coming winter. Dreaming Wolf knew from his talks with Ike that life in the wagon camps was hard. Even so, those young ones found occasion to laugh.

Their mothers did more. When the Wolf and his companions walked to their horses, they found a party of women waiting with kettles of food.

"You can't leave just yet," the one called Sudie argued. "You helped us in our hour of need, and we'd be poor neighbors to dismiss you without at least feeding you."

"Some of you look in need of a feed, too," a fat woman said, pinching Ike's bony shoulder.

"We should leave," Dreaming Wolf urged.

"I got only tinned beans for our supper," Louis

119

explained. "Smell those pots! You can't mean to turn away from a feast like this?"

"*Nah nih?*" Stone Lance asked. "Will you starve Hairy Chin?"

"No," Dreaming Wolf said, relenting. "But after eating, we must make our camp by the spring."

"Sure," Louis said, grinning as he accepted a tin plate.

"Never could abide the noise of a wagon camp," Ike added, helping Sudie set down her kettle.

Dreaming Wolf gazed at the wondrous array of baked breads and found himself grinning, too. Not even Mary Freneau could assemble such wonders. And even if the meat was a little greasy, it was nevertheless tasty. He ate as if emerging from the long winter fast of a grizzly.

Ten

That night, camped beside the bubbling spring on a hillside overlooking Shell River, Dreaming Wolf found himself gazing at the flickering fires of the wagon camp. Those people were not so unlike his own. They cared for their little ones. They struggled to survive the hardships life brought. The strong prevailed, and the weak broke down like that abandoned wagon and were left behind.

"They'll have a hard time getting to Oregon, those folks," Tom observed as he rolled out his blankets. "Winter's bound to catch 'em in the passes. They'd be smart to camp down on the plains and wait for next spring."

"I told their captain that," Louis confessed. "He said they were bound to go on. Stubborn fellow! They won't get there."

"Too few scouts," Tom grumbled. "Men that make the crossing tend to stay out West. Good country there, I'm told. The companies with smart scouts head out early, just after the grass greens.

The late ones find sparse grazing, and they fall behind."

"Soon there'll be no grass at all along Shell River," Dreaming Wolf declared. "Already the *wihio* wagons chase the game far north and south. Our people are splitting apart even now. It's hard for me to cry for these wagon people, knowing they spoil this good country."

"But you don't ride with Talkin' Stick," Ike observed.

"I find no joy in killing," Dreaming Wolf explained.

"No, it's not a thing you can warm to," Ike said, gazing at the moon. "I think one day I might like bein' a trail scout. Showin' others the way. Warnin' of the dangers. Helpin' 'em find their dreams."

"My brother Peter tried it," Tom said, laughing. "Lucky for him he had cousins to save his hide from the Lakotas."

"Iron Wolf was riding with a raiding party determined to avenge a wrong," Dreaming Wolf explained. "My brother saw Young Corn Hair, and the two were able to make a peace. It was a good thing, I believe, but very rare. Mostly the angry words fly, and the killing follows."

They spoke a while longer, mostly of hunting elk before the snows choked the sky. Then each found what rest he could manage on that lonely hillside.

Dreaming Wolf found little peace that night. His dreams were visited by phantom shapes, and he found himself drifting along Shell River, watching a war lance paint the earth red with blood. The weeping of women tormented his ears, and the lonely cries of little ones haunted the hills.

Then Trickster appeared, disguised as he often was as a gray-backed coyote.

"This is my doing," he cackled. "See how I turn man upon his brothers? How foolish is the two-legged creature to think himself better than the animals! Only he preys upon himself. See how man kills his own sons, how brothers strike each other! Seeing it, I can only laugh!"

Dreaming Wolf found nothing amusing in the dream. Corpses lay scattered across the valley. Arms, legs, heads . . . mutilated flesh. It sickened him, and he awoke in wide-eyed terror.

"Nah nih?" Stone Lance whispered.

The Wolf didn't answer. Instead he rushed off past the horses, fell to his knees, and was sick. He heaved until his insides were afire. His head seemed to be exploding. Even now he saw the bloody nightmare. It wouldn't go away!

"You've had a dream," Stone Lance observed when the Wolf finally returned. "Tell me what you saw."

"Death," Dreaming Wolf explained.

"Here?"

"There," the Wolf answered, pointing toward the valley beyond Fort John. "Blood everywhere. Men mutilated."

"Tsis tsis tas?"

"I don't know," Dreaming Wolf said, shivering

123

as the cold gripped him. "Blood is blood, no matter what color the skin."

"Was it a battle, then?" Stone Lance asked.

"I saw no fighting, *See' was' sin mit*. Only butchery."

Stone Lance frowned a reply, and the cousins sat together beside the stream and waited for dawn.

Not long after the sun broke the eastern horizon, Dreaming Wolf and Stone Lance knelt beside a small fire and made the morning prayers. Ike Williams and the Freneaus were there, too, listening to the ancient words and smoking the ceremonial pipe.

"It will be good to swim with our cousins again," Stone Lance said after Dreaming Wolf emptied the pipe.

"I don't think we'll be swimming this morning," Tom said, frowning as he pointed to a party of frightened wagon men approaching from the river.

"More trouble?" Louis asked. "Can't have lost another wagon."

"Look at their faces," Stone Lance urged. "I see fear."

Dreaming Wolf turned and stared out at the far valley, but he spotted no sign of riders. *If not Talking Stick . . .*

They didn't have long to wonder about the source of the trouble. The wagon captain, a white-haired preacher named Tobias Gafford, explained it.

"We've got boys missing," Gafford said, shuffling his feet. "Six in all. Oldest is twelve. They were all of them down at the river with you last night, and we thought maybe they came up here to share your camp."

"No, sir," Louis assured them. "We haven't seen or heard anybody."

"I was afeared of that," a second man muttered. "My Joe was boastin' to some friends how he'd seen buffalo yesterday. My rifle's gone. I think maybe he and them others went off to shoot game."

"There's little enough danger in that," Louis declared. "Can't any of them gone far afoot."

"Nor are we goin' to find 'em walking, Mr. Freneau," Gafford said. "We've asked enough of you already, but if you're not beyond doing us another favor, we'd be forever grateful if you'd find 'em. They'll get themselves lost out there certain."

"There's worse things than bein' lost, too," Ike said, tensing. "I'm goin' to have myself a look. Anybody comin' along?"

"I'll ready my horse," Stone Lance said, touching Dreaming Wolf's elbow. "There's no time to waste."

"Tom?" Louis asked.

"Been fool enough already for ten men," Tom said, laughing. "You tell the womenfolks we'll expect some more stew, though."

"It'll be waiting for you," Gafford promised. "God go with you."

"We're apt to need Him," Ike declared.

125

Yes, Dreaming Wolf silently agreed. *Trickster's out there. As is Talking Stick.*

The Wolf didn't share his dream with the others. Already Stone Lance's face reflected concern, but even he could only guess what horrors had visited his cousin's dream. They spread out across the yellow-brown plain, searching for some trace of the missing boys. For a time, Dreaming Wolf suspected it was hopeless. Then Stone Lance announced he'd found the trail.

"This way!" the Lance shouted, motioning northward. The five of them rode off at a gallop.

At first they spied nothing. By and by, indentations made by boot heels marked the trail, though, and finally Ike pointed to a flash of something in a stand of cottonwoods ahead. They rode with renewed vigor toward the trees. But where they'd hoped to find the missing boys, they saw only shirts hanging in cottonwood branches. Discarded boots and stockings. Small pouches of cold biscuits and dried meat.

"They can't have gone swimmin'," Tom cried. "There's no water up here."

"They didn't. Look there," Stone Lance said, pointing to tracks left by unshod ponies.

"No, there," Ike said, pointing to a line of horsemen emerging from a nearby ravine.

"Oh, Lord," Tom said, sighing as the wagon boys stumbled out into view. Stripped to the waist and barefoot, they appeared particularly helpless. And completely terrified.

"Young fools," Louis grumbled. "I imagine

they're expectin' the wagon people instead of us, too."

"It's Talkin' Stick," Ike said as the chief rode out ahead of the others. "He'll butcher 'em."

"We have to do something," Louis said, turning to his cousins.

"You and Tom stay here," Dreaming Wolf said, frowning. *"See' was' sin mit,* see they remain. Only one man's needed to speak. It's for me to do."

"Be careful, Wolf," Ike urged.

Dreaming Wolf rode out, holding his right hand out as a sign of good intentions. He intended to meet with the chief alone, but Stone Lance rode along.

"As you rode with my father," the Lance explained.

Dreaming Wolf wanted to send the boy back. But Stone Lance was a young boy no longer. It was his right to come.

"You keep bad company," Talking Stick observed as the two young men drew near. *"Wihio! You smell of them!"*

"Ayyyy!" the Crazy Dogs accompanying Talking Stick howled.

"They're my cousins," Dreaming Wolf said, gazing fiercely at the Crazy Dogs. "My father, who keeps the Arrows, took their father as a brother. Recognize them, brothers. They have slept in my lodge, and I in theirs. They are kin, and the man who harms them will have my family as enemies!"

"They're not wagon people," Talking Stick said, laughing. "We don't care about them. If we wish to kill them, we know the way to Fort John. No, we expected the fathers of these field mice to come looking for them."

The Crazy Dogs jabbed their captives with the blunt ends of their lances and pelted them with small stones.

"So, you make war on children?" Dreaming Wolf asked.

"They are as old as the brother they killed at Shell River," Talking Stick barked. "Old enough to die."

"Is that what your dreams have told you to do?" the Wolf asked. "Kill the helpless? Take their scalps? Where's the honor in it? A man can step on an ant easily enough. Should that prove his courage?"

"They don't merit your defense," Thunder Coat argued, waving a piece of chalk rock in the air. "See how they etch their words in the earth! Their wagons cut the land. They kill our game and foul our streams. It's right they should die!"

"I hate these things they've done, too," Dreaming Wolf agreed. "And if they were soldiers, I would fight them. When they raise a rifle, I do. But these boys can bring us no harm. Look. See them for what they are. Helpless. Once we would have carried such boys to our camp and adopted them as brothers."

"*Wihio* captives only bring trouble," Thunder Coat declared.

"Yes," Dreaming Wolf said, nodding. "But killing them? We can't eat them. Their hair's too fine and short to make worthy trophies. Better to trade them for something useful."

"Trade?" Thunder Coat asked. "Ah, we can consider that."

"Can you forget our brother?" Talking Stick raged. "Our father?"

"I have seen good rifles in the wagon camp," Thunder Coat argued. "We need them. The blood of these children means nothing."

"A rifle for each of them then," Talking Stick demanded. "Go, tell your *wihio* friends of our offer."

"You'll bring the boys to their camp?"

"When the sun's straight up," Talking Stick vowed. "Have the rifles waiting."

Dreaming Wolf nodded, but before he could leave, Stone Lance spoke up.

"These boys must not be harmed," the Lance added. "You agree?"

The angry stare with which Talking Stick replied chilled Dreaming Wolf's heart.

"They'll be alive," the Stick answered.

"Unharmed," Stone Lance insisted. "Agreed?"

"Agreed," Thunder Coat answered. "Have the rifles waiting."

"They will be," Dreaming Wolf said, nudging his horse into a trot. "It's well you followed, *See' was' sin mit,*" he told the Lance once they were out of Talking Stick's sight. "You read his heart. I believe he meant to kill them."

"Some are too easily read," Stone Lance replied. "Now, we must collect the rifles."

The wagon people were reluctant to turn over weapons to men likely to be future enemies, and some argued against the exchange.

"What will happen to my boy if we don't hand over the rifles?" a dark-haired farmer asked.

"Talking Stick will murder them as you watch," Stone Lance explained.

"The dyin' won't we easy, either, mister," Ike added. "I've seen that one work. Best give over the rifles."

Some continued to argue, but once Talking Stick appeared with his hundred followers, most grew mute with terror. When a pair of Crazy Dogs rode out, holding one of the boys between them, all dissent ceased. The boy was stripped bare, and wet rawhide was wrapped around his throat so that he struggled to breathe.

"I've heard they cut a man up so his own ma wouldn't know him," Gafford said, falling on his knees. "Get the rifles ready. We have no choice."

Dreaming Wolf took the rifles out himself, and Talking Stick accepted the weapons reluctantly.

"Warn the *wihio* there will be no trading next time," the Stick muttered. "Only killing."

"They know that," Dreaming Wolf answered icily. He then took charge of the captives. Stone Lance rode over to the one held by the Crazy Dogs, sliced the choking strip, and offered the boy a buffalo hide to cover himself. The two cousins then escorted the *wihio* boys back to their families.

While mothers took charge of the wayward children, the Freneaus stepped out with a handful of wagon people. They spread a blanket on the ground and placed food, finely-woven blankets, looking glasses, and other assorted items they wished to trade. Talking Stick, looking on, shouted angrily, but many of his companions dismounted and brought hides and moccasins to exchange. For a time, *Tsis tsis tas* and *wihio* traded and ate and laughed together.

"This is how it was in the early days," Louis observed.

"Ne' hyo has spoken of it," Dreaming Wolf replied. "Too often our people trade for whiskey, or are cheated. Killed even."

"That makes it hard on honest traders," Louis said, shaking his head.

"Honest traders?" Tom asked, laughing. "You mean the ones less likely to steal your teeth, don't you?"

"A man's entitled to a profit," Louis insisted.

They laughed a bit and argued considerably more. Dreaming Wolf left them and walked out past the traders to where Stone Lance and Ike Williams stood, watching a band of Crazy Dogs on the distant hillside.

"It wasn't as you dreamed, *Nah nih,*" Stone Lance said when he noticed his cousin's approach.

"Not this time," Dreaming Wolf answered. "Did you see Talking Stick? His eyes carried no love for these wagon people."

"He would've killed those boys if not for you," Ike said, gazing somberly at his companions.

131

"Rifles or no rifles. It's the way he is."

"There's reason," Dreaming Wolf argued.

"I've heard it, all about his dead father and brother," Ike said, spitting. "I lost a father, too, remember? That give me an excuse to shoot any Indian I see?"

"When my mother died," Dreaming Wolf said, "I was filled with sadness. Anger. I cast it off in the sweat lodge and restored the harmony of my world. A man only walks his path. He doesn't determine what he'll find there. Talking Stick believes he will make the world over as he chooses, but it won't happen. Seeing that, he simply grows angrier."

"He's a dangerous man, even without a hundred men followin' him," Ike declared. "You watch him, Stone Lance. Wolf. He's none too happy with you two just now, either."

Dreaming Wolf sighed. It was a disturbing thought.

They swam the river a final time that evening with the wagon boys. Next dawn, after making the required prayers, Dreaming Wolf and Stone Lance bade their cousins farewell. The wagon people were already snaking their way on to Fort John, and the Freneaus were eager to ready themselves for these new customers.

"It's a fine thing we did here," Louis observed as he mounted his horse. "Restoring boys to their families. Leading the lost home."

"No one ever found Sudie's husband," Ike noted. "But I guess we did what we could."

"We were lucky," Tom declared. "If we'd come upon Talking Stick instead of you two, there'd be need of a new trader at Fort John."

"Yes," Dreaming Wolf agreed. "Lucky. We stood between two angry bulls, and both listened. Next time?"

"Next time we'll have to choose sides," Stone Lance predicted.

"Could you ride with Talkin' Stick?" Ike asked.

"We have," Dreaming Wolf answered. "Because we speak your words and have lived in your fort, don't imagine we're not *Tsis tsis tas.*"

"I hope we don't find ourselves enemies," Ike said, swallowing hard. "I owe you. But even burned brown by the summer sun, I'm a white man. *Wihio.* I can't forget that anymore'n you can ignore who you are."

"Whatever follows, we've shared good days," Dreaming Wolf said, gripping the hands of each departing friend in turn. "A difficult time is coming, but it will never change what has been."

"Never," Louis agreed, and the others nodded.

Eleven

Dreaming Wolf and Stone Lance returned to the *Hev a tan iu* camp late that evening. Talking Stick's party had already arrived, and many of the People gazed warily at the latecomers.

"There they are," whispered Talking Stick's eldest son, Four Toes. "The *wihio* hearts."

Four Toes was but a boy of fourteen summers, and Dreaming Wolf ignored the insult. Stone Lance swung his pony over and glared.

"I was there, too," Buffalo Calf, Four Toes's younger brother, declared. "We both saw how you spoke for the *wihio*. We would have killed them!"

"You?" Stone Lance asked. "When did you ever count coup on an enemy? A boy should have chin hairs to pluck before he talks up. Otherwise he sounds like a coyote who burned his toes in a campfire."

A small band of boys were standing nearby, and they laughed at the Lance's words. Buffalo Calf, who was small for a boy of twelve summers, scowled. His brother was no happier. Four Toes was so called because of a toe badly burned as a child.

"You can't talk to us that way!" Four Toes shouted. "You who hide in Arrow Lodge, avoiding the young men's camp. When did you ever ride to war with my father? No, we've all seen how you prefer to live at the *wihio* fort. What do you do there? Make the trader's fire? Cook his food? Are you a woman?"

Stone Lance would have struck Four Toes had not Dreaming Wolf intervened.

"Stop!" the Wolf howled. "We'll bring no disharmony into the *Hev a tan iu* camp. Maybe you'll meet my brother at the river, Four Toes. It's a good place to wrestle. You're taller and heavier, so perhaps Stone Lance won't batter you too much."

The others laughed again, and Four Toes nodded his acceptance of the challenge.

"Remember to come," Four Toes added. "There are no *wihio* to hide with this time."

"Hide?" the Lance asked. "When did Stone Lance hide? My place, like my father's, is at the front. Except when the enemy is pursuing."

Four Toes began a reply, but Stone Lance turned his horse, and the words were choked by a blanket of dust.

Later, at Arrow Lodge, Dreaming Wolf told his father both of the quarrel with Four Toes and the trouble on Shell River.

"Yes, it's not surprising," Stone Wolf told the young men. "My dreams have told of terrible days. I have seen a great white sea sweeping Bull Buffalo from the valleys he has always walked. I've seen strange white blankets falling from the sky to choke life from the little ones. I saw a forest of thin trees fill the nearby hills. Only when I came close did I see they were burial scaffolds. The dying cries of old friends tormented my soul, and I hungered to share their walk on Hanging Road."

"You've dreamed of white seas before," Dreaming Wolf noted. "It's the coming of the *wihio*."

"No, this was different," Stone Wolf insisted.

"How, *Ne' hyo?*" Dreaming Wolf asked.

"It had the taste of ice, and it chilled my very heart. It's a ghost sickness, *Naha'*. It will kill us all."

"We'll be careful," Stone Lance vowed. "We'll avoid the *wihio*."

"There's no escaping," Stone Wolf argued. "It will creep upon us by night. Not even the sharpest-eyed scout will see it. One morning we will rise and make the morning prayers. By nightfall, the dying will have begun."

It was a chilling vision, and Stone Wolf did everything he knew to protect the People from it. Those next several days he smoked and prayed and made medicine. Twice he sat alone in the hills, starving himself and cutting his flesh.

"Man Above, show me a path the *Tsis tsis tas*

136

can walk," Stone Wolf pleaded.

"Ne' hyo?" Dreaming Wolf called the morning he watched Stone Lance thrash Four Toes at the river. "What can I do to help? Shall I pound a buffalo horn to make medicine?"

"There's nothing either of us can do," Stone Wolf answered. "There's no turning this peril. It will find us."

Afterward, as Dreaming Wolf led small parties of young men out to hunt Bull Buffalo, he warily avoided the *wihio* wagon camps that occasionally appeared beside Shell River. It was late in the season for a successful crossing, and the people and animals were often wretched sights.

"Look at them!" Otter Foot said, pointing to one band. "Their horses are nothing more than hairy sticks!"

Dreaming Wolf noted the children were no better. It appeared the *Tsis tsis tas* would not be the only ones to know dying that winter.

The Plum Moon was dying and the cotton-woods were losing their leaves the day Dreaming Wolf spied the white sheet people. He, Stone Lance, and five others were returning from hunting dragging a travois bearing the meat cut from three large bulls, and the Wolf's first thought was to see the meat safely to camp. It was only when he noticed the sheets set up outside the wagon camp that his father's vision flooded his thoughts. Frowning, he waved his companions away.

"What is it?" Bent Arrow cried. "Look, they're gesturing to us!"

"Waving us away," Stone Lance said as he stared at the white flags billowing in the autumn breeze. "Look at their eyes! See how fearful they are."

"They can't be afraid of us," Otter Foot argued.

"Not *of* us," Dreaming Wolf said, fighting to steady himself. *"For* us."

"But . . ." Otter Foot started to argue.

"We must go," Dreaming Wolf insisted. "It's death to stay."

"We must warn the others, too," Stone Lance suggested. "They should know of the danger."

Dreaming Wolf agreed. He hoped this time the chiefs might heed Stone Wolf's warning and keep the hot bloods under control. The survival of the People depended upon it.

Even as Dreaming Wolf and Stone Lance rode into the camp dragging their travois, small parties of young men were collecting ponies.

"Wihio!" Four Toes shouted, waving a lance.

"They have many horses," his cousin, White Tail, added. "We'll steal them!"

"Stop!" Dreaming Wolf called. "These people should be avoided."

138

"They carry sickness," Stone Lance added.

Stone Wolf stepped outside Arrow Lodge and greeted his sons. It took Dreaming Wolf only a few moments to convince the Arrow-keeper that here were the people of his vision.

"Hear me!" Stone Wolf shouted in a voice more deep and powerful than many of the younger men had ever heard. "I speak with the weight of *Mahuts*. You must not go near this place. You must take nothing from these people. Ghost fevers walk with them, and it is your death to come near."

"Old women's stories for scaring children!" Four Toes said, laughing. "Your voice carries no weight with us, old man!"

"Quiet!" Dancing Lance shouted, glaring at the boy. "Who are you to know anything? From the moment Sweet Medicine brought *Mahuts* to the People, the Arrows have guided our actions. Stone Wolf's dreams have led us from many perils."

"*Ne' hyo,* tell him what weight that old man's words carry among the chiefs," Four Toes said when Talking Stick stepped out to speak with the Arrow-keeper.

"Yes, tell them," Stone Wolf urged. His eyes bored into the chief's chest, and it was not Talking Stick who returned the gaze. No, here was the boy, White Horn, who had learned the medicine cures walking his fourteenth summer beside Stone Wolf.

"Naha'," Talking Stick said, turning to his son, "you are young and foolish. You don't understand the power that walks in a man's dreams. If Stone Wolf speaks of ghost sickness, I believe it. So many times we've sat with the *wihio,* trading and smoking. All the time, the invisible dagger of death is killing us. You say these white flags came to you in a dream?"

"Yes," Stone Wolf answered.

"It's a *wihio* sign," Dreaming Wolf explained. "It means they have sickness. It warns others to stay away."

"And it can hurt us even so?" the Stick asked.

"I've heard how it passes out of the *wihio* onto everything he owns," Stone Lance said, frowning. "It lingers in the hearts of the dead so that even the burial places are haunted."

"You must not take the *wihio* horses then," Talking Stick said sourly. "You must not treat or trade with these wagon people. Don't disturb their camp or take anything they leave behind."

The young men sighed and turned away.

"Return your ponies to the herd," Thunder Coat added. "Until these *wihio* and their ghost sickness leave, it's best all remain close to our camp."

For once, the chiefs were in agreement. Leaders of the soldier societies were told to post guards around the horses.

"No one must go there," Talking Stick insisted. "If some young fool rides off to steal a pony or

140

count coup, we may all come to suffer."

For those who had lost relatives to the dreaded spotted sickness of past years, the Stick's admonition brought fresh recollections. Mothers held their small ones closer, and old people spoke of the dying times or showed the scars left by the demon fevers.

Dreaming Wolf noted the precautions and smiled his approval.

"Ne' hyo, they have heard you," he told Stone Wolf. "Your dreams have been honored."

"Some have heard," Stone Wolf agreed. "The danger remains, though. I saw more than peril. I witnessed death."

Dreaming Wolf studied his father's eyes. Despair walked there.

"We will help watch the camp," Stone Lance pledged. "Dreaming Wolf, I, the other Foxes. We'll keep the hot bloods from bringing this new sickness into our camp."

"It's good you try," Stone Wolf said, nodding his head wearily. "I'll smoke and pray. Perhaps Man Above will honor your efforts with success."

Dreaming Wolf sighed. His father spoke without confidence. The Arrow-keeper had known too much death and disappointment!

The Foxes maintained their vigil over the pony herd two nights before yielding the responsibility to the Crazy Dogs.

141

"We should stay for a time and watch," Stone Lance suggested, but Otter Foot and Raven's Wing were tired, and Dreaming Wolf motioned his cousin back toward camp.

"Look at them," the Lance complained. "They're laughing. Hear them taunt each other? They're sure to ride to Shell River!"

"If that's their choice, we can't stop it," Dreaming Wolf argued. "Even a Fox has to sleep. There are too many of them anyway."

"Can you forget your father's dream?"

"No, but haven't you looked deeply into his eyes? He knows it's Man Above who will decide what will happen. Not you. Not me."

"Look there," Stone Lance urged. "Four Toes. He'll ride off and bring the ghost sickness."

"There are others there to stop him."

"Who among them would stand against Talking Stick's son? No, they place no weight in Stone Wolf's words, so they'll let the People die."

"Nothing lasts long," Dreaming Wolf whispered. "Perhaps it's our time to climb Hanging Road."

"I'm ready. But I have sisters. It's for them I worry."

"It's not in our power to change what will be, *See' was' sin mit,*" Dreaming Wolf lamented. "We must take to our beds and find some rest. If the sickness comes, we'll have little rest."

"If?"

"When," Dreaming Wolf said sourly. "Come. It's time."

142

"It was a boy's prank," Antler explained later, when the dying began. "Four Toes said we weren't men. We listened to fools and dreamers while there were good things to take from the *wihio* camp. I was a fool, and now my brothers have died."

That night, Antler told the chiefs, the Crazy Dogs rode off to the white sheet people's camp. The *wihio* kept a good guard over their wagons, but on a nearby hill many good things lay in a heap. The young Crazy Dogs took some clothes, knives, even a kettle. Four Toes then found the graves.

There were thirty in all, each with a cross of cottonwood limbs to mark it. Four Toes dug up the first body with his lance. It was a young woman, but although she was thin and frail, she bore no spots or blisters.

"It's only hunger that torments them," Four Toes had said.

The others joined him, and soon one body after another was dragged from its shallow trench. Corpses were stripped of rings and other ornaments. Younger boys then tore off their clothes and began hacking off limbs. Some of the smaller corpses were hung on saplings. Heads were severed, and limbs were hacked off.

The Crazy Dogs were missed at dawn, when

River Fork and Bent Arrow had accompanied Dancing Lance to guard the pony herd.

"Where are the watchers?" Dancing Lance had asked.

Following a pony trail south and east, the three Foxes saw Four Toes and Buffalo Calf dragging *wihio* corpses behind their horses. Waving frantically and racing out to prevent them from carrying the sickness to the camp, Dancing Lance successfully forced the Crazy Dogs to leave the bodies behind. Bent Arrow chased after the others, but in the darkness the renegades eluded capture and returned to the camp. With them they brought death.

Prairie Bonnet, Talking Stick's young daughter, was the first to grow sick. Her small forehead burned with fever, and she couldn't keep food in her stomach. She writhed in pain, crying out in youthful terror. It took her only a day and a night to die.

"Fools!" Stone Wolf said after his medicine failed to restore the girl's health. "I have no power to turn this ghost sickness. I warned you!"

Talking Stick chose to place the fault with the Arrow-keeper.

"Where are your powers, old man?" Talking Stick screamed. "My daughter is dead. Your Arrow medicine is useless. You say you guard the welfare of the People, but you're useless. A white-haired dreamer!"

Stone Wolf raised no argument. No words

could console a man who mourned a dead daughter. He understood that far too well.

"Man Above," he prayed that night under the stars, "save us from the mistakes of our young men. They hurry us to our deaths!"

Dancing Lance told the assembled chiefs that very thing.

"I've seen the butchery near the *wihio* camp," the Lance said bitterly. "Arrows shot into bodies. Many dead marked as a warrior might cut the enemy slain in fair battle. You cowards! You can't find a live man you can fight, so you mutilate ghosts. Now the shades stalk us all!"

So it seemed, for hardly had the mourning for Prairie Bonnet begun when Buffalo Calf collapsed. Four Toes, too, took the fever, as did their mother, Cornstalk Woman. In four days' time, all were dead.

It was the same elsewhere, especially among the Crazy Dogs. Thunder Coat lost his family, too. Antler alone survived of his seven brothers and four sisters. His aunts, uncles, cousins, and grandparents all climbed Hanging Road.

"It's my doing!" he screamed as he hacked off his hair and cut the little fingers of both hands off at the first joint. "I brought the ghost sickness to them. Why am I spared?"

As the fever spread, Stone Wolf devoted himself to tending the sick. He offered what medicine he suspected might aid the struggle to recover. He erected a sweat lodge. Grass Snake,

145

Whirlwind's young son, told how the *wihio* had recovered the bodies of their dead and were burning them and their clothes.

"The bodies must not be marked," Stone Wolf insisted, for the spirits required them for the long walk to the other side. The *Tsis tsis tas,* like many Plains peoples, believed any injury done a corpse would leave its shade crippled or mutilated in like manner.

"Even so, we should destroy their possessions," Dreaming Wolf argued.

Men like Talking Stick and Thunder Coat, who had already placed wives and children on burial scaffolds, found the burning of their lodges particularly painful.

"There's nothing left of them now," the Stick said, sinking to his knees. "All that I loved is dead. I am a man alone. Empty."

"We are a people abandoned," Thunder Coat added. "Death fills our eyes, as it does those of a bleeding buffalo."

When Stone Wolf, too, took ill, the People despaired. Young warriors rode out alone or in pairs to seek out *wihio* wagon camps. If they found one, they would ride out and shoot arrows into wagons or make suicide charges. Some vowed terrible sacrifices if a relative recovered.

"Man Above," Dreaming Wolf prayed as he stood on a hillside, watching the sun rise. *"Ne' hyo* is dying. Stone Lance is feverish, and Hoop Woman doesn't eat. Only the little girls are growing better. Help me restore my father to the medicine trail. Give me your help. I have no power to drive the ghost sickness from him."

But as the nights grew colder, Stone Wolf became thinner. Death lingered nearby. When Dreaming Wolf brought his father to *Mahuts,* Stone Wolf examined the Arrows.

"See, *Naha'?*" the old man muttered.

"Yes," Dreaming Wolf answered. There were small red flakes on the points of the Arrows. The People were in great peril.

"They must be renewed," Stone Wolf explained. "You will do it."

"How?" Dreaming Wolf cried. *"Ne' hyo,* I don't know what's to be done. You must fight the fever and return to us. We need your medicine. Your power. Your wisdom."

"No," Stone Wolf said, sighing as fever tormented him. "They have done us no good. The burden's been too great for me to carry. Another must try."

Twelve

Hot, feverish death continued to torment the *Hev a tan iu*. There seemed no end to it, and Dreaming Wolf worried there might be no one left when the ghost sickness finally departed.

"*Heammawihio,* hear me!" he cried. "Save your people!"

Dreaming Wolf and Stone Lance performed rituals. They passed long mornings in the sweat lodge, fighting to drive the evil odors from the bodies of the sick and restore the harmony that had once filled the Rope Men's camp. Nothing affected the unseen killer as it stalked new victims.

Red Hoop and Little Hoop, who had recovered from a brief sickness, boiled over with fever again.

"This is no spotted sickness that strikes only once," Stone Wolf observed. "It will haunt us until there are no more *Hev a tan iu* to walk the earth."

It was a terrifying notion.

"Nah nih, my sisters are dying," Stone Lance lamented when he accompanied Dreaming Wolf to the river that next day to make the morning prayers. "We have no medicine that can stop it."

"Some of the sick have grown better," Dreaming Wolf argued. "Sit with your sisters. Talk to them. Bathe their bodies with a cooling cloth. And give them only boiled water to drink, for the smoke often drives out the bad humors."

"Nah' koa is doing that," the Lance noted.

"You must take some of her burden," Dreaming Wolf said, frowning. "Hoop Woman is growing weaker. She doesn't eat enough. She's needed, too, *See' was' sin mit."*

"I remember how your mother starved herself so that we would have food to eat," Stone Lance said, remembering it. "It's the same with *Nah' koa.* She wishes to take my sisters' torments onto herself."

"It's not like hunger, this sickness."

"No, it's like the torture of many Crow knives. They cut off a little flesh at a time, allowing a man to linger, bleeding. Only when there is nothing left does he find death."

And even then, Dreaming Wolf suspected, there would be no peace. When they rested a small body on its burial scaffold, the wasted flesh and contorted face spoke only of pain.

Little Hoop was the next to die. Stone Lance wrapped his sister in an elk hide and carried her to the scaffold Dreaming Wolf had built on the ridge overlooking Shell River. It was a fine, green place.

"Here, sister, rest," Stone Lance urged. Hoop Woman dropped to her knees, sobbing, while Stone Wolf sang an ancient medicine chant. Red Hoop remained in her lodge, too weak to rise even to bid her sister farewell.

"She had only eleven summers to walk the world," Stone Lance said, gazing skyward. "She never knew woman's lodge. Why have you taken our sun from us, *Heammawihio?*"

"Who can know such things?" Stone Wolf asked, offering his nephew a reassuring hand. "Man Above's ways are beyond our understanding."

"We'll all of us perish," the Lance muttered as he studied his mother's weary eyes. "All of us."

In the days that followed, Dreaming Wolf, too, believed the long walk of the People might have come to an end. Red Hoop joined her sister on the ridge, and Hoop Woman, despairing, rarely spoke. She no longer cooked food or worked hides. Instead she sat beside a fire and stared at the twisting flames.

"We're a people lost," Stone Wolf said. "A people lost."

When the ghost sickness struck Hoop Woman, Stone Wolf cut strips of flesh from his arms, hoping the blood would purify his soul and hurry a dream. The Arrow-keeper hung necklaces of elk teeth around her neck and sprinkled pounded buffalo horn across her tormented forehead. Finally he sat before *Mahuts,* offering eagle feathers as he invoked the sacred power of the Arrows. They gave no answers he wished to hear, though.

"Nah' koa will die," Stone Lance whispered when he studied his uncle's dispirited face.

"There's nothing we can do?" Dreaming Wolf asked.

"Her daughters call to her from the other side," Stone Wolf explained. "Their song is too sweet. Their need for her too great. Don't cry for them, Nephew. Younger Wolf has surely missed his family. They'll soon be together once more."

"Yes," Stone Lance answered. "All the Rope Men may come to walk Hanging Road before the snows come."

The morning Hoop Woman breathed her last, Stone Lance walked out to the river and cut his hair. He tore his shirt and screamed at the sky.

"Heammawihio, why?" the young man called.

But the ways of the Great Mystery were past comprehension. No word, no sign, no whisper of understanding softened the hurt. If he hadn't had the task of building a scaffold to occupy his hands, Stone Lance might have gone mad. Even so, when he helped Dreaming Wolf place Hoop Woman's withered body on its platform beside her daughters, he trembled. His knees buckled, and afterward he collapsed. Lying there on the cold, rocky ground, he appeared to be little more than a shadow of the cheerful, wide-eyed young man who had greeted the summer.

Stone Lance remained behind when the others returned to the camp. As he stared at the river with solemn, haunted eyes, he seemed terribly lost.

"Leave him to his solitude," Stone Wolf urged when Dreaming Wolf turned back.

"Ne' hyo, the grief's too heavy to bear alone," Dreaming Wolf argued. "We've shared too many dangers. I should help him carry his burden."

"He's no child," Stone Wolf insisted. "He knows the mourning prayers, and he can speak them in his own way. There are times when we all need to walk alone."

Dreaming Wolf reluctantly turned and started back to Arrow Lodge. He didn't believe Stone Wolf understood the icy touch of loneliness. When grief overwhelmed a man, it was good to have others near.

While Stone Lance remained on the ridge, concluding his private mourning, Dreaming Wolf helped Stone Wolf empty the Arrow Lodge of Hoop Woman's possessions. Elk robes and buffalo hides, clay pots and beaded moccasins. . . . There were so few things to represent a lifetime's walk upon the earth. They were piled atop a mound of dry wood and prepared for burning.

The other belongings — even the medicine pouches and sacred articles — were cleansed in cedar smoke. Stone Wolf even fanned the purifying smoke over Arrow Lodge itself, whispering the old prayers as he worked. Afterward he smoked, pondering the difficult days that were coming.

"We'll journey to *Noahvose,*" the Arrow-keeper told Dreaming Wolf. "We'll pray and sacrifice. Perhaps Man Above will show us a path to walk."

Dreaming Wolf nodded, but his heart held no hope. Too many had died. And when Stone Lance returned, they lit the fire together which carried away the possessions of the one who had been mother to both of them those past two years.

"Yahaaaa!" Stone Lance screamed as he drew out a knife and cut the flesh of his arms. *"Nah' koa* is gone!"

"Yahaaaa!" Dreaming Wolf echoed. "Our hearts are heavy with her passing."

"What will we do?" the Lance asked, turning to Stone Wolf. "The world has grown cold and empty. Half our lodges are ashes. We're dying!"

"We'll seek a dream," the Arrow-keeper said, clasping his nephew's bleeding arms. "We'll find a path to walk."

"Will we, *Ne' hyo?*" Dreaming Wolf asked.

"We must," Stone Wolf declared. "It's our obligation."

They struck Arrow Lodge after making the dawn prayers that next morning. Dreaming Wolf and Stone Lance broke down the lodge and packed it on a travois. Stone Wolf himself brought horses from the pony herd. Before the Arrow-keeper could leave, though, Talking Stick and Thunder Coat appeared. Dressed in mourning rags, with their hair cut short, the proud chiefs bore little resemblance to the finely attired men who had so often challenged Stone Wolf's advice in the council.

"Uncle, where are you going?" Talking Stick asked.

Stone Wolf paused for a moment. He didn't see a broken man. Instead the eyes of the boy, White Horn, who had come to share Arrow Lodge and learn the medicine trail gazed somberly at him.

"I go to seek a dream," Stone Wolf explained.

"You would carry *Mahuts* from the People?" Thunder Coat asked. "Now, when we need the protection of the Arrows most of all!"

"This is a place for dying," Stone Wolf told them. "Leave it behind you. I go to *Noahvose*, hoping to invoke the spirits in that sacred place. There, where Sweet Medicine first brought *Ma-*

huts to the People, we may be given a path where we can walk safely. A place where children can grow tall, and the sick will regain the harmony they have lost."

"I have no children," Thunder Coat observed.

"We are lost, all of us," Talking Stick added. "The power of the medicine Arrows is broken. Soon the *Tsis tsis tas* will be no more."

"It may be as you say," Dreaming Wolf admitted as he took charge of the ponies. "But while *Ne' hyo* breathes, there is hope. His dreams have saved the People before. We have to try."

"It's your folly that's brought us to this," Talking Stick said, glaring at Stone Wolf.

"No, it was your son who introduced the ghost sickness to our camp," Dreaming Wolf answered. "Let *Ne' hyo* go and save us from it."

"Go," Thunder Coat said, drawing his brother aside. "If it was Four Toes who invited death among us, he has paid for it. Go and make medicine. Find a cure before we all join him on Hanging Road."

"I will do all I know," Stone Wolf vowed. "If Man Above wills it, the People may yet survive."

Thunder Coat nodded and pointed to the east with a mutilated left hand. Two fingers had been cut in mourning.

"Old man, dream of war," Talking Stick mut-

155

tered. The boyish sadness fled from his eyes, and a new fiery hatred blazed in its place. "Show us how to sweep the *wihio* into memory. He's killed our children. We'll slay his. He's . . ."

Thunder Coat silenced his brother and urged Stone Wolf's departure. "It's the madness," Thunder Coat explained. "It floods our camp."

Stone Wolf frowned. Dreaming Wolf glanced at Stone Lance and nodded. They all understood that much. And more.

The journey to *Noahvose* required long days of difficult going. The old trail alongside Shell River was cut by deep wagon ruts, and the grass which once fed ponies was now gnawed to the roots.

"Soon this place will be barren as winter rock," Stone Lance declared.

"Bull Buffalo can't fatten where there's no grass," Dreaming Wolf added. "Perhaps those who have died are the lucky ones, *Ne' hyo*. The *wihio* will bring the slow death to the rest of us."

"It's the white cloud of my dream," Stone Wolf lamented.

"Soon you'll have another dream," Dreaming Wolf said, mustering his spirits and forcing a smile onto his face. "Many times, despair has haunted us. Our Arrow-keeper has led the

People from dark valleys to sunlit hills before. Ayyyy! It will be that way again!"

"Yes!" Stone Lance agreed.

Stone Wolf tried to reflect their confidence, but age and weariness etched his face with a hundred deep crevices, and he sighed. *Heamma-wihio* would decide what would be. A man, after all, was but a two-legged creature at best.

Not far from the charred prairie where the *wihio* had burned their dead, Dreaming Wolf saw the first of the crazy women. *Hev a tan iu* mothers who had placed husbands and children on scaffolds and watched their lodges vanish in curling clouds of cedar smoke now walked the emptiness of the plain alone, bare-footed, and often naked. They clawed the earth like animals and ran about, howling and waving their arms.

"That's Mountain Dawn," Dreaming Wolf said, pointing to a crazed old woman who was jabbing a broken arrow shaft into the discarded shoe of a *wihio*.

"She had four sons," Stone Wolf muttered, remembering. "All are dead now."

"Winter will bring her peace," Dreaming Wolf observed. "Or the sickness will find her."

"Already she walks with the spirits," Stone Wolf explained as he urged his pony along. It was better to be past that haunted place.

* * *

It was the day after, shortly after midday, when Stone Lance grew feverish.

"Ne' hyo, See' was' sin mit has the ghost sickness," Dreaming Wolf called to his father.

"We must stop then," Stone Wolf said, drawing his pony to a halt.

"No, go on," Stone Lance pleaded. "You must save the People. You must make the medicine prayers before all the Rope Men are dead."

"Noahvose is a place of great power," Stone Wolf noted, "but perhaps Man Above wishes us to suffer here, to invite the dream on Shell River where the ghost sickness first struck at our hearts."

Dreaming Wolf didn't know. His only concern was for the tormented body of his cousin. Even before Dreaming Wolf could dismount, Stone Lance rolled off his horse and sprawled, helpless, in the dusty earth.

"See to him," Stone Wolf said as he turned the horse dragging Arrow Lodge's travois toward the nearby ridge. "I'll prepare a camp. Bring him along slowly."

Dreaming Wolf did as instructed, but it seemed strange. Why had Stone Wolf not seen to the Lance? Wasn't the Arrow-keeper famous for his medicine cures? Making camp would tax the old man's strength. But, of course, there was no questioning Stone Wolf. He would have reasons for acting in this way.

Dreaming Wolf helped his cousin back atop

158

the horse and tied his writhing body there. Then, leading both Stone Lance's pony and his own horse, Dreaming Wolf followed the trail left by the travois. Up and up, ever higher, they plodded along. Finally, near the summit of the ridge, Dreaming Wolf saw a fire blazing. The horses grazed nearby, but Arrow Lodge remained packed on its travois. Only a few medicine bags had been removed.

"Make a bed for him beside the fire," Stone Wolf suggested, pointing to an appropriate place. "Then join my prayers."

Dreaming Wolf unbound Stone Lance and helped him to the fire. Then Dreaming Wolf saw to the horses and made beds for Stone Wolf and himself, as well as for the Lance.

"Now I can smoke," Stone Wolf said, drawing out a pipe. As he invoked Earth and Sky and the spirits of the cardinal directions, the Arrow-keeper's weary gaze fell upon the tormented face of his nephew. Stone Lance's brow was bubbling with sweat, and he shivered as the sickness gripped him.

"Touch the pipe to his lips," Stone Lance said when he passed the pipe to his son. Dreaming Wolf smoked, then placed the pipe to his tormented cousin's mouth. Stone Wolf then accepted the pipe and smoked again. The old man drew the sacred smoke into his lungs and exhaled it into the crisp mountain air.

"*Heammawihio,* I come to ask a dream," the

159

Arrow-keeper whispered. Afterward, he sang an old chant and bared himself. Dreaming Wolf, too, stripped, and the two of them danced beside their stricken companion.

"I will cut myself," Stone Wolf explained when he ceased his song and knelt beside the fire once more. "I'll eat nothing. I must concern myself with the welfare of the People."

"And Stone Lance?" Dreaming Wolf asked, shaking.

"You must help him through the dark night of his sickness, *Naha'*. You know all I can teach you. Use your power to bring him back to us. He'll be needed in the difficult winter that's coming."

"Ne' hyo, I have no power to drive off this sickness," Dreaming Wolf cried. "The old chants and the many medicines we've made failed to drive the fever from Hoop Woman and the girls."

"He's strong," Stone Wolf argued. "You are bonded, the two of you. Join your heart to his, and the two of you will defeat this dark cloud. Trust yourself to do it."

"Ne' hyo?"

"Naha', you're a boy no longer," Stone Wolf insisted. "You have walked man's road too many days. Give him your strength. Call him back from the other side. Restore the harmony that's left him. You'll require company on the road you must walk."

160

"I know," Dreaming Wolf said, gazing at the fever-racked body of his cousin. "Don't worry, *Ne' hyo*. He didn't let me fall to the Crows. I'll bring him back from this ghost sickness."

Stone Wolf nodded somberly. He then resumed his chanting and left Dreaming Wolf to begin the medicine cure.

Thirteen

Dreaming Wolf labored long and hard to drive the ghost sickness from his young cousin. He fed Stone Lance only a broth made of freshly killed prairie hen. As for water, Dreaming Wolf located a small spring near the summit of the ridge, and its cool, sparkling liquid seemed to fill the Lance with new life.

"Heammawihio," Dreaming Wolf prayed each night, "drive off this demon sickness. Bring him back from the other side to us. He's needed."

Stone Wolf, too, worked hard. He prayed, danced, and chanted, invoking every spirit in hopes of finding a vision. A hundred times the Arrow-keeper cut the flesh of his arms and chest, but his dreams remained empty. He saw only the dark void of a cloud-choked heaven.

"The sky has hidden its light," Stone Wolf remarked as he sat with his son, gazing overhead. "Where are the moon and stars? Swallowed by the darkness."

"Is it a sign, *Ne' hyo?*" Dreaming Wolf asked. "Will the People be eaten by their grief? Will the ghost sickness carry all of us away?"

"No," Stone Wolf declared. "Even now, Stone Lance brightens. You remain unbothered. We'll find a way to restore our power, *Naha'*. We must!"

But as the days of fasting and exhausting effort mounted, Stone Wolf himself grew feverish.

"The fever may bring on a vision," the Arrow-keeper objected when Dreaming Wolf wrapped the old man in buffalo hides and offered him broth.

"No, *Ne' hyo,*" Dreaming Wolf argued. "The dream isn't coming. You must not die."

Stone Wolf gazed at his son with troubled eyes. Dreaming Wolf knew his father welcomed death before failure. All hope of a vision faded when he accepted the broth. But Dreaming Wolf smiled gratefully.

"You'll grow stronger, *Ne' hyo,* as Stone Lance has," Dreaming Wolf predicted confidently. "The People won't die."

In truth, Dreaming Wolf had doubts, but when Stone Lance cracked open his eyes and joined in the morning prayers that next day, the world itself seemed brighter.

"You've come back," Dreaming Wolf told his cousin. "Ayyyy! Man Above has answered my prayer."

"It was your need that drew me back," the Lance said. "My father told me the story of your bow."

"Yes?"

"How when he lay bleeding, his shield arm hacked away, you came to him and asked for a bow. He promised to make it, and honor forced him to rise and do that one final task. In doing it, he regained his pride and became Younger Wolf once more."

"I asked for no bow from you, *See' was' sin mit,*" Dreaming Wolf noted.

"You asked for nothing," Stone Lance admitted. "I heard the sweet songs of my mother and sisters. They held out their soft fingers to me, and I wanted to join them. *Ne' hyo* stood higher up on the trail, gazing sternly. 'I've seen your winter count, *Naha',*' he told me, 'and your days are not at an end. Go, help your cousin carry the burdens of the People.' Your words then grew louder, and I knew I must return."

"It's good," Dreaming Wolf said, gripping the Lance's young hands. "We'll ride side by side again."

"And did your father find his dream?"

"No," Dreaming Wolf admitted. "Perhaps, when we reach *Noahvose,* it will come."

"Perhaps," the Lance agreed. "Or it may come to you instead."

* * *

164

Dreaming Wolf suspected afterward that in his brief walk on the other side, Stone Lance might well have seen some hint of tomorrow. How else would he have known of the dream?

It came that very night, uninvited and unexpected. At first, there was only darkness. Then, storming from the center of an immense explosion of yellow flame, thundered Bull Buffalo.

"Have you forgotten the helpless ones?" he shouted. "Where are the men who once called themselves *Tsis tsis tas?* Are there none left who stand two-footed as men? Have they all become yellow dogs to hide their tails and yap at each other?"

Dreaming Wolf then felt himself stepping out onto a thundercloud. He approached Bull Buffalo naked and small, as men had always stood before the spirits.

"I haven't forgotten," the Wolf whispered respectfully.

"What's this?" Bull Buffalo fumed. "A mouse? Speak as a man speaks, and I will hear."

"I have forgotten nothing!" Dreaming Wolf shouted.

"Others have," Bull Buffalo said, tearing at the earthlike cloud with his forefoot.

"Yes, and we have suffered for their ignorance. *Ne' hyo* has warned, but always they have turned to their own purposes. It's a sad day when wisdom is ignored."

"When men are deaf to warnings, and they are too blind to see the sacred road before their feet, then they must leave the earth to others," Bull Buffalo suggested. "Once Sweet Medicine gave power to the *Tsis tsis tas*. He issued stern prophecies. Each has come to pass because his words were ignored. Now my children feel the sting of *wihio* bullets. Men kill who don't make the sacred prayers, who ignore the proper ceremonies. If this continues, I will no longer walk the world. The helpless will starve, for there will be no meat to feed them. Trees will vanish, and rivers will dry up. The world will be like a smoked ash, barren and lifeless."

"That must never come to pass!" Dreaming Wolf cried. "The People cannot die! We must not vanish like the Mandan, living on only in the memory of grandmothers' stories."

"Then you must fight to stop these bad things," Bull Buffalo demanded. "You must restore the old power, insist the appropriate prayers be made. Hunt so that meat is made ready for winter's need. Only in this manner can the People regain their strength. Only then will it be possible to survive."

"I'll do it all," Dreaming Wolf vowed.

"Then there is hope, *Naha'*. Stand tall, and speak with the voice given you by the power of your medicine dreams. I will come again and show you a path." Bull Buffalo pawed the ground once more, snorted gray smoke, and charged. Dreaming Wolf threw his arms out to his sides and waited for horns to tear at his chest. Instead the spirit vanished, and a voice whispered, "You've done well, my son. You have courage, and that, above all, is required. Remember my words."

Darkness then enveloped the vision, and Dreaming Wolf slept until morning. When he awoke, he discovered Stone Lance had already kindled a fire. Stone Wolf sat beside the flickering flame. readying a pipe.

"Ne' hyo, your suffering is over," Dreaming Wolf noted.

"Yes, the dream came," Stone Wolf noted. "My prayer was answered."

"What did you see?" Dreaming Wolf asked.

"I?" the Arrow-keeper asked. "The dream filled your sleep, *Naha'*."

"How did you know?" Dreaming Wolf asked, gazing first at his father before turning toward Stone Lance. "Both of you?"

"We read it in your movements," Stone Lance explained. "We heard you speak. Now you must share your recollection of the vision."

"Yes," Stone Wolf agreed. "I'll help you understand."

"The message is easily comprehended," Dreaming Wolf said. He then described the images he'd seen and recounted the words of Bull Buffalo. Each warning was noted gravely.

"It's clear what we must do," Stone Wolf declared. "Our journey is at an end. We'll return to the People and tell them of Bull Buffalo's admonition. Then we must hunt so that the helpless ones will not suffer when the snows come."

"What of the *wihio?*" Stone Lance asked. "Should we fight him?"

"We must be careful not to bring his sickness back among the People," Stone Wolf replied. "We must turn away from his guns and iron pots. We'll erect a new sweat lodge and help the men purify themselves. As we turn back to the old ways, we'll revive the ancient power held by the *Tsis tsis tas.*"

"Many will retain their guns," Dreaming Wolf argued. "The chiefs have never heeded such advice before."

"Never have we known such death," Stone Wolf argued. "Who can ignore the empty lodges, the riderless horses, and the deserted camps? I will not be the only one to speak, either. You, my son, will stand tall as you explain your vision."

Dreaming Wolf nodded, but he wasn't certain of any of it. Nevertheless, they packed up the camp and readied the horses. After making the morning prayers, they attached the travois to one pony and placed their horn saddles atop

168

others. Then they began the long ride west-ward, toward what remained of the *Hev a tan iu* camps.

Three long, seemingly endless days they rode. Dreaming Wolf led the way, and he was careful to keep the small party away from curious parties of Crow hunters or small bands of *wihio* traders. The Wolf also avoided the old *wihio* wagon camps, for he feared even now the ghost sickness lingered there. They carried enough spring water to satisfy their needs, so he saw no need to travel the rutted Shell River road.

Dreaming Wolf was somewhat relieved that the crazy women had vanished, but the forests of scaffolds on the ridges had grown even larger. Many of the Rope Men remained sick, and what was worse, visitors from other bands had spread the fever to their people, too.

Dancing Lance was the first to greet the re-turning Arrow-keeper.

"Have you found a path we can walk, Uncle?" Dancing Lance asked.

"Dreaming Wolf has had a vision," Stone Wolf explained. "He will stand with me in the council and explain."

"There are few chiefs left to make a coun-cil," Dancing Lance noted. "Even Whirlwind is sick now, and many of his people are dead."

"We should leave this cursed place," Dreaming Wolf advised. "There are good springs north of here, on Horse Creek."

"Crows camp there," Dancing Lance argued. "We are too weak to face an enemy."

"Crows are on Shell River, too," Stone Lance complained. "Their scouts will have seen the new scaffolds of the many dead. Soon all will know our sorrow."

"We'll be less troubled on Horse Creek," Stone Wolf suggested. "There's game there, and good grass for the ponies. Our hunters can stay near, and camp can be made on easily defended hillsides."

"We must leave," Dreaming Wolf insisted. "There can be no camping where the ghost sickness has visited. Even leaving, we should purify the People. A new sweat lodge can be erected nearby, away from the foul odor of death. Everything we own must be cleansed in cedar smoke or burned."

"It's a lot to do," Dancing Lance said, frowning. "We're weak now. Those able will be overburdened."

"Is it so much?" Stone Lance asked. "Shall we allow the People to die?"

So it was that Dancing Lance assembled the remaining Fox Warriors and sent them to explain his decision. Thunder Coat and Talking Stick, together with a few Crazy Dogs, argued against the need for such extreme precautions, but those who had survived held a great dread for the ghost sickness, and their voices were many and loud.

"We may yet save the *Hev a tan iu,*" Dreaming Wolf said as he and Stone Lance constructed the sweat lodge.

"It's your doing, *Nah nih,*" the Lance observed. "Your dream has offered us hope."

"It will be harder to convince the chiefs to heed Bull Buffalo's other admonitions," Dreaming Wolf grumbled. "To take a sweat and wave smoke over one's possessions isn't so much. To abandon rifles and iron pots will be hard for many."

"Some won't do it."

"I know," Dreaming Wolf said, frowning. "And there will be many who urge revenge on the *wihio*. That will bring us only more dying."

"Are you certain the dream forbade such a raid? It seems to me we should sweep the strange ones from our country."

"Even our cousins at Shell River?"

"Shell River is ours no longer," Stone Lance observed. "But these good hills and swift rivers are different. If we find *wihio* here, we should punish them."

"Are you so hungry for killing, *See' was' sin mit?*" Dreaming Wolf asked. "Would you bloody your lance?"

"I could pass my old age in peace and never miss the stench of death, *Nah nih*. But others vow vengeance. Antler has taken up a Crazy Dog lance, and he means to make a suicide charge. Others are of like mind. There will be a fight."

"And death."

"Yes, that, too. *Nah nih,* your father has always argued against what is bound to be, and the chiefs turned against him. If you, too, stand in their path, they will turn aside from your words."

"What you say is true," Dreaming Wolf confessed. "But if we only honor that part of the dream that's easy, will we avoid the terrible fate Bull Buffalo spoke of?"

"We can only do what's possible."

"Yes, but will it be enough?" Dreaming Wolf asked.

Even as he sat in the sweat lodge with other young men, Dreaming Wolf knew it would be as Stone Lance had predicted. Men readied their weapons for war, and the chiefs instructed boys as young as twelve in the power of medicine charms and the need to follow the soldier chiefs in battle.

"Watch them and learn!" Dancing Lance urged. "Don't rush to your death! We are few, and each man must save himself for the obligations he must carry this winter."

While the women and surviving old people

escorted the children among the pony drags, parties of warriors rode out to scout the nearby hills and find meat for the cook fires. Bull Buffalo provided for the People's needs. Later, in the hills, deer and antelope proved abundant.

"This is a good place!" Talking Stick boasted as he rode among the young men, waving his painted lance. "Ayyyy! We'll soon be strong once more!"

Some boys shouted, but the women yelled taunts, and some of the warriors turned away, scowling.

"It was his son who brought death among the People," many whispered.

"If he hadn't ignored *Mahuts,* we might have avoided this summer of death," Otter Foot observed.

Nevertheless, when Talking Stick and Thunder Coat carried a pipe through the newly erected camp, many flocked to their sides.

"There are *wihio* camped on Horse Creek," Thunder Coat explained. "Not many, but enough to foul the water and spread death in this good country as they did on Shell River."

"We should kill them all!" Talking Stick argued.

"You spoke this way before, and we found only death," Dancing Lance reminded them. "Remember the old ways. Take presents to *Mahuts.* Invite the favor of the Arrows. Then we can make strong medicine and paint ourselves. When the proper preparations are completed, the *wihio* can feel the sting of our arrows."

"Yes," others called. "Consult *Mahuts*. Go and talk to Stone Wolf."

Talking Stick grumbled and kicked the earth, but Thunder Coat readily agreed. Accompanied by Antler, whose blood was hot for revenge, the two chiefs brought their pipe to Arrow Lodge.

Dreaming Wolf would long remember that day, for he sat with his father when the chiefs offered their eagle-feather presents. He smoked the pipe with them and listened as Talking Stick patiently explained the proposed raid. For once, the Stick was calm, and his reverent manner drew a smile from Stone Wolf.

"Once, not so long ago, you sat here, learning the power of *Mahuts'* medicine," Stone Wolf said as he emptied the pipe's ashes beside the fire. "The Arrows hold great power, but even they cannot protect a man who ignores their advice."

Stone Wolf then allowed Talking Stick to speak to the Arrows, but instead of moving through the sacred smoke as always before, they remained rigid after the chief had urged *Mahuts'* aid for the war party.

"Something is wrong," Talking Stick noted.

Stone Wolf rose and gazed warily at the Arrows. An uneasy feeling flooded the lodge, and

Antler rubbed his hands together to cast off an odd chill.

"Look," Stone Wolf said, turning the Arrows so that the light of the fire illuminated the points. Small flakes of blood stained the flint points.

"It's the sickness," Thunder Coat said. "The sacred Arrows share the People's torment."

"You must not strike the enemy," Stone Wolf advised. "Our power is broken, and we cannot renew the Arrows before next summer. Winter will be hard, and the young men must devote their efforts to hunting."

"Old man, will you always use your tricks to fight us?" Talking Stick demanded. "Don't you know we will fight the *wihio* anyway?"

"Are you blind? Don't you see the blood?" Dreaming Wolf asked, touching one of the arrowheads. The blood was fresh, and it ran down his finger. "Don't you understand anything? *Ne' hyo* warned you before, and you ignored him. You bring death again and again to us."

"I have already vowed to die," Antler said, rising before the Stick could answer. "I will ride ahead and die. Then, if others would share my fate, they may charge, too. I hear this warning of death, and I see *Mahuts* can't urge it. But I intend to fight the *wihio* on Horse Creek even if I must ride alone."

"You won't," Talking Stick promised.

"And the young men who will hurry their deaths?" Stone Wolf asked.

"Already many of us climb Hanging Road," Antler noted. "We'll leave behind us the pain that is life. On the other side, friends wait to welcome us."

Fourteen

Dreaming Wolf watched with dismay as Thunder Coat and Talking Stick walked among the young men, taunting them, inciting them to action.

"Are we to let the *wihio* fill our camps with death once more?" the Stick shouted. "Where are the Elks? The Bowstrings? Can only Crazy Dogs fight? What has become of the brave hearts who once called themselves Foxes?"

"We are here," Otter Foot responded. "Our chief says the Arrows are fouled. It's for us to wait."

"As a woman waits," Thunder Coat said, laughing. "Look beneath your breechclouts! See if you are men!"

"Feel the sides of your heads!" Dancing Lance answered. "Have you ears? You always speak of fighting, Talking Stick. You say your dreams hold power and promise success. When have we seen your power? When have you known success? Stone Wolf argues against this

177

raid, and we've seen what happens when the Arrow-keeper is ignored. Many die. You walk alone because your sons have climbed Hanging Road. I wish my sons to grow taller before I build their scaffolds!"

"Yes!" others cried. "Listen to the Arrow-keeper."

"Old men are always content to wait," Talking Stick declared angrily. "Their fighting days are over. They've counted coup and won favor. They have many horses to give for a wife. Among us are many who desire to walk man's road. They would fight the enemies of the People. Stand tall, brothers, and let yourselves be known!"

Antler was the first to step over beside Talking Stick, but not the last. Many others followed.

"It's easy for you to die, Antler," River Fork said sourly. "We all know who broke the admonition and brought the *wihio* sickness into your lodge. You wear the guilt of it like a bloody shirt for all to see. Do you ask the rest of us to join you? To die?"

"I will charge the enemy," Antler explained. "I will ride down on them alone. If there are those who wish to follow, I'm glad of it. But even if no one else leaves our camp, I'll go."

"Are we *Hev a tan iu?*" Thunder Coat asked. "Can we watch this brave heart draw the fire of our enemy with no hope of knowing his sacrifice has bought our victory?"

"The *wihio* should pay for my dead brother's life," Bent Arrow argued. "I'll fight."

Others, too, shouted their intentions to ride.

"If it's to be done, we should make medicine," Dancing Lance declared. "We should paint our faces and decorate our ponies. The shield carriers should lead the way and turn the *wihio* bullets."

"Will you join us, then?" Thunder Coat asked.

"I won't let a young Fox ride to his death unaided," Dancing Lance replied. "We must gather in our warrior societies and smoke. We'll make medicine charms and dance."

"While the *wihio* escapes?" Antler asked.

"Where would they go?" Dancing Lance asked. "They've come to hunt, and none will leave until they have meat."

"He's right," Thunder Coat agreed. "Even so, scouts should go and watch the enemy camp."

"I'll go," Antler volunteered.

"Then it's for me to follow," young Lizard Tail argued. "I, too, have lost all my family."

"You're too young," Dancing Lance argued.

"I'm not," Bent Arrow said, stepping out from the others. "I have felt the sting of Crow arrows, and I am a Fox. I won't act without caution, and I can be trusted not to run away."

"He's a good choice," Dancing Lance agreed.

"Then that, at least, is decided," Talking Stick muttered. "Go, but keep your eyes open.

179

We must know what the *wihio* are doing."

"You will," Antler vowed.

But if who would watch the *wihio* camp was easily decided, nothing else was. The soldier bands had lost many of their chiefs, and they quarreled among themselves as to whom should be the head men. Some of the older fighters insisted the young ones remain behind.

"What could that one do to harm a *wihio?*" Walks in the Sun asked. "Only yesterday he was sucking his mother's breast!"

The boy in question, Whirlwind's eleven-year-old son Grass Snake, barked an angry reply. Clearly, though, the child had to be left. He lacked the strength to hold a war lance, and he was no famous shot with a bow.

Finally, a party of twenty men did form. Most were Elks and Crazy Dogs, but Dancing Lance and Raven's Wing were there to represent the Foxes.

"Who will provide the bulletproof medicine?" Dancing Lance asked when the band prepared to mount their horses.

"My brother and I carry shields," Talking Stick boasted. "Antler will draw the bullets onto himself. We'll strike hard and fast, before the *wihio* can reload."

"You're fools," Dancing Lance grumbled. "Antler's charge won't break the wall of barrels and rocks they've put around their camp. Your ponies will be repulsed, and when you charge on foot, the *wihio* will kill you."

"What should we do, then?" Talking Stick asked. "Make the *wihio* vanish?"

"Blind them," Dancing Lance argued. "As in the old times, use horn powder to paint yourselves. Sunlight will dance on its surface, and the enemy will be blinded."

"We must speak the ancient prayers and perform a war dance, too," Dreaming Wolf found himself suggesting.

"It's a fine notion," Dancing Lance agreed. "But are you joining this fight, Wolf?"

"We're Foxes," Stone Lance said, stepping to his cousin's side. "We always choose the difficult things to do."

"Ayyyy!" the young men howled. "With these good men with us, we can't fail."

Dreaming Wolf glanced at Dancing Lance and frowned. Neither of them thought this raid a good idea, and now both were lending it their efforts. Worse, although Talking Stick and Thunder Coat nodded at their suggestions, the chiefs ignored caution and plunged into battle unprepared. No prayers were spoken, and no dance was held. Instead, the Stick ordered horses readied. Soon Thunder Coat was forming the warriors into three lines.

"Talking Stick will lead the first, and the second band will ride with me," Thunder Coat announced. "The others will follow Dancing Lance."

"Ayyyy!" the young men shouted. "It's a good plan."

It wasn't, though. Half the warriors joined Dancing Lance, and only three led their horses to where Talking Stick stood waiting. Those three were the youngest, and only Black Beaver had ridden to battle before. He was yet to see his fourteenth winter.

"I'm no older," Stone Lance said when Dreaming Wolf grumbled that the boys were all too young.

"The Stick will lead them all to their deaths," Dreaming Wolf complained.

"Then we must ride with them," Stone Lance said, frowning. "I'm Younger Wolf's son, after all, and you carry the bow he made."

"Nothing lives long," Dreaming Wolf whispered. "I'm at your side, *See' was' sin mit.*"

They rode out in their three ragged lines, quietly singing old warrior songs and braving up for the fight. Once they joined the small camp Bent Arrow and Antler had made overlooking the *wihio* camp, the raiders dismounted and painted their faces. While the chiefs discussed their plans, the others tied medicine charms behind ears or braided feathers in their hair. Once a plan was settled upon, each fighter tied his pony's tail and silently spoke a final medicine prayer.

"I'm to go first," Antler reminded his companions as he mounted his horse. The young

182

man had painted his face black as night, and his chest bore other death signs. He kicked his pony into a gallop and raced off down the hill, screaming at the startled *wihio* hunters.

For a brief instant, Dreaming Wolf thought Antler might dash through the confused whites and escape unharmed. But as he closed on the stone and barrel wall, three shots rang out. The pony went down, and Antler slammed into a barrel, breaking it apart with a war ax as he screamed furiously. Already he had been hit twice by bullets, and a burly *wihio* rushed over and shoved a shotgun into young Antler's face. The gun exploded, tearing Antler's head from his shoulders. What remained of the brave heart fell to the earth.

"Ayyyy!" Talking Stick screamed, waving his lance. "There was a brave death. Who will follow me and win such honor!"

The Stick raced off down the hill, and his young companions followed. Dreaming Wolf and Stone Lance had difficulty keeping up at first, but when they grew closer, Talking Stick held back. Black Beaver raced ahead and was blasted from his horse by a volley of rifle fire. Two young companions had their horses shot, and the third slumped across his pony's neck, shot through the side.

"Brave up!" Stone Lance called to the two dismounted boys. "I'm coming!"

The Lance then kicked his pony into a gallop

and raced to the nearest boy. Pausing but an instant, Stone Lance pulled the youngster up behind him and raced away. Dreaming Wolf watched with approval, then repeated his cousin's effort. The second boy climbed up and was safely carried away. Only Black Beaver remained. There was no helping him.

"Once more you led us well!" Dreaming Wolf shouted at Talking Stick.

The Stick, stung by the words, raised his lance and charged the enemy alone. It was a wild, reckless ride, and it won nothing but a grudging admiration from his companions. Talking Stick raised his shield and seemingly turned the *wihio* bullets. His horse whined as it was struck again and again. Talking Stick himself had a braid of hair shot away and a silver charm torn from his ear.

"Brave up!" Thunder Coat howled when his brother returned. "We're next."

Thunder Coat led a party of young Elks toward the *wihio,* but the whites were no longer alarmed. They held their fire, and they aimed well. When their rifles barked, the charging Rope Men vanished in smoke and dust. Only four emerged alive. Led by Thunder Coat, they fled in panic, leaving their arms behind.

"Your shield!" Talking Stick shouted.

Stone Lance howled furiously and charged toward the discarded shield. Weaving his way magically between flying bullets, he managed to reach down and clasp the shield. Then his horse screamed as bullets tore into its heart.

Dreaming Wolf raced to rescue his cousin, and the three *wihio* who had left the safety of their rock and barrel wall quickly retreated. The Wolf halted his horse and drew his shaken cousin up behind him. They then completed their escape.

"We must not leave our brothers to be mutilated!" Dancing Lance argued as Thunder Coat mounted a spare pony and started to depart.

"We can at least return them to camp," Dreaming Wolf added.

"They are nothing," Talking Stick complained. "We've done enough. Ayyyy! The *wihio* hunters will remember this day and wet themselves!"

"What should they fear?" Stone Lance asked. "They've killed us. Look and see who's bleeding?"

"Who will follow me?" Dancing Lance called.

Those still able to ride nudged their ponies onward, and the band made a final charge. Again, Stone Lance had a pony shot from beneath him, but, using Thunder Coat's shield to deflect the *wihio* bullets, he crawled to Antler and dragged the young man's bloody corpse back up the hill. The other dead were also recovered, and although some of the living had to walk in order to tie the dead across ponies, all started homeward.

* * *

It was only a short distance back to the camp, and the abrupt return of the raiders surprised the boys watching the pony herd. Two called out in alarm while a third raced to the camp to summon help.

"They think we're raiding Crows," Dreaming Wolf told Dancing Lance. "Have we changed so much that no one recognizes us?"

Perhaps we have, Dreaming Wolf thought as he gazed at his companions. Their clothes were in disarray, and sweat wove streaks through their war paint. Many bled from wounds. Although Dreaming Wolf had no holes in him, his hair had become unbound and flew behind him like a horse's tail. Behind him, Stone Lance trembled with exhaustion. Battered and torn from two hard falls, the Lance had miraculously escaped the stinging bullets.

Thunder Coat and Talking Stick rode ten paces ahead of the others. Stone Lance had returned Thunder Coat's shield, and the chief now carried it on a limp left arm. The life seemed to drain from the brothers, and they had no words to cheer their weary followers.

"Look, it's Talking Stick!" Grass Snake called from the camp.

"They aren't Crows," Grass Snake's young sister, Flute, complained. "Our warriors have returned."

A crowd soon assembled to welcome the returning band, but the welcoming howls were quickly muted. Instead, mourning wails rose from wives and sisters as the dead were taken down from the ponies. The wounded gathered near Arrow Lodge, and Stone Wolf began examining their injuries.

"What's happened?" men called.

"Surely the *wihio* are all dead, but where are their scalps?" River Fork asked. "Haven't you brought back their ponies?"

"We took no horses," Dancing Lance answered. Turning to Talking Stick and Thunder Coat, the Fox chief waited for either to explain. Neither spoke.

"Antler was the first to fall," Dreaming Wolf said, staring bitterly at the headless corpse that lay, untended, beside Arrow Lodge. "He was alone, and he welcomed death. Too many others fell, though, and for what purpose?"

"They won honor," Talking Stick argued.

"Black Beaver was little more than a boy," Dancing Lance said, frowning. "You led him to his death, Talking Stick. You made no preparations!"

"We surprised them," Talking Stick insisted. "They . . ."

"What?" Dreaming Wolf asked. "You said before we frightened them! How? They stood and shot us down. They remain as they were before, camped on Horse Creek. You say we scared them. No, they're laughing at us the way a mountain cat laughs at a rabbit. The rabbit can be brave, but he will soon be dead anyway. You listen to no one, and it is you who has returned unhurt. No medicine and rage are poor strategy. Good friends are dead, and what has it gained us?"

"They'll be remembered," Thunder Coat argued. "Their brave heart deeds will be sung around many council fires."

"I hope so," Dancing Lance said, glaring at the other chiefs. "Perhaps we others may remember their pointless sacrifice and insist the sacred prayers be spoken before we ride out to war. We've ignored *Mahuts* too often and suffered for it. Let's learn from these deaths."

"If *Mahuts* had ridden with us . . ." Talking Stick began.

"Silence!" Dancing Lance shouted. "We need no more words from you! A man who leads others to their deaths and then holds back has no honor, and his words are worthless."

"You have no right to speak that way to me!" the Stick screamed. "You saw my charge!"

"We saw everything," Dancing Lance replied. "And some of us will long remember it."

"Many of us," Bent Arrow added.

Fifteen

After the wounded were treated and the dead were mourned, the Fox Warriors met in council to recount brave heart deeds and plan a final buffalo hunt.

"No one counted coup on the *wihio*," Dancing Lance lamented, "but many performed well. We left no dead behind. Some proved the power of their medicine, for many bullets were turned. Others proved the sharpness of their eyes while watching the enemy camp."

Dancing Lance then spoke of Bent Arrow's vigilance. The Arrow, who already bore the scars of wounds inflicted by the Crows, displayed a shirt twice nicked by *wihio* bullets. The Foxes howled their approval, and Dancing Lance tied a hawk feather in the young man's hair.

"One among us showed he is among the bravest of the brave, though," Bent Arrow spoke as he turned to reclaim his place in the circle of warriors. "He's young, but all of us have watched him. Once a thirteenth summer would have been passed holding a brother's ponies or swimming the creek with his age-mates, but no longer. The People require fighters, and so Stone Lance has joined our band, standing first among us."

"Ayyyy!" the others cried. "He's a brave heart."

"This young one charged the enemy," Dancing Lance explained. "He rode into the heart of the *wihio* bullets, singing the ancient songs and relying on his medicine. When Thunder Coat lost his shield, it was Stone Lance who retrieved it. When others thought to flee, leaving the dead and wounded behind, Stone Lance rode through the stinging bullets to claim Antler. Twice his pony was shot from under him!"

The others howled louder, and Stone Lance felt their eyes fall on him.

"Come forward, brother," Dancing Lance called, and Dreaming Wolf helped his cousin rise. As the others sang the Fox song, Stone Lance walked to the chief and stood stiffly while Dancing Lance tied two eagle feathers in his hair. "He doesn't stand tall in the way some men measure themselves," the chief observed, "but it's a man's heart that counts. Here is a man who walks as his father walked, devoting himself to his brothers. Ayyyy! Here's a man of the People!"

"There's another!" Stone Lance shouted.

"Yes, we know of him," Dancing Lance replied. "Even a brave heart may fall, and so it was at Horse Creek. Stone Lance, who rescued the fallen shield, required rescuing himself. His cousin, Dreaming Wolf, who warned loudly the peril of ignoring the medicine prayers, rode swiftly to rescue this brave heart."

"Ayyyy!" the Foxes shouted. "Another brave heart is honored."

Now came Dreaming Wolf's turn to stand before his friends, listening to their account of his rescue. When the last words were spoken, Dancing Lance tied an eagle feather in the Wolf's hair and rested a heavy hand on his shoulder.

"Here is our future, brothers," Dancing Lance explained. "These two know the power of the Arrow medicine, and we can trust their words. Heed them. Rely on their far-seeing eyes. So long as we keep our hearts pure and devote ourselves to the helpless ones, the Foxes will enjoy success."

Dreaming Wolf warmed at the notion. Standing beside Stone Lance, glowing in the admiration of friends and elders, he felt new hope surge through his insides. Perhaps they would be the two to lead the *Tsis tsis tas* out of their nightmare into a better future.

The Foxes passed those last days before the first snow hunting and butchering meat. Bull

Buffalo was elusive, though, and too few deer and elk fell to Fox arrows. Worse, the other warrior societies continued to harass the *wihio* hunters and ignore their responsibilities.

"This will be another starving winter," Stone Wolf told the council. He was right.

Even as the first powdery snow fell on the *Hev a tan iu* camp, children began to whine. There weren't enough warm buffalo hides to replace those burned to drive off the ghost sickness. Too many felt the icy fingers of winter. Soon hunger struck, and the suffering of the helpless ones began.

"*Heammawihio,* help us," Dreaming Wolf prayed as snow cloaked the hills. "Give us the true aim. Send elk and deer to warm and clothe the helpless ones."

But there was never enough. As the Hard Face Moon filled the heavens, the dying began.

First were the very old. They gave over their warm hides to grandchildren and stepped out, ragged and barefoot, into the snows to find their deaths. Day after day, the pony boys came across them, their stiff bodies sheathed in glittering ice.

Little ones, too, climbed Hanging Road. Few born survived their first night, for mothers lacked the strength to bring healthy infants into the light.

"They're fortunate," Dancing Lance said as he sat beside Stone Wolf's warming fire. "Winter-born children never grow tall and strong as others do, and they would only have known the torments that visit life."

Dreaming Wolf couldn't accept that. He read the same grief in the mothers' eyes that followed the death of any child, and if their fathers were less likely to weep openly, the hurt was nevertheless present in their eyes.

Whenever the snows relented, and the sun climbed high in the morning sky, Dreaming Wolf would lead a party of hunters into the thickets along Horse Creek. Usually they would find a deer or perhaps rabbits. It was never enough, but fresh meat was a tonic to those who shared it, and the hunt freed the Wolf and his companions from the gloom which hung over the *Hev a tan iu* camp like a teetering boulder.

Eventually winter passed. Cold and hunger had thinned the band, but many had managed to survive.

"Once, twenty deaths would have torn at my heart," Stone Wolf said as he kindled a cook fire. "Now I feel only relief that more were not taken from us."

"We must insist the hunt is carried out in the old way," Dreaming Wolf said as he added sticks to the fire. "You must remind the People of the sacred path and bring them back to it."

"It's too much to ask," Stone Wolf answered. "I'm a man growing old with too many burdens. There's no sweetness to life. Only dying."

"That will change," Dreaming Wolf argued. "The bands will assemble to remake the earth. Iron Wolf and Goes Ahead may have sons to show you."

"There will be no New Life Lodge this summer," Stone Wolf explained. "Instead we must renew *Mahuts*. Soon I'll journey to *Noahvose* and replace the stained points. Afterward, we'll restore the power of the Arrows."

"Then we'll be strong once more," Dreaming Wolf boasted.

"My dreams say otherwise," Stone Wolf grumbled. "It's the chiefs who will choose the People's path, and I fear they have no eyes to see the danger awaiting us."

"They'll listen to you now, *Ne' hyo,*" Dreaming Wolf said, stoking the fire. "They will remember the raids on the *wihio*. They'll count the dead. Even a fool can see we must put our feet upon a new path."

"Some know only hatred," Stone Wolf argued. "Their voices will be loudest, *Naha'*. Soon I, like my brother, will be only a memory to be whispered on long nights by grandfathers."

"Never!"

"It's true, *Naha'*. When we needed a dream, it didn't come to me. No, you received the vision. It's for you to take up the fight."

Dreaming Wolf gazed deeply into his father's

weary eyes. For the first time, the Arrow-keeper appeared ready to surrender.

"I'm little more than a boy," Dreaming Wolf argued. "No one will listen."

"Sweet Medicine was just a boy when he first spoke to the People," Stone Wolf recounted. "You'll speak with power, *Naha'*. You will know the medicine secrets, and they will mark you."

Dreaming Wolf felt none of his father's confidence. If the chiefs ignored a famous man like Stone Wolf, why would they heed the words of a boy of seventeen summers?

Not long afterward, Stone Wolf met with the *Hev a tan iu* chiefs. He dressed in his finest war shirt and buckskin leggings, and he wore the buffalo horn bonnet passed to him long ago.

"The snows are melting," the Arrow-keeper explained to the grim-faced men seated around the council fire. "Soon the grasses will green, and the cottonwoods will grow new leaves."

"All this we know," Talking Stick grumbled. "We're not children to be taught the seasons."

"Quiet," Dancing Lance insisted. "Listen. Let Stone Wolf speak."

"Yes," Whirlwind agreed. "His words have always held wisdom."

"I spoke before of *Mahuts*," Stone Wolf continued. "As always when they are flecked with blood, the People have suffered. Their power must be restored. I will go to *Noahvose*, the sacred heart of the world, and make them over. You must send word to the many bands that the Arrows will be renewed."

"Yes," Dancing Lance agreed. "All the bands will gather, and we'll grow strong."

"It's appropriate," Thunder Coat declared. "We have suffered without the aid of the Arrows."

"It's decided then," Dancing Lance said, nodding to Stone Wolf. "Who will go with you, Uncle?"

"My son and nephew," Stone Wolf replied, glancing at each in turn.

"Cubs!" Talking Stick cried. "An old man and two boys. If the Pawnees find you, *Mahuts* will be lost to us once more."

"The Crazy Dogs would ride with you," Thunder Coat suggested.

"The young men should hunt," Stone Wolf argued. "There's too much hunger in our lodges. I may be old, but I won my shield in battle as a young man. If there's fighting to be done, I can do it. Dreaming Wolf and Stone Lance wear coup feathers in their hair."

"Cubs!" Talking Stick growled.

"I'm small, yes," Stone Lance replied, "but I've left no companion to die alone. *Nah nih* and I have never turned from danger as some

196

have. *Mahuts* will be safe."

"A large party would surely attract the attention of our enemies," Dreaming Wolf added. "Lakotas camp in the sacred hills now, and they have always been our brothers. There's nothing to fear there."

It wasn't entirely true, and all of them knew it. Still, Dreaming Wolf knew there was a purpose to his father's decision to go alone, and he trusted Stone Wolf's actions above all else.

Reluctantly, and in spite of Talking Stick's repeated complaints, the chiefs agreed to assemble the bands while Stone Wolf remade the Arrows.

"Hear me, old man," Talking Stick said when the council disbanded, "guard the Arrows well. We're in need of their power."

Dreaming Wolf scowled. He thought to ask the Stick who most resembled a whining cub, but thought better of insulting a chief. A son should follow, and Stone Wolf was certain to choose a wise path.

Stone Wolf waited only until the snow melted from the buffalo valleys and the horses fattened before setting off toward *Noahvose*. The eastward journey required ten days, and the Arrowkeeper devoted the long ride to sharing the old, half-forgotten stories with his son and nephew. Later, as they climbed the wooded hills toward *Noahvose,* Stone Wolf collected medicine herbs and tested his young companions' knowledge of their use.

"Soon you two will be medicine men," Stone Wolf reminded them. "Draw your power from earth and sky. Maintain the harmony of the world, and weave your way gently through it."

"Yes, *Ne' hyo*," Dreaming Wolf responded. "Haven't we always done so?"

"You have," the Arrow-keeper admitted. He studied the serious frown etched on his son's face and Stone Lance's equally sober countenance. "The People will prosper with your help. It warms my heart to know it will be so."

Not until they climbed *Noahvose* itself did Stone Wolf share the mysterious prayers and ancient chants that accompanied the remaking of *Mahuts*. The shafts, yellow with age, were freed of their tainted points, and the withered fletchings were likewise replaced. Eagle tail feathers were cut to the proper size, and Dreaming Wolf helped his father fix them in place with pine sap. New points were formed of black flint and secured with deer sinew. When all signs of pollution were removed, the Arrows were purified in the smoke of cedar bark and sweet grass, scented with sage.

"Ayyyy!" Stone Wolf howled. "It's good. *Mahuts* may now be renewed."

"The power of the *Tsis tsis tas* will be restored," Dreaming Wolf added. "Our heart will be strong once more."

"What must we do now, Uncle?" Stone Lance asked. "I've seen parties of Pawnees on Shell River, and Rees sometimes visit these hills."

"The spirits of our fathers protect us here," Stone Wolf explained. "Here the ghost of Sweet Medicine walks with the shades of the old ones. Touches the Sky climbed Hanging Road here. Cloud Dancer, my grandfather, knew this sacred mountain. There's nothing to fear."

"Will we wait for the bands, then?" Stone Lance asked.

"Yes, we'll wait," Stone Wolf answered. "And as the days pass, we'll hunt and share this remembered time."

"You'll teach us more about the medicine trail, *Ne' hyo?*" Dreaming Wolf asked.

"I've showed you all that I know," Stone Wolf explained. "You must find the rest in your heart and in your dreams. *Heammawihio* walks here, too. Often he's spoken to me when I've come to *Noahvose.*"

"*Ne' hyo,* you've told us many things," Stone Lance said, stepping closer to his uncle. "And yet I read something else, something unspoken, in your eyes. What is it? Why did you bring us here alone?"

"*Ne' hyo?*" Dreaming Wolf asked.

"We have come to share this time on *Noahvose* because the People will soon rely on you," Stone Wolf explained. "My days are numbered. I have carried too great a burden for too

199

long. The chiefs will lift it soon."

"No," Dreaming Wolf gasped. "We're too young. There's too much we don't know."

"The world is changing, *Naha',*" Stone Wolf replied. "No man, not even an Arrow-keeper, can hold it still. I cannot change what's to be. I can only prepare you for it."

As he had so many times before, Stone Wolf had clearly seen the future. When the ten bands gathered later that summer to renew the Arrows, Stone Wolf walked with a brisker step. He performed the required prayers and saw to every detail of the ceremony. Dreaming Wolf and Stone Lance were at his side, learning, but it was Stone Wolf who directed the ritual.

After the Arrows were renewed, and the bands had completed the final dance, the chiefs met to plan the buffalo hunt. New chiefs were elected to replace those who had died, and many boys were welcomed into the warrior societies. The chiefs spoke of those things and more. Then Talking Stick rose and turned to Stone Wolf.

"Uncle, our power is restored," the Stick began. "You have used the old prayers to bring *Mahuts* back to us, and all of us owe you a great debt."

"It was my obligation," Stone Wolf answered, displaying no emotion.

"No man has kept the Arrows more faithfully," Thunder Coat added. "Always you've conducted the required ceremonies, and you have invited hardship in their name."

"Before, in the old days, it was thought best that *Mahuts* be kept by an old man," Talking Stick said, gazing past Stone Wolf toward *Noahvose*. "White hair brought wisdom, it was thought. But the People now need energy, vitality. You tell us of the dangers we may find, but when have you promised our war parties success? You're tired, and it's time a younger man lifted your burdens."

"It can wait," Stone Wolf argued. "My son is young."

"Too young," Thunder Coat declared. "And you are too old."

"There's much that must be passed on to an Arrow-keeper," Stone Wolf explained. "Prayers. Ceremonies. Cures."

"Who else could keep *Mahuts* safe?" Dancing Lance demanded to know. "Stone Wolf is old, yes, but he's not dying. His sons are brave hearts, and they will be older soon."

"There's another who is prepared to accept the burden," Thunder Coat argued. "When my brother was young, he walked the medicine trail. He shares the Arrow knowledge. He's sponsored New Life Lodge, and he's led the young men in battle. He's worthy of the honor and responsibility."

"Talking Stick?" Whirlwind asked. "Arrow-keeper?"

"It isn't possible!" Iron Wolf cried from the far side of the council. *"Ne' hyo* is old, but he isn't foolish like the Stick. *Mahuts* requires a man of the People to insure their safety."

"Are you prepared to take the burden onto yourself?" Dancing Lance asked.

Iron Wolf gazed at Stone Wolf, and the Arrow-keeper stood.

"My sons are devoted to the People," Stone Wolf announced with great pride. "but Iron Wolf has a young wife and many young men who rely on him to lead them. Goes Ahead, my other son, is no different. My youngest son knows the medicine trail best, and already his dreams hold power. It's to him we should turn."

"Even a brave heart who has known but seventeen summers is too young to carry such a burden," Dancing Lance declared.

"Ne' hyo isn't dead," Dreaming Wolf insisted. *"Mahuts* remain safe in his care."

"He's too old," Thunder Coat grumbled. "It's for Talking Stick to do. His dreams carry power, too, and he will lead us to reclaim our old place as masters of all this good country."

The chiefs argued loudly the choice, but Thunder Coat argued powerfully, and he swayed the others to his opinion.

"My brother will lift the burden from your

202

shoulders, Uncle," Thunder Coat told Stone Wolf. "The People owe you much. You'll always be welcome in our council. Come, sit with us as an old man chief."

"I will never again sit with you in council," Stone Wolf replied. "My days are coming to an end, and I wish only to keep a simple lodge and make medicine. Perhaps I'll craft shields for the young men and make arrows for the children. It's right a grandfather should act in this way."

The chiefs nodded. Afterward, Stone Wolf emptied Arrow Lodge of his possessions and led Dreaming Wolf and Stone Lance aside.

"Ne' hyo, how can you let this happen?" Dreaming Wolf cried. "Talking Stick will lead the People to their death."

"Even when he was White Horn, I knew he would one day keep *Mahuts,"* Stone Wolf explained.

"Then why did you prepare us?" Dreaming Wolf asked. "Why did you teach us the ritual, the prayers?"

"Nothing lasts long," Stone Wolf told them. "Not trees. Not even Bull Buffalo. Talking Stick's days will come to an end, too, and the People will need good men to restore what has been taken away."

"Ne' hyo?" Dreaming Wolf cried.

"Your day is coming," Stone Wolf said, drawing them near. "The rest remains cloudy, but

I'm certain you must one day restore the heart of the People."

"Yes, *Ne' hyo*," Dreaming Wolf vowed.

"We'll do it," Stone Lance promised.

"Then I can rest," Stone Wolf told them. "Soon I'll join the Great Mystery, but first there will be hunting and good days to share. Ayyyy! I feel reborn."

Dreaming Wolf tried to smile, but he couldn't match his father's optimism. Talking Stick was sure to bring difficult trials to the *Tsis tsis tas*. No one could find such a notion cheering.

Sixteen

Even as the warrior societies met to organize the buffalo hunt, Talking Stick was forming a war party.

"Have you learned nothing?" Dancing Lance cried. "First we must hunt Bull Buffalo. We should put the starving winters behind us."

"There can be no living with the *wihio* in our country," Talking Stick argued. "Ayyyy! We must tie up our ponies' tails and paint our faces. Then, when *wihio* bones are baking in the summer sun, we can hunt."

"Brothers, don't listen to this madness!" Dancing Lance shouted. "We must turn back to the old ways and regain our strength."

"No, our feet have found a new path," Talking Stick insisted. "You said to me before that I did not consult *Mahuts*. Who now turns from their advice? The Arrows are remade, and their power now rides with me. Who will follow?"

Young men howled loudly as they hurried to

join the raiding party. Dancing Lance and Whirlwind managed to sway only older men, mostly Fox Warriors long accustomed to their chiefs' good words.

"You surrendered your burden too soon," Dancing Lance told Stone Wolf. "Talking Stick bends even *Mahuts* to his will."

"Perhaps the Arrows direct him," Stone Wolf suggested.

"To ignore the needs of the helpless?" Dreaming Wolf asked. "To neglect our responsibilities? I will never believe that."

"Then you must organize the hunting and hope Bull Buffalo will be generous," Stone Wolf advised. "Without the Buffalo Arrows to lead us, we must rely on the strong arms of our men."

"You could help us perform appropriate prayers," Dancing Lance suggested.

"I can do that much," Stone Wolf agreed. *"Naha'* and Stone Lance will ride with you, and I have passed into their care the old knowledge. Maybe it will be enough."

"I pray so," Dancing Lance said, sighing. Doubt flooded his face.

Stone Wolf thus directed the medicine prayers a final time. Dreaming Wolf and Stone Lance helped, and all three joined the twenty determined hunters who struck a buffalo herd west of *Noahvose*. In spite of the prayers, the hunters brought down only a few animals. With

such a small party, even great men like Whirlwind and Dancing Lance were unable to contain
the herd. Gradually, the buffalo outdistanced
the exhausted hunters and the defenseless camps
that trailed along behind.

"We should ride ahead and continue the
hunt," Otter Foot urged.

"This is Crow country," Whirlwind lamented.
"We can't leave our wives and children here
with only pony boys to defend them. Enough
have died."

Instead the camps broke into small bands.
Men rode out to shoot elk, deer, and antelope.
Boys caught fish in the nearby streams. No one
doubted hunger would stalk the land when the
snows came, and what could be spared was
smoked and set aside. It wouldn't be enough.

"Perhaps it's appropriate our path grows steep
and narrow," Stone Wolf told his son and
nephew. "When there are so many fools among
us, we earn such suffering."

"Can anyone forget the sickness?" Stone
Lance cried. "The hunger?"

"Some remember and vow it won't return,"
Dreaming Wolf noted. "Others recall only the
pain, and it drives them to strike out at an enemy. Talking Stick no longer has sons to feed,
so why should he concern himself over others?"

"Aren't all of us a family?" Stone Lance
asked. "My mother and father are gone, but I
feel kinship for the helpless ones."

"You're a man of the People," Stone Wolf observed. "The Stick is a man haunted by his mistakes. He knows only hatred, and it distorts all he sees."

"Will any of us survive the death he'll bring to us?" Dreaming Wolf asked.

"Who can say?" Stone Wolf asked. "Perhaps your dreams, *Naha'*, will show you a new, better path. I only know the ache of weary bones. My heart is tired, and I want to rest."

Dreaming Wolf frowned. Since abandoning Arrow Lodge to Talking Stick, the three of them had resided in the hunters' camp. Now they passed their nights in the young men's lodge.

"We would be welcome among Iron Wolf's relations," Stone Lance suggested.

"You should go there," Stone Wolf advised the young men. "I will turn east. It's time I climbed *Noahvose* a final time."

"No, *Ne' hyo*," Dreaming Wolf argued. "The People need you."

"I would only be another old man to feed this winter," Stone Wolf argued. "My bones are brittle, and the cold winds torment them. Summer is a better time to climb Hanging Road."

"It's foolish to hurry yourself there," Stone Lance complained. "With Talking Stick to guide us, we'll all of us begin the long walk soon."

"No, you have summers to hunt Bull Buffalo," Stone Wolf told them. "You should know

208

a woman's touch and see the birthing of tall sons."

"They'll need a grandfather," Dreaming Wolf said, gazing intently at his father's wrinkled forehead.

"You can share the old stories with them," Stone Wolf answered. "The memory of what I was. It's all that remains of me."

"And who will craft their first arrows?" Stone Lance asked.

"An uncle can do it," Stone Lance suggested. "I have only a small task left to perform, and to do it I must climb into the heart of the world and greet *Heammawihio*. The Great Mystery has one secret left to share."

There was no lodge to dismantle, and no mountain of possessions to pack. Stone Wolf brought forward the poorest of the pony boys, and Dreaming Wolf presented each a horse.

"In honor of the old ones," Stone Wolf explained. "Once, a man who had more than he needed felt the obligation to share. In this way, one named Wolf Boy once received a pony. Now the sacred hoop that is life has brought me wealth, and I wish to pass it into the hands of those who deserve it."

"Ayyyy!" the boys howled. "He's a man of the People!"

"Long after you've left us," a boy of twelve

summers named Little Mane vowed, "we'll recount your coups, Uncle. The *Hev a tan iu* will always remember the shield-giver, Stone Wolf."

"Ayyyy!" the others shouted. "We'll always remember!"

Stone Lance then readied the six remaining horses possessed by his uncle for the long ride east. Stone Wolf walked among the lodges, seeing to the medicine needs of the sick and speaking a few final words to old friends. It was clearly a final parting, but only Dancing Lance spoke of a farewell.

"We'll hunt Bull Buffalo together again," Dancing Lance promised. "Silver Arm and Younger Wolf already stalk the herd, and the old ones make the ancient prayers."

"Yes, we'll hunt again," Stone Wolf said, clasping the chief's hand. "On the other side."

The ride to *Noahvose* was a slow one, for Stone Wolf didn't hurry it. Instead, he passed the days recounting the events of his boyhood. He told of the Crow fights and the fine days passed with his *wihio* relations, the Freneaus.

"Those who walked with me in those times are all gone now," Stone Wolf said, frowning. "Dove Woman, who gave me sons. Dawn Dancer, the child of the Crow woman, who left us so many winters ago."

"My mother and sisters will be glad to see

210

you, Uncle," Stone Lance whispered. "But the People will find winter colder without your wisdom to guide them."

"I leave sons and a nephew to lead the way," Stone Wolf replied. "I have only a little left to do. The rest will be your burden to carry."

When the sun died in the western hills, and the stars brightened the darkness overhead, Stone Wolf spoke of making medicine. He insisted his young companions repeat the old medicine prayers, and he instructed them in the making of powerful amulets.

"We've made these charms many times, *Ne' hyo*," Dreaming Wolf said when he noticed his father tiring. "We know what to do."

"The time will come when this old knowledge is needed, *Naha'*," Stone Wolf replied. "You must not only make medicine. You must teach the young to do it. If they turn away from the stone-pointed lance and the medicine arrows, bring them back. My old bow lacks the range of a *wihio* rifle, and its points can't cut deep like the iron points some prefer, but my aim was always straight. My arrows found Bull Buffalo. The People grew strong from the meat of my many kills."

Only when they reached *Noahvose* and climbed the shoulders of the sacred butte did Stone Wolf give over to his young companions the greatest of his medicine.

"When I leave this scarred and withered

211

body," Stone Wolf said, "you will place my shield upon my scaffold. This was the first of the Buffalo Shields, and it turned many arrows. It will walk Hanging Road with me so that I may turn the darkness from our People."

"We'll do it," Dreaming Wolf vowed. Disappointment showered his face, for he had long hoped he might receive the shield upon his father's death.

"We'll build a fire and smoke the pipe," Stone Wolf continued, "and I will seek a dream. It's necessary to make medicine and give the power of the dream to the shield. Even as I once dreamed of Bull Buffalo and White Buffalo Cow, you will come to see other images. These you will paint on the shield's outer skin so that it can turn death from the man who carries the shield."

"Yes, *Ne' hyo,* but what else is there to do?" Dreaming Wolf asked. "I've watched you craft many shields, and I've helped cut the hides and scrape away the hair. You give them more than the power of your dreams."

"Yes, *Naha',*" Stone Wolf agreed. "I will show the rest as we shape the last of the Buffalo Shields."

"Ne' hyo?"

"If a man is to safeguard the People, he must have all the power I can give him," Stone Wolf explained. "I must make two shields here, where they may receive *Noahvose's* power. As I show

212

you and Stone Lance, each will mold a shield for the other. You've always been bonded, the two of you. Each shield will carry the power of three, for it will flow from my knowledge and your devotion."

"Yes, *Ne' hyo,*" Dreaming Wolf said, warming at the notion of his father's final gift. Sharing it with Stone Lance would help ease the suffering a father's departure was certain to bring.

They performed each step of the shield-making as Stone Wolf instructed. First he sent the young men down into the valley to hunt Bull Buffalo. They hadn't spied a single animal while approaching the sacred hills, but Dreaming Wolf wasn't surprised to discover a small herd grazing north of Shell River. Stone Wolf was rarely wrong. Dreaming Wolf killed a great black bull, and Stone Lance struck down a second. They dragged the carcasses up the mountain and cut away the skins. Then, while Stone Lance cooked the meat, Dreaming Wolf prepared the tough hides. An elk was afterward slain to make a cover, and for the first time in many summers Dreaming Wolf felt himself grow fat.

"We'll smoke the buffalo meat so it may drive off the winter's starving," Stone Lance promised.

"Give some of the meat over to the wolves, Nephew," Stone Wolf urged. "Put some good pieces high in the tree for the eagles to eat.

213

Their help will make the shields stronger."

Stone Lance nodded. He quickly set the meat out for the creatures, and afterward found eagle feathers to decorate the shields. Stone Wolf later located a wolf's skeleton from which he took six teeth.

"These hold Wolf's power," Stone Wolf explained. "They will guide you on the hunt."

"And the eagle's feathers?" Stone Lance asked.

"Will give you far-seeing eyes," Stone Wolf explained. "They will be good shields. Your medicine will be strong."

Finally, after the hides were dried and stretched over steaming coals, Dreaming Wolf laced them over their hoop frames. Only then did Stone Wolf teach them the medicine prayers and invite a dream.

"See how I fashion the charms," Stone Wolf told the young men. "I mark them with my blood to show the sacrifice a man of the People makes. Now I must dream."

Three times the sun rose and fell, and Stone Wolf ate nothing. He danced and prayed, accepting only a little water as he hurried the dream. The third night, he cut his flesh, and as the blood ran down his belly and across his bare thighs, his eyes widened.

"*Heammawihio,* walk with me!" he shouted. "Show me the path ahead."

Dreaming Wolf had matched his father's sacrifices those three days, and he, too, uttered the old prayers. No sooner did Stone Wolf collapse beside the fire than his son joined him. Each dreamed in his own fashion, for even a father might be different from a son. But it was to both that a remembered dream came.

Only upon awakening did Stone Wolf accept something to eat. Stone Lance, who had remained alert to tend the fire and guard against intruders, provided dried buffalo meat and a soup made of wild onions and turnips. Dreaming Wolf, too, rejoined the world.

"You, too, saw the future," Stone Wolf told his son.

"Yes, *Ne' hyo,*" Dreaming Wolf agreed. "You'll speak of your dream first?"

"I will," Stone Wolf agreed. "You must wait until later, when I am walking Hanging Road, to share yours."

Stone Lance started to object, but his uncle muted any argument with a wave of the hand.

"It will be as you say, Uncle," the Lance agreed as he passed a bowl of broth into Dreaming Wolf's hands. "We'll hear of your dream now. There will be time for *Nah nih* to speak later."

Stone Wolf waited until after they had eaten to ready his medicine paint. Then, sitting beside the first of the shields, he spoke of the vision.

"When the world was young," Stone Wolf began, "Eagle flew across the land, dancing on

215

the wind and gazing with pity on the naked, hairless creature that walked on two legs. Bear and Wolf, likewise, laughed at the weak animal that would raise himself above his merits. 'You believe because you can speak that Man Above values you over others,' they said. 'Hear us. Your tongue will bring you trouble. You'll quarrel with your brothers, and the day will come when you will hunt your own kind.' "

"Man remained weak until he was given the Medicine Bow," Stone Lance observed.

"Yes, Man Above did value him," Stone Wolf agreed. "He sent many dreams to show Man the sacred path. Prophets like Sweet Medicine came to offer advice and warn of future peril. Man accepted the gifts of the Medicine Bow, of *Mahuts,* of Horse and the Buffalo Shield. Again and again, he ignored the warnings. He brought death and sickness to the land. Now he walks in danger, forgetting who he was. He'll suffer for it."

Dreaming Wolf gazed at the wonderful image of an eagle filling the center of the shield. Wolf and Bear were below, climbing *Noahvose*. The sacred Arrows floated on a cloud. Even unfinished, the shield possessed an aura of power.

"You see how I have painted what I saw," Stone Wolf said, nodding to his son when the image was complete. "This is what you'll do with the other."

"Now?" Dreaming Wolf asked.

"No, later, after I'm gone," Stone Wolf instructed. "I leave you my medicine paints to do it. Now I'm tired."

"I'll bring you hides," Stone Lance offered. "You should rest."

"Up there," Stone Wolf said, pointing to a clearing near the mouth of a small cave. "There, where Sweet Medicine received *Mahuts,* you should build my scaffold. Hang my shield beside my head. Make the appropriate prayers, and mourn the required three days. Then, *Naha',*" Stone Wolf added as he gripped his son's hands, "you must share your dream and make Stone Lance's shield. You both may need this strong medicine for what you must do."

"Yes, *Ne' hyo,*" Dreaming Wolf promised.

"We'll do it," Stone Lance vowed.

"Then I can rest well, knowing there are good men to watch over my people," Stone Wolf said. "Ayyyy! It's good I've lived to see it."

Stone Wolf then walked over to a boulder and sat quietly. He sang an old chant and sang a bit. Then, almost silently, he whispered, "Nothing lives long. Only the earth and the mountains."

His eyes closed, and he started the long walk up Hanging Road.

Seventeen

Dreaming Wolf and Stone Lance built the scaffold in a clearing near the cave. Many times, Stone Wolf had spoken of his grandfather, old Cloud Dancer, and the place where the old man had climbed Hanging Road.

"Now you're with him, *Ne' hyo,*" Dreaming Wolf whispered as he laid his father's withered body on its burial platform.

"Speak to Younger Wolf, my father, of us," Stone Lance added. "My sisters and *Nah' koa* will help you up the steep climbs."

"Yes," Dreaming Wolf agreed. "You won't be alone on the other side."

The cousins then spoke the mourning prayers and cut their hair. Each night, they sat beside the fire, singing the ancient prayers and hurrying Stone Wolf's shade up Hanging Road. Only when three days had passed did Dreaming Wolf perform the pipe ritual and instruct the Lance to bring the unpainted shield close.

"*Nah nih,* here it is," Stone Lance said, setting the medicine shield on its stand near the glowing embers of the fire. "Now you'll share the vision?"

"Yes," Dreaming Wolf said. "First I will pray to Man Above that I may speak of it clearly so that you, too, can understand the path we must walk."

"It's only for you to set your foot on the road, *Nah nih*. I will follow."

"That was appropriate when you were a boy," the Wolf noted. "Now you must choose for yourself."

"I did even then," Stone Lance assured his cousin. "I'm not tall now. I wasn't yet plucking my chin hairs when we first rode together. *Ne' hyo* once told me a man should follow someone who has proven his devotion to the People, though, and so I have. It's as the old one said. We're bound, the two of us. Whatever you saw in your dream, it's for us to face together."

Dreaming Wolf nodded. He then whispered his prayer and turned toward his eager-eyed cousin.

"*Ne' hyo* spoke of what he saw," the Wolf explained. "I, too, saw Eagle, Bear, and Wolf."

Dreaming Wolf dabbed paint and began decorating the shield. It seemed a twin of the first in the beginning, but instead of the Arrows floating on a cloud, he depicted White Buffalo Cow instead.

"This is what I saw clearest," Dreaming Wolf

explained. "Dark clouds choking the sun. Fierce winds tormenting the People with their icy touch. And through it all emerged White Buffalo Cow, singing a mourning song for her many lost children.

"*Haah te quah,*" she seemed to be saying.

"I don't know those words," Stone Lance said.

"I don't recognize the chant, *See' was' sin mit,* but my dream told me their meaning. White Buffalo Cow marked the death of her sons, the thunder beasts. No longer will Bull Buffalo know these valleys. And with his death will come the end of the *Tsis tsis tas.*"

"This is the future?" Stone Lance asked anxiously.

"Once, *Ne' hyo* spoke to me of dreams," the Wolf said, darkening the cloud that surrounded White Buffalo Cow. "He said that a man's medicine can show what will be, or what can be."

"How can you know which?"

"*Ne' hyo* said my heart would tell me."

"And what does your heart say, *Nah nih?*"

"This is a warning," Dreaming Wolf explained. "So long as we ignore the ancient ways, turning away from the medicine trail and neglecting the needs of the helpless ones, we will encounter more misfortune."

"What can we do to stop it?" Stone Lance asked. "We're only a little older than the pony boys."

"We've counted coup," Dreaming Wolf insisted. "We've performed brave heart deeds. Even small as we are, we stand high in the eyes of our age-mates."

"A chief can tie feathers in my hair, and it's a fine thing, *Nah nih*. But will it turn the bad hearts away from war's road? Will Talking Stick take note of our advice when he forsook Stone Wolf?"

"No," Dreaming Wolf agreed. "But there are many who already grieve for sons slain following the Stick. Others, too, will soon discover the peril he leads us to. Talking Stick's power has never stood against our enemies, and he won't always lead the young men. When his day has passed, we must guide the People back to the sacred path."

"Will there be a People to lead?"

"That's our obligation, *See' was' sin mit*," Dreaming Wolf explained. "We must ensure the survival of our people. We can't let the bad hearts bring the *Tsis tsis tas* to their death."

That was a daunting task for grown men, and the cousins sighed as they felt the weight of the obligation resting on their shoulders. Still, they had shields to turn away the greatest dangers, and their hearts were eager to try.

They remained on *Noahvose* two more days, making medicine and tying powerful charms on the shields. Then, leaving two ponies to aid Stone Wolf's climb up Hanging Road, they mounted their horses and turned south toward Shell River in search of their people.

Those first days were difficult ones for Dreaming Wolf. No longer was there a father or a chief to follow. Instead, he knew a wrong choice would bring peril to Stone Lance as well as to himself.

"Man Above, show me the way," Dreaming Wolf prayed each morning. But in truth he traveled the north bank of Shell River westward mostly because he knew the country. No dream guided his feet.

Dreaming Wolf found the Shell River country changed. The *wihio* wagon bands had left deep ruts in the trail, and spring rains had further mutilated the land. In places, there wasn't enough grass to feed a prairie dog. Whenever the road climbed a ridge, the cousins passed piles of *wihio* belongings. Great wooden beds and all manner of chests lay broken and battered beside the trail. Books, clothes, chairs, and even an iron stove littered the ground.

There were worse reminders of the *wihio* wagon people. Graves scratched in the sandy ground were often disturbed by animals. Sometimes, the bones of a small child were scattered across a hillside. Other times, a ghostly foot or hand would protrude from the eroded earth.

"It's a trail of death," Stone Lance observed. "We should avoid it. The ghost sickness may haunt this country."

"Perhaps," Dreaming Wolf said, turning northward away from the river.

"I don't understand these people," the Lance grumbled. "What makes a man leave his world and journey so far?"

"Who can say?" Dreaming Wolf replied. "I could never cut myself off from the sacred hoop of the People. Our cousins, Yellow Rope and White-haired Frog, came among us in search of peace. To escape the *wihio* madness. But these wagon people are all crazy!"

After riding Shell River alone three days, Dreaming Wolf finally spotted a thin wisp of smoke in the distance.

"Go slowly, *Nah nih,*" Stone Lance warned as he strung his bow. "Pawnees come here in summer."

"Crows, too, sometimes," Dreaming Wolf noted. "There's only one fire, though."

"Scouts?"

"Or a small hunting party. Probably Lakota. Arapaho maybe. Or *Tsis tsis tas.*"

Dreaming Wolf continued his approach, but he, too, strung his bow, and he warily studied the nearby hills. The smoke rose from the far side of a low hill, and when the Wolf reached the rise and gazed at the river, he halted his pony and motioned for Stone Lance to stop.

"*Wihio,*" the Lance said when he drew up alongside his cousin.

"Yes, but it's no wagon camp," Dreaming

Wolf observed. "One wagon, yes, with two, maybe three, men."

"Let's turn north," Stone Lance urged. "I've known *wihio* to shoot at visitors."

"Not these *wihio*," Dreaming Wolf said, noticing three young men splashing their way toward the bank. They appeared fearful for a moment. Then one raised his hand in greeting.

"It's the Frog," Stone Lance said, laughing.

"Yellow Rope is there, too," Dreaming Wolf said as he nudged his pony onward. "Our cousins!"

Tom and Louis Freneau paused only long enough to pull on trousers before rushing to greet their cousins. Hairy Chin Ike Williams followed more cautiously. He alone carried a rifle.

"Are we enemies, Hairy Chin?" Stone Lance asked as he set aside his bow and jumped down from his pony. "Or have you grown *wihio* crazy while we've been away?"

"We've had some trouble lately," young Ike replied.

"Talking Stick killed two traders on Horse Creek," Louis explained. "Everybody's nervous."

"You've come far from Fort John," Dreaming Wolf noted.

"Gone to bring up supplies before the wagons start their run," Louis said as Dreaming Wolf dismounted. "Be a lot of 'em. Gold's been found in California."

"That's not welcome news," the Wolf said,

224

scowling. "Already they spoil the country."

"Good for business, though," Louis argued. "Be a lot of wagons passing through, but no reason for 'em to stay."

"They'll bring their sicknesses," Stone Lance grumbled. "They've killed enough of us already."

"Been folks killed on both sides," Ike complained. "One batch of wagons had the cholera, and they hung up sheets to keep people away. A band of Indians dug up the dead and spread it anyway."

"Yes," Stone Lance said, gazing at the earth. "It came to our camp. *Nah' koa,* Red Hoop, Little Hoop. . . . They all climbed Hanging Road."

"Many good men died," Dreaming Wolf added. "Talking Stick and Thunder Coat lost their whole families. Those two won't be treating with anyone."

"Can't say I welcome that news," Louis said. "There's talk of bringing out soldiers to deal with the raiding. Once that happens, the old ways will be finished. They'll put up forts, build regular roads, and pretty soon towns are sure to follow. Won't need old traders like me and Tom then."

"Be a need for army scouts, though," Ike said. "By then I'll have some size."

"You'd fight my people?" Stone Lance asked.

"Your people killed my father," Ike said, "or did you forget?"

"I thought that wound had healed," the Lance said, stepping closer. "We're brothers."

"Takes more'n a swim in the river to make you brothers," Ike argued. "Been friends, though."

"We'll hunt," Dreaming Wolf suggested. "Then we can smoke and invite a dream. Perhaps I can find you a good name."

"First me," Tom insisted. "I don't much resemble a frog anymore."

"Don't need to waste time huntin', either," Ike added. "We've got a pile of trout up here ready for bonin' and fryin'. Aren't afraid of such honest work, are you, Lance?"

"No," Stone Lance said, matching the grin on his young companion's face.

It was later, after frying the fish and filling their bellies, that Dreaming Wolf told the Freneaus of Stone Wolf's dying.

"He was the last of the old ones," Louis observed. "It means there's no voice left to argue peace."

"Or understanding," Tom added. "Be real war now."

"Maybe we'd be better to stay at Ash Hollow with Charlie," Louis said, shaking his head. "We could use interpreters. Might be good for you to join us."

"Be safer," Ike argued.

"I carry a shield now," Stone Lance said, rising. "I'm a boy no longer. My obligation carries me back to my people."

"Wolf?" Louis asked.

"He's right," Dreaming Wolf agreed. "The time for swimming rivers is past. We're *Hev a tan iu.*"

"Where will you go, though?" Tom asked. "From what you've said, Talking Stick won't welcome you."

"We must join Two Moons's band," Stone Lance said. *"Nah nih's* brothers ride with him. Iron Wolf and Goes Ahead would be glad to have us with them."

"Their camp isn't far from here," Louis said, pointing northward. "A day's ride north, and another day west. If they haven't moved."

"If they've come so near Shell River, Talking Stick must be camped even closer."

"He killed the traders, remember?" Ike asked. "We saw some of his scouts two days back. They would have stolen our horses if we hadn't kept a good watch on them."

"We've got good rifles, too," Louis boasted. "I don't think the Stick's got much stomach for fighting anybody that shoots back. He does his best work scalping babies and sleeping traders."

"He often fights without honor," Stone Lance agreed, "but he now carries *Mahuts.* He's a man of power. Don't judge him without teeth. He's no camp dog who's content to chew scraps. He might find a wagon of trade goods worth a hard fight."

227

"I'll keep it in mind," Louis replied. "You consider he might think you're betraying him by visiting our camp?"

"He's spoken of our *wihio* relations before," Dreaming Wolf admitted. "He would kindle anger against us, but we have many friends. Our hearts are well known among the *Hev a tan iu.*"

"You spoke the last time we were together of being caught between two sides," Louis said, studying his cousins. "I'm afraid that time's come. I have no choice myself. I wouldn't be welcome among my brothers, the Cheyenne."

"Would I be welcome among the *wihio?*" Dreaming Wolf asked. "No, we were born to different worlds, we cousins."

"Figure it'll come to fightin'?" Ike asked.

"Hasn't it already?" the Lance asked.

They remained with the Freneaus that night, but when the five of them made the dawn prayers together, Dreaming Wolf suspected it was for the final time. He'd dreamed of fire scorching the prairie, and he smelled an odor of death even as they swam Shell River.

"Did you find us names?" Tom asked when they splashed out of the river.

"Yes," Dreaming Wolf answered. "We must smoke and make a giveaway."

"Not much to give away, nor anyone to give it to," Louis said, "but we'll do as you consider best."

The Wolf nodded, and once the pipe ritual

had been completed, the cousins swapped ponies.

"Here's our cousin, White-haired Frog," Stone Lance began. "It's a boy's name, and he needs it no longer. He throws it away to anyone who would take it."

"Now he should carry a man's name," Dreaming Wolf insisted. "In my dream I saw a great bull elk painted white as snow. Many horns crowned his head. Here, then, is my cousin, White Elk."

"And me?" Ike asked.

"I also saw you in my dream, little brother," the Wolf said. "It's not for a stranger to give you a name. Only a relative can do it."

"You just called me brother, didn't you?" Ike asked.

"Yes, and it's appropriate," Dreaming Wolf explained. "I would invite you into our family. In my dream I saw you flying over this good country alone, a red-tailed hawk, seeing everything as you crossed the heavens. Come, *See' was' sin mit,* and become Lone Hawk."

"Lone Hawk," Ike said, nodding solemnly. "It's a good name. Better yet, I've got brothers."

Dreaming Wolf embraced the slight-shouldered *wihio,* and Ike greeted Stone Lance even more warmly.

"It's been rare good fortune we happened across each other out here," Louis noted.

"Ah, luck," Dreaming Wolf said, laughing.

"It's part of your *wihio* craziness. All that happens is part of the sacred hoop. A man's life is woven like a basket, and all that happens is intended to bring him to his path's end."

"Then I guess when we make the dawn prayer, we should thank Man Above for directin' us both down Shell River," Ike said, gazing briefly at the river. "Sometimes, hearin' you four tell the old stories about your fathers and the old days, I truly wish I'd met you then. We would have chased buffalo and camped out on the plain. Had fine times."

"Our time is now," Dreaming Wolf insisted.

"It's not such a good time, is it?" Ike asked. "But maybe we'll be findin' each other again by and by."

"The world turns," Dreaming Wolf said. "All trails cross each other."

"Sure," Ike said.

"You won't ride with us to the Hollow?" Louis asked.

"No, we have obligations," the Wolf answered.

"Then go with our best," Tom said. "And keep an eye out for trouble. Seems like lately that's what mostly rides this road."

Eighteen

As Dreaming Wolf and Stone Lance rode north, they discovered the truth of Lone Hawk Ike's words. The sun had yet to complete its overhead climb when Dreaming Wolf's pony snorted and stomped nervously. The Wolf instinctively turned off the well-worn trail and concealed himself in a nearby ravine. Stone Lance followed, and the two cousins gazed anxiously at the trail they had so recently abandoned.

The cause for their alarm soon revealed itself. Two bare-chested boys wearing their hair in a single narrow strip from the crown back toward the neck galloped by. Even if they hadn't spoken, Dreaming Wolf would have identified them by their dress and the odd markings on their ponies.

"Pawnees," the Wolf whispered.

"Yes," Stone Lance agreed. "Only two. We can run them."

"There are never only two Pawnees on Shell

River," Dreaming Wolf warned. "Especially boys. This is our country, and the Pawnees don't dare to come here in small bands. No, they've come to hunt Bull Buffalo, and there will be more of them."

Dreaming Wolf was right. A dozen older men appeared on the road, jabbering in their odd language about something. Their leader stopped for a moment and glanced around. He took note of tracks in the dusty trail, but the boys reappeared, setting the chief at ease. The Pawnees then shouted a few taunts at the distant hills and laughed to themselves.

"They can't expect us to charge them?" Stone Lance asked. "They are too many."

"I'm tempted," Dreaming Wolf confessed. "Two shield carriers are certain to run fourteen Pawnees, after all. But there are probably more of them."

In truth, a whole camp of them soon appeared. Dreaming Wolf estimated as many as fifty warriors, and he didn't bother calculating the number of women and little ones.

"Something's wrong," Stone Lance observed. "The Pawnees never bring their women into this country."

"It's the *wihio*," Dreaming Wolf explained. "The wagon people chase Bull Buffalo from Shell River. They've come north to hunt."

"They're more likely to find themselves hunted, *Nah nih*. The Lakotas hate Pawnees, and they hold the sacred hills here to be their most honored place. They'll surely kill these Pawnees."

"If they're nearby. Many Lakota bands summer in the Big Horn country or up on Elk River, hunting and raiding the Crow pony herds."

"If Two Moons's camp is near, we should warn him of these Pawnees. There are so many of them, and your brothers might be in peril."

"Someone already is," Dreaming Wolf said, pointing to two young *Tsis tsis tas* captives being driven along by an old Pawnee woman. Stripped bare and taunted by rock-throwing children, the boys did their best to stay ahead of the sharp-tongued woman's stick.

"I know that one," Stone Lance said, pointing to the nearest.

"Rock Turtle," Dreaming Wolf muttered. "He's our brothers' wives' cousin. I remember him from the wedding feast."

"He's ridden into peril. These boys are too old to be adopted into the tribe, *Nah nih.*"

"They'll be tortured."

"No," Stone Lance objected. "Not if we're clever."

The cousins exchanged grins, and as they hid in the ravine, they made plans for a rescue.

The Pawnees made their camp along Shell River that night, not far from where the Freneaus had rested the night before. Pony boys ran out to watch the horses, and women busied themselves cooking and attending to their children. The captives were bound to a cottonwood. There, helpless to prevent it, they were showered with food scraps and poked with sticks and bird arrows by small Pawnee boys and girls.

"Look at the camp!" Stone Lance gasped as Dreaming Wolf led his ponies from the ravine. "They are too many, *Nah nih*. We must have been too long in the sun. Or too long among the *wihio*. We've become crazy."

"Look at how the old woman is sharpening her knife," Dreaming Wolf whispered. "Once I came upon a man who had been tortured by the Crows. Every piece that could be cut from him was gone. His eyes and tongue even! He lived a long time, bleeding slowly and suffering. If we can't rescue them, we can at least provide them a chance to die fighting."

"And us?"

"Nothing lives long," the Wolf said as he climbed atop his pony. He led his spare horse along, hoping Rock Turtle or his young companion might escape atop the animal. Stone Lance sighed and mounted his pony, too. The Lance also brought along his spare horse.

They rode for a time in the shadows, unnoticed. The Pawnee camp was alive with singing and laughter. A band of warriors was performing some sort of scalp dance, and Dreaming

Wolf feared the two young captives were not the only *Tsis tsis tas* to have suffered.

"You go on the right," Dreaming Wolf said, scowling at the dancing Pawnees as he slid his left arm through the straps of his shield. "I will charge on the left."

Stone Lance strapped his shield on and notched an arrow on his bowstring. Dreaming Wolf held a stone-tipped lance. Satisfied they were ready, the Wolf raised his lance and shouted an unearthly war cry. The cousins then charged the Pawnee camp.

In the darkness, four charging ponies were mistaken for a hundred, and as Dreaming Wolf upset kettles and tore down smoking racks, startled Pawnees scurried for safety. Two warriors raced to block his path, and the Wolf clubbed the first one across the forehead, knocking him senseless. The other fired an arrow, but the shield easily deflected it. Dreaming Wolf then thrust his lance into the Pawnee's chest and left him to bleed out his life in the dusty prairie.

Stone Lance was the first to reach the captives. He managed to drive off the little tormentors and chase the old woman away. Then, jumping to the earth, he cut the captives' bonds and urged them to mount the spare ponies.

"Ayyyy!" Rock Turtle screamed as he leaped on a surprised Pawnee boy and helped himself to the young man's clothing. The second young *Tsis tsis tas* covered himself with a buffalo hide and climbed atop the spare pony Dreaming Wolf was holding in readiness.

"Hurry!" Stone Lance shouted as the Turtle dressed. "They won't remain confused long."

"Where are the others?" Rock Turtle asked. "My brothers? *Ne' hyo?*"

"We're alone," Dreaming Wolf said as Rock Turtle finally pulled himself onto the waiting pony. "Now follow me out of here."

"Follow you?" Rock Turtle cried. "Ayyyy! I know you, Wolf. You don't know our camps. It's for me to lead the way."

"He's right," Stone Lance readily agreed.

"Then lead!" Dreaming Wolf urged as a Pawnee arrow flew past his shoulder.

"Ayyyy!" Rock Turtle screamed as he kicked his horse into a gallop. He rode right through the center of the Pawnee camp, driving frightened children in every direction. Then he attacked the pony herd, scattering horses and running twenty of the best northward.

"I suppose we should have something to show for our efforts," Dreaming Wolf observed as he glanced back at the confused Pawnee pony boys.

"If they weren't so much trouble, I would have brought along some of those Pawnees," Rock Turtle declared. "I would show them how it feels to be poked and prodded, to have pieces cut from their bodies!"

"It's no good making war on the helpless

ones," Dreaming Wolf argued. "Maybe when we've returned and rested, we'll come back and take the other horses."

"Maybe," Rock Turtle wearily agreed.

When Rock Turtle and his companion, Stalker, entered the Windpipe camp that next morning, they were greeted with howls of amazement.

"We were rescued by the bravest of the brave hearts!" Rock Turtle declared.

"Talking Stick found you, then," the Turtle's older brother, Panther Claw, observed. "But where is he? We should offer the chief food."

"It wasn't him," Rock Turtle grumbled. "He left us alone with the ponies to face thirty Pawnees. We alone of five survived, and the Pawnees would have killed us, slowly and painfully, if Dreaming Wolf and Stone Lance hadn't come."

"Who?" the Claw cried.

"Dreaming Wolf," Stalker explained. "The son of the old Arrow-keeper. Even now he's driving the horses we took to the herd."

"His cousin, Stone Lance, freed us," Rock Turtle added. "They charged the camp alone, two against two hundred. Their shields turned the Pawnee arrows, and their medicine spread fear and confusion. Ayyyy! They ran the enemy!"

"Only two?" Panther Claw said, shaking his head. "Charging the camp alone? They must have powerful medicine. Or their spirits are disturbed. Crazy."

"We couldn't ignore your brother's need," Dreaming Wolf explained as he dismounted. *"Ne' hyo* taught me well the obligations a man carries."

"Man?" Two Moons asked as he arrived with a small band of followers. "You are only boys yourselves. You did well freeing these pony boys, but now the Pawnees are certain to fall on us. We must move the camp and send men to slow the enemy."

"If you think it's necessary," Dreaming Wolf said, "but I think the Pawnees more likely to cross Shell River and hurry back to their camps in the southern country. By now they'll suspect a hundred men raided their camp. Soon it will be a thousand! They showed no eagerness to chase us."

"Then we won't disturb the camp," Two Moons declared, nodding solemnly. "Even so, I'll send men to watch."

"It's only prudent," Dreaming Wolf admitted. "I'll go myself."

"You must rest," a familiar voice insisted. Dreaming Wolf turned and found himself confronted by Running Doe, Iron Wolf's young wife.

"She's right," Rock Turtle agreed. "We rode all

night. They're tired."

"And certainly hungry," Two Moons noted. "We'll eat something. Then you'll rest. Afterward we can smoke and hear of this brave heart rescue."

"Come." Running Doe urged. "We have room for you in our lodge. Your brother will soon return from hunting, and we will make a giveaway. It's only right when brothers are brought back together."

"Or cousins," Stone Lance whispered.

"Certainly," Running Doe agreed.

The rescuers were soon stuffed with food brought by grateful relatives, and many fine gifts were given away to honor the return of the captives. Dreaming Wolf greeted many of the Windpipes, and he promised to lead the young men after Bull Buffalo. He didn't remember too many of them later, for he slept long and well in Iron Wolf's lodge.

The days that followed were among the best Dreaming Wolf could remember. Iron Wolf and Goes Ahead returned from the hunt to greet their younger brother. The Windpipe Fox Warriors met in council and praised the rescuers by sponsoring a feast. And each evening, as the sun sank lower in the western sky, Dreaming Wolf walked beside a nearby pond with Singing Doe.

"All the People praise your courage," she whispered. "No one among us, not even the chiefs, is certain he would have acted as bravely."

"Anyone who saw what was awaiting those boys would have acted," Dreaming Wolf argued.

"My father has warmed to you," she continued. "Rock Turtle's my cousin. Our family owes you a great debt."

"It was my obligation," the Wolf insisted. "Nothing is owed. We should put an end to this feasting and resume the hunting."

"Can you step away from this greatness you've won?"

"What have I won if the People starve this winter? There will be time for singing warrior songs and recounting coups when the snows come. Now's the time for hunting."

"Some would say it's also time for courting," Singing Doe suggested. "We've spoken of the future before. Once you were unsure what you would become, but now it's clear. You have power, Wolf, and everyone recognizes it. First you'll lead the young men. Next you'll be called to be a chief among the Foxes. Finally, you will sit in the council of forty-four."

"I hope one day to keep *Mahuts,* even as *Ne' hyo,* and his grandfather before him, did," Dreaming Wolf explained.

"Talking Stick is now Arrow-keeper," she reminded him. "He is not an old man yet, and there's talk he may choose a young wife. There may yet be sons."

"It was his sons who brought the ghost sickness to us," Dreaming Wolf grumbled. "He neglects the People. Where has he gone when the hunt requires his efforts? Elsewhere. It's for the Buffalo Arrows to lead the hunters, but they are absent."

"Once the Arrow-keeper stood high in the eyes of all," she observed. "He was a great man. Now he is someone to be blamed for every failure, chastised for each shortcoming. It's no road to seek!"

"Perhaps not," Dreaming Wolf admitted. "But I'm my father's son. *Ne' hyo* instructed me in the medicine cures, and he intended that I should keep the Arrows. If that's for another to do, then my obligation remains to *Mahuts,* and to the People. I must do what I can to insure both prosper."

Those words were much on Dreaming Wolf's mind that night when he burrowed his way into the buffalo hides Running Doe had made into his bed. Nearby, Stone Lance dozed peacefully. The Wolf, though, failed to find peace.

The dream crept upon him like an uninvited guest. It tore him from the quiet of a pleasant late-summer evening. Soon his head filled with images, and he trembled as each revelation followed the one before.

As had happened often before, it began with a sensation of flying above the world. He was a hawk, perhaps, or even a cloud. It didn't matter. That wasn't important.

Next the dream filled with light. Blazing yellow lightning tore at a pale blue sky. Then, proudly soaring overhead, a white-tailed eagle appeared. Its grace and majesty were beyond belief. Discord then exploded through his head. Frenzied voices shouted meaningless arguments. Finally, the eagle swept close to earth in an effort to silence the voices and restore the harmony of the world. But an arrow suddenly tore through the heavens and pierced the heart of the eagle. That wondrously powerful bird shuddered and then plunged downward into a dark sea.

Dreaming Wolf awoke in a sweat. Stone Lance sat at his side, bathing his tormented forehead.

"You had a dream," the Lance explained. "A vision. You must have seen terrible things. We must summon the council and tell them."

"No," Dreaming Wolf argued. "Not for a time."

"What did you see?" Stone Lance asked.

"An old dream my father before me saw," Dreaming Wolf explained. "Once, long ago, when your father led the young men, *Ne' hyo* saw this vision. A bold eagle shot from the sky."

"He saw it when Porcupine, your brother, was killed."

"It foretells the death of a chief," Dreaming

Wolf noted. "But who? Two Moons? Iron Wolf? Who can make sense of it?"

"Tell the chiefs," Stone Lance urged. "Let them decide."

Both cousins knew it was a poor choice at best, but Dreaming Wolf considered it best. Then, the following night, the dream returned.

"I must go and consult the Arrows," Dreaming Wolf announced. "Perhaps *Mahuts* has an answer."

"Once the Arrows contained enormous power," Iron Wolf argued. "Now they reflect only Talking Stick's high opinion of himself."

"I must warn him, *Nah nih*," Dreaming Wolf insisted. "He may be the chief who is in danger."

"And you would shield him? You, who have suffered as much as anyone from this madman? No, stay here in my lodge and share the hunt. We'll need your medicine power."

"It's what I hoped to do," Dreaming Wolf confessed, "but how can I ignore the welfare of others? I must ride and speak to Talking Stick."

"They won't listen!" Singing Doe complained as she made her way to Dreaming Wolf's side.

"Perhaps they won't," Dreaming Wolf agreed. "Man Above gives me eyes to see, though. Can I ignore what I know?"

Nineteen

Dreaming Wolf's intent was to ride alone south and west, seeking out Talking Stick's camp. He would deliver his warning and depart. But as he sat with Stone Lance beside a small fire, making the dawn prayers, the Wolf knew he would not be the only one to leave Two Moons's camp.

"Remember your father's words," Stone Lance urged. "We're bonded, you and I. It's for you to dream and me to follow."

"I've never enjoyed solitude," Dreaming Wolf confessed. "I welcome the company."

Later, after washing the summer dust from their bodies in the shallow stream that flowed past the camp, they discovered word of their imminent departure had spread. Rock Turtle stood waiting with ten ponies. Dreaming Wolf readily recognized the four he and the Lance had departed *Noahvose* with. The others had been captured from the Pawnees.

"It's wise for a man to have a spare pony," the Turtle declared, grinning. "He may come upon a boy in need of rescuing."

"A spare, yes," Dreaming Wolf agreed. "Ten?"

"Ah, you didn't imagine you would ride alone," Stalker said, joining them. Shortly, Panther Claw arrived with provisions.

"You should remain here, with your families," Dreaming Wolf told the boys.

"I'm as old as Stone Lance," Panther Claw argued. "I may not carry a shield, but I know where Talking Stick is camped. I can guide you there."

"And these two?" the Wolf asked, turning to the younger boys.

"We owe you a debt," Rock Turtle replied.

"We're not tall," Stalker added, "but you won't find us lacking. We've hunted Bull Buffalo and we've faced the enemy. We won't wet ourselves if fighting's called for."

"I go to prevent a fight," Dreaming Wolf insisted.

"We know," Panther Claw said, frowning. "You've climbed *Noahvose,* and spirits speak to you in dreams. We know Talking Stick, too. You may more easily turn the sun from its path than change his mind."

"We're going," Rock Turtle added.

"I feel like I'm leading an army of children out to count coup on a buffalo calf," Dreaming Wolf said, sighing. "There's danger waiting! I already carried a heavy burden, and now you place your lives on my shoulders as well."

"Don't feel it's a burden," Rock Turtle suggested. "We were dead, Stalker and I, in the Pawnee camp. You gave us back our lives. If we lose them now, it can only be Man Above's doing."

"And you?" Dreaming Wolf asked, turning to Panther Claw.

"I would have ridden against the Pawnees to find my brother," the Claw answered. "A man alone has little chance. If I fight now, I'll share the peril with brave hearts."

"There's no keeping them back," Stone Lance told his cousin. "If they know the way, they can hurry us to Talking Stick."

"Well, you're foolish, all of you," Dreaming Wolf grumbled, "but I was much the same myself. Let's ready the ponies and begin. Our brothers are in peril, and we should warn them before death overtakes them."

There remained only a few brief farewells. Singing Doe came to urge caution and contribute dried meat and fresh berries. Iron Wolf and Goes Ahead came along to offer quivers of arrows.

"We would ride with you, *See' was' sin mit,*" Iron Wolf said, "but we have responsibilities here."

"It's right you stay," Dreaming Wolf replied. "Bring nephews into the world to ride with us.

246

Give the People grandsons of Stone Wolf to lead them upon the sacred path."

"It's for us to do," Stone Lance added. "Look! We are enough already. Five *Tsis tsis tas!* Who would stand against us?"

Panther Claw howled, and the cry was taken up by the men of Two Moons's camp. Dreaming Wolf gazed at the intense eyes of his young companions and grinned. The thought of the five of them charging the enemy was too ridiculous to imagine. They must all of them be crazy!

"Heammawihio protects the crazy ones," Stone Wolf had once told his son. Dreaming Wolf hoped it was so. They would need such looking after.

"Ayyyy! They're Foxes!" Iron Wolf shouted.

"It's for them to do the difficult things!" Goes Ahead added.

In truth, only the two shield carriers were Fox Warriors. Panther Claw had joined the Bowstrings, and the younger boys had yet to be invited into any of the soldier society camps. In the old days, someone would have said as much. But in the old days, five boys would never have ridden out on such a journey alone. There would have been men to walk man's road, and pony boys would have minded the herds.

It was Panther Claw who led the way, for he

had glimpsed Talking Stick's band only two days before.

"They rode a ridge overlooking Shell River," Panther Claw explained. "I saw thirty, maybe more."

"And they saw you?" Dreaming Wolf asked.

"No, they had eyes only for the river," Panther Claw replied. "I judged it was a scouting party, or maybe they were hunting Bull Buffalo as we were."

"If it had been Pawnees, your dreams would have come to pass," Stone Lance told Dreaming Wolf. "It's like Talking Stick to ride, unaware, into danger."

"To lead others into it," Dreaming Wolf grumbled as he motioned Panther Claw on. They rode faster, with greater purpose. Instead of resting their ponies, they switched mounts and kept going, pausing only to water the animals and chew some of the dried meat.

"It wasn't far from here," Panther Claw announced when they wove their way up a low ridge not far from Shell River.

"There!" Stone Lance said, waving toward a curl of gray smoke. "They must be over the ridge."

Dreaming Wolf took the lead, and the little band surged onward. When they finally topped the ridge, the Wolf halted. Below he could see the valley cut by Shell River. The distant Medicine Bow country marked the southern horizon.

A small herd of buffalo grazed to the west, unbothered by hunters.

"It's not them," Stone Lance said, pointing to the source of the smoke. A *wihio* wagon camp spread out in a wide circle on the north bank of the river. Listening carefully, Dreaming Wolf detected the faint chorus of a song. Children splashed about in the shallows, their pale bodies appearing oddly out of place in that land of reds and yellows.

"There," Dreaming Wolf said, pointing to a line of riders approaching from the east.

"Talking Stick," Panther Claw noted. "He carries the Arrows."

"Yes," Dreaming Wolf agreed. His chest ached, and he glared at the chief. To invite the power of the Man Arrows against a wagon camp! *Mahuts* had led the People into battle only a few times, and then it was in times of great peril. When Bull had turned them against the Pawnees, the Arrows had been lost.

"I count twenty. Where are the rest of them?" Stone Lance asked.

"Look to the west," Dreaming Wolf said. Thunder Coat approached with a larger body of men from the opposite direction. As Talking Stick rode out to treat with the *wihio* wagon chiefs, his brother readied the others. They would charge the *wihio* from the back.

"It's a good plan," Panther Claw said, "but the sun's against them. They should have struck

249

tomorrow, at dawn. The *wihio* would have been sleepy, and the sun would have blinded them."

"They carry *Mahuts*," Stalker insisted. "The Arrows will blind the wagon people."

"Only if the proper preparations have been made," Dreaming Wolf argued. "When has Talking Stick ever made medicine in the old, sacred way? They will not have made the prayers, and the Stick won't have found a vision. Man Above would surely have warned him of the danger as he did me!"

"What will you do?" Panther Claw asked warily.

"Watch and wait," Dreaming Wolf replied. "Hope I'm wrong."

He wasn't, though. The *wihio* chiefs stepped out, rifles in hand, to meet the fierce-looking enemy. Talking Stick carried the old painted lance, and it was decorated with light-haired scalps. Others beside him held guns and bows ready.

The *wihio* called out, and for a moment Talking Stick seemed to welcome them. Two *Tsis tsis tas* spread out a blanket, and the leaders sat to talk. Then Talking Stick rose and waved his lance. Thunder Coat charged the wagons with his fifty screaming warriors while the *Tsis tsis tas* overpowered the surprised wagon chiefs.

Cries of fear and despair rose from the wagon camp, but many of the men remained calm. As Thunder Coat's onrushing warriors drew close, a volley of rifle fire tore the late-afternoon air. Horses fell, throwing their riders forward toward the wagons. Men cried out in pain as lead balls splintered bone and pierced vitals. The charge was turned back in disorder. Only a third of the riders remained mounted, and some of them were hurt. Several men were dead, and others crowded beside Thunder Coat a stone's throw from the encircled wagons.

"Leave!" Stone Lance shouted. "Flee. His medicine is broken!"

The remaining warriors were deaf to the warning, though. The barking of rifles and the taunts of the survivors filled the air. They made a second charge, and the rifles again spit fiery death. Only two fell this time, though, and many of the fallen were rescued.

Talking Stick now mounted his pony and raised his painted lance. The Medicine Arrows were tied there, and his companions cheered to see them. Talking Stick screamed and charged the *wihio* camp, but the rifles drove him away. One ball severed the thong holding the Arrows, and *Mahuts* fell to the dusty earth.

"Ayyyy!" Dreaming Wolf screamed. "Wait for me here," he told his young companions. Then he slapped his horse into a gallop and charged down the ridge.

Briefly, for only a moment, quiet seemed to settle over the land. The stunned *Tsis tsis tas* fought to regain their senses, and the *wihio* re-

251

loaded rifles in expectation of another charge.

Dreaming Wolf's mind worked furiously to take in the scene before him. Each *wihio* seemed to have three or four rifles with which to fire. Women and boys did the reloading, leaving their husbands and fathers to shoot. In this way, fifty *wihio* were as a hundred or more would have been. Clearly there was no breaking such a well-armed line.

The Wolf charged past a band of young Crazy Dogs and on to where a dazed Talking Stick stared at his lance. On and on Dreaming Wolf rode, out toward the *wihio*. Now the whine of bullets rose to meet him. He held high his shield, and its medicine turned the balls. One did nick his horse's rump, and two others managed to tear his clothes. Only a single one found flesh, though, stinging his right ear.

He swung wide past *Mahuts* and slowed his pony. Then, bending low and extending his right arm as far as was possible, he closed his fingers and snatched the Arrows.

Behind him the disheartened *Tsis tsis tas* howled and waved their bows. Even as Dreaming Wolf raced away to safety, the others formed a fresh line behind their chief.

"Brave up!" Talking Stick cried. "See how *Mahuts* has made Dreaming Wolf bulletproof? Come and strike hard at the enemy!"

If Dreaming Wolf was bulletproof, the others had no faith their chief could protect them in like manner. Only two riders turned toward the wagon camp, and they retreated when Talking Stick hung back.

"What are you waiting for?" the Stick shouted. "Are you women to hide from the enemy?"

"Lead us, brave heart!" Otter Foot shouted as he greeted Dreaming Wolf. "We require only an example."

"Then I'll give you one," Talking Stick said, quirting his pony. The weary animal raced toward the *wihio* wagons, and Talking Stick hugged the horse's neck, avoiding a volley of bullets. The chief got to within a few feet of the wagons before firing his rifle into the face of a hairy-faced *wihio*. Talking Stick continued on, breaking through a wall of barrels and striking down a boy with his lance.

"Do we follow?" Otter Foot asked.

"Look around you," Bent Arrow urged, holding a shattered arm. "We're broken like old, discarded arrows. If there are men with the heart to ride, they should save the brave hearts there."

All eyes turned to where Thunder Coat and his wounded companions lay, exchanging fire with the wagon people. Talking Stick, who might at least have rescued one of them, returned to safety carrying the scalp of the wagon boy to prove his power.

"Bent Arrow's right," Dreaming Wolf said, touching his bloody ear. With disdain, he smeared the blood across his chest, then painted twin lines below his eyes.

"I'll follow," Otter Foot pledged.

"I, too!" others shouted.

"Not you," Dreaming Wolf said as he passed *Mahuts* into Bent Arrow's care. "You've bled enough, old friend. This is for us to do."

There were five who followed Dreaming Wolf into the buzzing nest of *wihio* bullets. Leading the way, Dreaming Wolf held his shield at an angle, catching the dying sun. The glare troubled the *wihio* riflemen, and their aim was poor. The Wolf drew a weary Raven's Wing up behind him, then turned with the others to shield the flight of those able to walk.

"Where's my brother?" Thunder Coat shouted angrily. "This was for Talking Stick to do!"

Dreaming Wolf felt an odd sensation, and he shuddered with an unearthly chill. Thunder Coat felt it as well. He gazed up into the Wolf's young eyes and nodded.

"Nothing lives long!" Thunder Coat screamed as he tore Otter Foot from a pony and mounted instead. "Only the earth and the mountains!"

Thunder Coat then reared the horse high onto its hind legs and charged the *wihio* camp. Alone, with nothing to distract the fearful wagon people, he rode into a wall of death.

"Here's your fallen chief," Stone Lance said as he arrived at his cousin's side.

"He's a chief no longer," Dreaming Wolf observed as he watched Thunder Coat torn from his horse.

"His was a suicide soldier's death," Otter Foot declared as he climbed up behind Stone Lance.

"Wasted," was all Dreaming Wolf could think to say as he rode from the bloody ground. "So much death, and what have we gained?"

"Look!" Talking Stick shouted wildly. "See how they hold back their fire. They're short of powder. We can run them now!"

"They're short of lead, yes," Otter Foot observed. "It's in our brothers, there, dead in this place."

"My brother's there, too!" Talking Stick screamed. His eyes were wild, and his gestures were odd. "Who will go and help me avenge him!"

"Haven't we enough men to mourn already?" Dreaming Wolf asked.

"I can break their power!" Talking Stick said, waving the *wihio* scalp. "I struck them hard once. Together, we can kill them all!"

"One scalp or a hundred," Bent Arrow said as he fought off his pain. "It's a poor price for the men killed here today. I need help to return to my family."

"It's for me to do," Otter Foot volunteered. "Someone must remain behind to recover the dead."

"It must be done," Raven's Wing said soberly. The angry survivors turned toward Talking

Stick. The chief, surrounded by the Crazy Dogs, stepped over and reclaimed the Arrows.

"I must make medicine," the Stick explained. "You can bring my brother to Arrow Lodge."

"We'll set him with his family," Raven's Wing explained. "With the forest of dead you have also forgotten. Ayyyy! It was a bad day you won your shield, Stick! A bad day for the *Tsis tsis tas!*"

Twenty

Dreaming Wolf sat sourly in the *Hev a tan iu* camp. He would rather have turned north and returned to his brothers. He longed to enter a sweat lodge and cleanse his tortured soul. The many wounded required medicine, though, so he and Stone Lance remained. Panther Claw, Rock Turtle, and Stalker had already left for Two Moons's camp, carrying with them the grim news of Thunder Coat's death.

"Our hearts are heavy with mourning," Dancing Lance had said when the bodies of the slain arrived. The *wihio* had not cut the bodies, but all were stripped bare, and the birds had gotten to them before their comrades.

"We might all have died," Otter Foot had argued, "if we had followed the false charms of Talking Stick."

"He sees many things," Raven's Wing had agreed, "but he leads us only to death. His own power is great, and he has proven his courage charging the enemy. But he has no devotion to his brothers. He brings them no protection, and

257

he leaves their bones to mark his failures."

Those who had not ridden to war with the Stick had been doubly shocked. Learning ten brave hearts had died was a blow, but hearing of Talking Stick's loss of the Arrows drew howls of disbelief.

"Always *Mahuts* have turned the power of the enemy from us," Whirlwind had observed. "Now even their power is lost to us."

"Not lost," Otter Foot had objected. "Dreaming Wolf came to us. He retrieved the Arrows."

"Where are they now?" Dancing Lance had called.

"I had them," Bent Arrow had explained wearily. His arm was strapped to his side, and his face was contorted with pain. Even so, he had recounted Dreaming Wolf's charges. Afterward, he had spoken of how Talking Stick had carried *Mahuts* away.

Now, long days afterward, the People had completed their mourning. Chiefs smoked and prayed in council, searching for a new direction. The wounded started the long recovery trail, and those still able set off in small parties to hunt.

Talking Stick was eight days absent from the People. When he returned, he showed no hint of remorse. His hair remained long, and no mourning scars marked his chest and arms.

"It's good so many chiefs are here," the Arrow-keeper said, dismounting his weary pony.

"One is missing," Whirlwind said frowning.

"He's missed," Talking Stick said, nodding

gravely. But if his brother's death weighed heavily on him, the Stick showed no evidence of it. "We must avenge those who've fallen," Talking Stick insisted. "I have been in the hills alone, smoking and praying. *Mahuts* have brought me a vision of much mourning in the *wihio* wagon camps. Not all are as strong as the ones we fought. I will show you others. We'll win easy victories against them. Ayyyy! We'll take many scalps! Stories of our power will reach all the peoples, and there will be trembling at our approach."

"Yes," Otter Foot agreed. "But who will be trembling?"

Others, too, laughed to hear such boasting. Sons and younger brothers of the slain welcomed the words, though, and Talking Stick still stood high in the eyes of the Crazy Dogs.

"We'll meet in council and consider your words," Whirlwind said, frowning.

"We must have more than words from you, though," Dancing Lance told the Stick. "We've bled too often, and we've lost too much. We can't continue to see our brave young men killed in senseless charges."

"My medicine will protect them!" Talking Stick insisted.

"As it protected your brother?" Bent Arrow asked. "I rode out, following your promises, and now I have only one arm with which to hunt. The other lies useless at my side, the bones shattered by lead balls you vowed to turn away.

I wore your charms, and you yourself painted my face. Your voice is loud, Talking Stick, but the words are empty. They didn't protect me at Shell River, and they won't save anyone foolish enough to ride with you now!"

"Yes!" others shouted. "We've buried enough good men!"

Whirlwind silenced them with a wave of his hand.

"Are we hungry dogs yapping at each other?" the chief asked. "No. We'll meet in council and consider what to do."

"It's best," Dancing Lance agreed. "People, trust us to do what's necessary."

"We honor you, Lance," Bent Arrow said, "but the days for trusting Talking Stick are finished. His dreams are full of lies. He would walk the land as a great prophet, but what gift has he brought us? Sweet Medicine came with *Mahuts* to raise the People high among all the tribes. Old Stone Wolf provided the Buffalo Shield. What has the Stick given us but hunger, sickness, and dying?"

"It's for the council to decide," Whirlwind answered. "It's your pain that speaks, Arrow. Rest, recover your strength."

"What use is a one-armed man?" Bent Arrow complained.

"I know of one who led the brave hearts," Stone Lance said proudly.

"Your father," Bent Arrow replied, nodding respectfully. "He was a great man already, though, and I'm only beginning my walk on man's road."

"It's not two arms that are required to face the difficult days ahead," Dreaming Wolf told his friend. "It's heart that's required. I'll help you gain strength, and you'll be a man to remember."

Bent Arrow frowned. Too many promises had been broken. He was past believing anyone.

"Put aside your pain for now," Whirlwind urged. "We'll meet and consider what to do. Then we'll decide."

"The chiefs are wise," one old woman declared. "Wait for them to meet and choose what's best."

"I won't follow a false prophet," Bent Arrow vowed. "I've suffered enough."

The *Hev a tan iu* chiefs met with those from other bands camped nearby. Two Moons and Iron Wolf rode in from the Windpipes, as other head men of the scattered northern bands did. Those bands who had made their summer camps in the southern country couldn't be reached. Even so, twenty chiefs met around a towering council fire.

Dreaming Wolf was surprised when Iron Wolf summoned him to the council.

"Nah nih?" Dreaming Wolf asked. "What business would I have among chiefs?"

"You're a boy no longer," Iron Wolf said,

laughing. "Everyone speaks of how you rescued the Arrows. You stand high in the eyes of the young men, and even the chiefs have heard of your dreams. They have questions for you."

"They have an Arrow-keeper to give their questions," Dreaming Wolf answered bitterly.

"Yes, but many have no ears for his words, *See' was' sin mit*. Come now. They mean to honor you."

Dreaming Wolf nodded. He paused only long enough to brush his hair and slip a beaded war shirt over his bony shoulders. He looked young enough. Bare-chested, he still resembled a pony boy.

"Come along," Iron Wolf urged. "You're pretty enough."

"A man must appear his best when sitting among the chiefs," Dreaming Wolf insisted. Satisfied he'd done everything possible to produce an appropriate appearance, he reluctantly followed his elder brother to the council.

"Welcome," Dancing Lance said, making a place for Dreaming Wolf beside him. "Another Fox is always welcome here."

"This is my brother, Dreaming Wolf," Iron Wolf told the others. "Some would consider a young man of seventeen summers too young to sit with us, but *See' was' sin mit* has always been a man of power. His dreams always foretell events. While still young, he distinguished himself among the Fox Warriors as a man of the People."

262

"Always the helpless ones have known his generosity," Whirlwind added. "My own sons have benefitted from his medicine, and that of his father."

"There was need," Talking Stick muttered. "When the old one kept *Mahuts*, the People suffered many misfortunes."

"Yes," Roaring Bear, a chief of the Eaters, agreed. "Many died in those days."

"And now?" Dreaming Wolf asked. Iron Wolf turned to urge silence, but Talking Stick's grinning face fueled a rare outburst. "Many times, other men blamed *Ne' hyo* for the sufferings of the People, but who neglected the hunt? How many times did he warn the council against some action which brought sickness or death? Look around you. My father is no longer here for you to blame! Who has tended *Mahuts* since Stone Wolf climbed Hanging Road? What bad heart has emptied our camps of their best men?"

"Silence!" Roaring Bear bellowed. "You are an invited guest. Your voice has no place in this council."

"Perhaps it should," Whirlwind argued. "I'm no old man, and yet who sits here other then Roaring Bear who can claim to be older? Talking Stick and I rode to hunt Bull Buffalo the first time together. I know him well. He would admit his raids on the *wihio* wagon people have brought little except grief to us."

"He's a brave man," Roaring Bear insisted.

263

"My sons ride with the Crazy Dogs, and many have seen his brave heart deeds."

"Ah, he makes many charges," Dancing Lance agreed. "He's quick to kill. And yet he's boasted of medicine that bends bullets. If so, they turn from him alone! How many times must we hear of how our Arrow-keeper lost *Mahuts?* Did he ride to save them? No. It remained for a boy to come, unbidden, and save them from the enemy. See how even now the *wihio* bullet's mark is on his ear!"

"So he also fails to turn the bullets," Roaring Bear observed. "And do the young men follow him?"

"They have," Dancing Lance continued. "He's a rescuer. A man who rides with this young one knows he won't be left to helplessly stand against the enemy if his horse is killed. Who brought Antler away from the Crows?"

"He's taken no scalps," Talking Stick growled. "He avoids fighting."

"Look at the coup feathers tied in his hair," Whirlwind suggested. "If he doesn't cut the hair off an enemy, it doesn't mean he fails to close with him."

"He's taken Crow scalps," Iron Wolf reminded them. "These he gave to his cousins, as is appropriate. They rest with them in a high place, for those girls have climbed Hanging Road."

"Enough of this arguing!" Roaring Bear shouted. "We accomplish nothing."

"He's right," Dreaming Wolf agreed, dropping

his eyes in respect. "We only disturb the harmony of this world. It's for us to restore that harmony, to return the People to the sacred path."

"This we'll only accomplish when the *wihio* are driven from Shell River," Talking Stick argued. "Listen. I've had a vision of a great battle. In it, we'll win victory over the pale-faced enemy."

"So you've said before," Dancing Lance grumbled.

"This time I have new medicine to use," Talking Stick declared. "Man Above appeared to me on a dark cloud, blowing a flute and gazing down at the barren plain. Bull Buffalo was gone. Elk and Deer had vanished. Only the bones of our brother creatures remained to mark their passing.

"*Wihio* were everywhere! They carved their rutted roads through even our most sacred places. They fouled the rivers with their leavings. The air bore their scent, even in the high places where wind and snow once purified the world.

" 'You must ride down and kill the destroyer of the world,' Man Above told me. 'Kill him! Erase him from your winter counts! Only when he's gone can the world regain its harmony.' "

"You would strike the wagon camps again?" Whirlwind cried in dismay.

"Again and again," Talking Stick argued. "We must kill them all."

"And what new medicine would you bring to protect the young men?" Iron Wolf asked.

"I will pound a powder from Bull Buffalo's horn and Elk's teeth. I'll add scented sage and purify it in sweet grass smoke. We'll take long sweats. We'll sing the old prayers, invoking *Heammawihio* to ride with us. Ayyyy! We'll renew the power of the shields, too."

"These aren't new to us," Iron Wolf observed. "Once, each war party performed the required ceremonies. Now men lead others into peril with empty promises."

"I've heard enough!" Roaring Bear complained.

"I'm no young brave heart brought to his first council," Iron Wolf said, glaring at the old man chief. "I'm Iron Wolf, who leads the Foxes. I sit here as a chief of the Windpipes, and my voice will be heard."

"Ayyyy!" the Windpipe chiefs shouted. "Listen to him!"

"All these old ways you speak of as something new," Iron Wolf continued. "Too long you've neglected what we've always known. You say in your dream Man Above sends us to strike the *wihio,* but you've said this often. If it was destined to be, why haven't the *wihio* been killed already?"

"How can we trust in your dreams?" Dancing Lance asked. "In your power?"

"Too many have already died," Whirlwind concluded. "Go and smoke on it, Arrow-keeper.

Bleed and fast. Invite a new dream. Bring medicine to us that will protect our young men, and truth that can lead the People back to the sacred path."

"Ayyyy!" Two Moons howled. "That would be good."

"Consult *Mahuts,*" Iron Wolf urged. "The Arrows have always guided our movements. It should be that way again."

"You haven't heard me," Talking Stick complained.

"We hear your empty words," Dancing Lance declared. "There are only a few who will follow them. Do as the council instructs and speak to us again."

"Later, when the hunting's completed," Two Moons suggested.

"After the *wihio* have ruined the country?" Talking Stick cried.

"I'll allow no starving this winter," Dancing Lance barked. "Bull Buffalo is nearby, eager to feed and clothe the helpless ones. We turn away from you, Talking Stick, and rely on our old benefactors."

"It's necessary," Iron Wolf agreed. "First we'll hunt. Then we'll consider making war on the *wihio.*"

"The war's here," Talking Stick growled.

"Yes, the old struggle has never left," Dancing Lance agreed. "We must feed the hungry. Make lodges to ward off winter's cold. That's the war we're fighting, Arrow-keeper."

Talking Stick glared at the chiefs, but they no longer were willing to listen to him. Instead Two Moons told of the scouts he had dispatched to watch the buffalo herd, and the chiefs organized the prayers and ceremonies that would be performed.

"Talking Stick can prepare the hunters," Roaring Bear suggested.

"I can't invoke Bull Buffalo and make medicine to kill *wihio*," the Stick said.

"My brother can prepare us," Iron Wolf boasted. "Have you seen the shield he carries? It holds great power."

"You know the ancient prayers?" Dancing Lance asked.

"I know what's to be done," Dreaming Wolf answered.

"Then it's good you have come among us," Dancing Lance declared. "You can perform the ceremonies, showing the young ones what's to be spoken before the hunt. Then all of us will have the true aim, and we'll enjoy success."

"We brought you here for another reason," Whirlwind explained.

"Uncle?" Dreaming Wolf asked, using the title out of respect rather than kinship.

Iron Wolf began by recounting his brother's rescue of the Pawnee captives. As each portion of the tale followed the one before, the chiefs grew more attentive. Finally, when the wild flight with the Pawnee ponies found their ears, even old Roaring Bear noted the courage of their young visitor.

Dancing Lance recounted the rescue of the Arrows, and Whirlwind told of Dreaming Wolf's devotion to the wounded.

"You were there and saw it all, Stick," Dancing Lance said, turning to the Arrow-keeper. "Tell us about it."

"I only know he brought *Mahuts* back into my care," Talking Stick muttered. "I was preparing to retrieve them with the Crazy Dogs when this boy appeared from nowhere and charged the wagons."

"He had time to see and act from far away, but you waited," Iron Wolf declared.

"I didn't notice the Arrows were gone," Talking Stick explained.

"Next he will tell us it snows only in summer," Whirlwind said, laughing.

"Believe what you will!" the Stick raged. "You sit here and insult your medicine chief, the keeper of *Mahuts*. I hold the power most sacred to the People, and you treat me no better than a fattening grandmother!"

Dreaming Wolf read the hurt in the Arrow-keeper's eyes. He recognized it. Stone Wolf, too, had suffered from the sting of hard words. It was enough to kindle sympathy in some. Dreaming Wolf found no pity for Talking Stick, though. The Stick had brought about too much suffering. If he, too, now felt the barbs of criticism, it was only justice.

Twenty-one

As the council fire burned down to embers, Dancing Lance drew Dreaming Wolf to his side.

"A brave man should be more easily recognized," the *Hev a tan iu* chief declared. He then drew out two eagle feathers and tied them in Dreaming Wolf's hair.

"You'll soon need a bonnet to hold these great honors," Iron Wolf observed afterward when they walked from the council.

"I'll never wear a bonnet," Dreaming Wolf replied. "My road is the medicine trail, and a modest man most easily walks it."

"If *Ne' hyo* was right, and hard days still lie ahead, the young men will need good chiefs to follow," Iron Wolf argued. "A bonnet isn't always worn boastfully. It can also crown the head of a quiet leader."

"*Ne' hyo* was rarely wrong," Dreaming Wolf observed. "Even so, you will more easily wear a chief's bonnet."

"I know you always thought you would be called upon to keep *Mahuts*."

"That's for an older man to do, *Nah nih*. I understand that. I only wish it were a better man."

"I do, too," Iron Wolf agreed.

With the council's business concluded, the chiefs returned to their individual bands to organize the hunting parties. It wasn't long thereafter that the scattered *Tsis tsis tas* bands assembled.

Dreaming Wolf met with the chiefs of the warrior societies and instructed them in the making of the ancient hunting prayers. Afterward, hunters performed the ritual dances, and pony boys as young as twelve summers were inducted into the societies.

Dreaming Wolf and Stone Lance devoted much of their time to visiting the wounded. Some already grew better. Others would be a long time mending still.

"I will never again hold a bow," Bent Arrow lamented, "but I can shape stone points. I've watched you. In time, I may come to learn some of the medicine cures."

"There are too few of us who know the old cures," Dreaming Wolf observed. "It would be good to share the sacred path with you."

Before the hunting parties dispersed across the plains, each man entered a sweat lodge to cast off any disharmony and purify his spirit. Some of the younger boys approached the sweat lodge nervously, but even they found that the fierce heat drove the evil humors from their bodies. As they listened to the old prayers, many nodded solemnly.

"Man Above, it's for the helpless ones I'll hunt," young Stalker vowed.

"*Heammawihio* honors such a pledge," Dreaming Wolf declared.

"I've been invited to join the Foxes," the boy explained. "We accept the difficult tasks."

"Yes," Dreaming Wolf agreed. "We do."

"We'll hunt Bull Buffalo together then," Stalker said, grinning. "Ayyyy! We'll kill many."

"Ah, I will ride with the *Hev a tan iu*," Dreaming Wolf explained.

"But Iron Wolf leads the Foxes," Stalker argued. "He's your brother!"

"He has married a Windpipe, and so he follows Two Moons," Dreaming Wolf explained.

"You and Stone Lance slept in his lodge," Stalker observed.

"Yes, we did," Stone Lance said, staring curiously at his cousin. "We don't belong among the Rope Men now. We should rejoin our brothers."

"Dancing Lance has asked us to stay," Dreaming Wolf said, sighing. "He worries that without us, the young men will again turn to Talking Stick."

"You only stay to safeguard *Mahuts,*" Stone Lance grumbled. "You feel the obligation."

"Yes," the Wolf confessed. "I do. Too long I

slept in Arrow Lodge. *Ne' hyo* expects us to look after the welfare of the People."

"We've done that," Stone Lance insisted. "Didn't we rescue the helpless ones? Haven't we hunted?"

"I can't explain why I must remain, *See' was' sin mit*. My heart calls on me to stay. We would be welcome in the young men's lodge, but Iron Wolf would be equally glad to have you riding with him."

"Have you forgotten the girl?" Stone Lance asked. "Singing Doe?"

"I've forgotten nothing," Dreaming Wolf replied. "But I must do what my dreams demand."

"You've had another dream?"

"Yes," Dreaming Wolf admitted. "I saw many buffalo fall to our arrows, and there was enough to eat. Dark clouds choked the sun then, and fire swept through our camps. I must prevent it."

"How?" Stone Lance asked. "Among your brothers, the Windpipes remember our rescue. They listen. But here . . ."

"We have friends," Dreaming Wolf insisted. "Otter Foot. Raven's Wing."

"Your age-mates," Stone Lance said, scowling. *"Nah nih,* I'm afraid we'll find only more death in this camp."

"It's dying I mean to prevent."

"Ah, but can you?"

The last sweltering days of the summer soon

273

melted into memory, and the hunting was finished for a time. The *Tsis tsis tas* bands smoked meat and worked hides into lodgeskins and clothing. Peace seemed to settle over the hills north of Shell River, and although small parties continued to harass the *wihio* wagon camps, few were killed on either side.

"We've done well," Stone Lance boasted as he walked with Dreaming Wolf through the *Hev a tan iu* camp. "See how round the children are growing? Even the old people have enough. We should go now."

"Go?" Dreaming Wolf asked.

"We should visit your brothers," Stone Lance declared. "We would be welcome there when the snows come. The young men's lodge is too empty a place to spend winter."

"I explained before," Dreaming Wolf said, frowning. "My place is here."

"Why, *Nah nih?*" Stone Lance cried. "Why?"

"I told you of my dream."

"You spoke of a fire. What does it mean?"

"I'm not certain," Dreaming Wolf admitted. "I do know, though, that it threatens the heart of the People. *Mahuts.*"

"I understand you feel an obligation," Stone Lance said, shuddering as he grasped his cousin's wrists in ironlike grips. "I, too, dream, though. And I have seen a flock of birds flying across the sky. They are brothers, these birds. Hawks, I think. An arrow flies skyward toward them, and one dives before the others. The arrow pierces its heart, and it falls."

"You think one of us is to die then," Dreaming Wolf noted. "We're all brothers here, though."

"But who is it who always rides ahead, who eagerly protects the helpless ones?"

"You think it's my death you've seen?"

"Yes," the Lance said, shivering as if an icy hand gripped his spine.

"I don't fear death, *See' was' sin mit*," Dreaming Wolf declared soberly.

"It's not a thing to dread, *Nah nih,* but life is precious. To give it up for a brother brings great honor, but to throw it away . . ."

"Throw it away?"

"You only help Talking Stick preserve his hold on the People by remaining here," Stone Lance declared. "Look how when everyone able to lift a bow was hunting, he busied himself pounding buffalo horns and elk teeth into medicine powder. How many times has he ridden out with the Crazy Dogs to strike the *wihio?* Ten? Twenty? He's a man of great medicine power, isn't he? He returns with the scalps of children. He rides down on boys swimming in the river! This is the greatness you would save."

"It's not for him I'm staying."

"Then why?" Stone Lance asked. "We have no relatives here and few friends. These are the people who turned away from your father's warnings. They don't heed your advice, either. We should go."

275

"Soon," Dreaming Wolf promised. "Before first snow."

"I hope it won't be too late," Stone Lance replied. "Death travels on fast wings."

When the plum moon rose high in the sky, Talking Stick sent riders to summon the chiefs to a new council. The Arrow-keeper, too, had dreamed. He saw many *wihio* wagons burning in a great fire, and he told the chiefs of a plan to strike hard at the hated enemy.

"I smell death on the wind," Iron Wolf told Dreaming Wolf afterward.

"Can't the chiefs stop him?" Dreaming Wolf cried.

"How, *See' was' sin mit?* The young men only hear the prophecy and imagine winning honor in battle."

"Doesn't anyone remember the Shell River fight?"

"Ah, there are many, especially among the Foxes. But we can't turn away when the other soldier societies are vowing to strike the enemy hard. Even those who would have spoken loudly against it have heard of your dream. 'These fires must be the same,' they say."

Dreaming Wolf sighed. It was as Stone Lance had warned. Talking Stick once again led the People into danger, and who was to blame? No one more than Dreaming Wolf himself.

Talking Stick sent out parties of Crazy Dogs

to scout the trail even before preparing the medicine prayers. Dreaming Wolf felt tricked by the Arrow-keeper, and he was quick to remind the chiefs of the necessary preparations.

"We waste too much time," Talking Stick complained.

"We'll have no more fights like Shell River," Whirlwind insisted. "You must send a pipe to each of the soldier societies. We'll pray and dance. You must offer what medicine you can to the young men. Older men must rely on what they have obtained."

And so the preparations continued. Boys so small they had yet to grow chin hairs painted their chests and tied elk charms behind their ears. Bands camped far to the north came to join in the fight.

"Ah, it will be long remembered, this day," Talking Stick boasted. "All the People will join together and sweep the *wihio* from our country!"

Many of the chiefs sighed, and some of the old men grumbled in disgust. The Arrow-keeper had made that boast too often. The younger men howled confidently, though. And when scouts arrived to tell of a large wagon camp to the west, a war party two hundred strong set out to do battle.

They were three days reaching the place where the *wihio* were camped. Along the way, stray wagons straggling behind the last of the westbound companies were attacked. The unfortu-

277

nate travelers often put up gallant fights, but they were always hopelessly outnumbered. Men and women were quickly killed, although some *Tsis tsis tas* made sport of killing them. As for the children, some of the younger ones were taken captive. A few were even sold to *wihio* traders for rifles and powder.

Dreaming Wolf disdained those unequal fights. He considered it little more than murder, and he soured to see the tortures the Crazy Dogs would sometimes perform. Flames devoured the wagons themselves, marking Shell River with towering funeral pyres of sorts.

"It's only the beginning of our firestorm!" Talking Stick boasted. His master stroke was yet to come.

Dreaming Wolf and Stone Lance rode with Dancing Lance and Whirlwind. The *Hev a tan iu* Foxes were the strongest band, but Talking Stick gave them only a small part of the fighting. They were to strike the wagon camp from the south while a line of Crazy Dog suicide soldiers made a frontal assault on the *wihio*s.

"It's a good plan!" Bull Heart, Roaring Bear's oldest son, declared. "We Crazy Dogs will run them!"

"It would be better to wait for dawn," Dancing Lance complained. "They have good guns, these *wihio,* and their wagons make good walls."

"Yes," Dreaming Wolf agreed as he studied the camp. "These aren't wagon people."

278

"It's said they look for a trail north," Whirl-wind explained. "Some are bluecoat soldiers. They bring no women and children with them, though."

"It's certain to be a hard fight," Stone Lance said. *"Nah nih,* remember my dream. Hold back."

"I'll remember," Dreaming Wolf promised. His eyes betrayed a great aversion for this fight. He dreaded killing bluecoats. Stone Wolf had warned that when a bluecoat was killed, three came to replace him.

"We must kill them all!" Talking Stick urged as he rode before the tense bands of *Tsis tsis tas.* "Spare no one. They must not live to bring others into the heart of our country!"

"Why attack at all?" Otter Foot taunted. "You could ride into their camp and talk them to death!"

The Crazy Dogs hurled insults at the young Fox, but Talking Stick silenced them.

"Now!" he shouted.

The Crazy Dogs howled as the five suicide soldiers lit torches and raced toward the *wihio* camp, screaming and waving their fiery bundles so that a line of sparks followed their ponies. The *wihio* waited until the Crazy Dogs were quite close before firing, and the volley slammed into the riders hard. Two Crazy Dogs fell instantly, their chests shattered by as many as five bullets. The others, too, were struck, and their horses were killed. Two of the brave young men

279

managed to crawl onward and hurl their lances into wagons. Flames quickly licked the canvas covers and consumed the dry beds. The grass, too, caught fire, and the *wihio* scrambled to extinguish the flames before they reached the powder supplies.

"Nothing lives long!" Talking Stick shouted as he waved his lance at the enemy.

"Only the earth and the mountains," Whirlwind said as he and Dancing Lance directed the Foxes toward the southern arc of the circled wagons. Screaming as they charged, the young Foxes charged the *wihio* camp. Only a shot or two met them as they surged up a slight rise and broke into the camp.

The fighting was furious. Bluecoats used their rifles as clubs to deflect lances and war axes. Some men grappled like boys wrestling in river mud. This was far more deadly fighting, though. Rarely did more than one man rise after such an encounter.

Dreaming Wolf remained atop his horse at first. Then, when a large *wihio* charged Otter Foot, the Wolf raced over, jumped from his pony, and stunned the fat *wihio* with a fierce blow across the back of the head.

"Ayyyy!" Otter Foot shouted as he counted coup on the helpless bluecoat. Raven's Wing, too, counted coup. Grass Snake, Whirlwind's young son, rushed over and cut the *wihio's* forelock away.

"Finish me," the bleeding soldier pleaded

when he stared up at his scalp.

Stone Lance then fired an arrow into the man's heart, killing him instantly.

Thereafter, it wasn't much of a fight. One group of bluecoats formed a square and fought on, but the others raced out onto the prairie or hid among the wagons. It was death to face a *Tsis tsis tas* in the open, as those who tried that quickly learned. And once the raiders began setting the wagons afire, the hiders, too, stood little chance.

Dreaming Wolf turned toward the last wagon in line. Two men were firing rifles from the bed, keeping their attackers at bay. Their aim was good, and already two Foxes lay bleeding.

"No!" Stone Lance called when Dreaming Wolf caught a riderless pony, mounted, and kicked it into a gallop. The horse flew toward the wagon, and he was able to deflect the single rifle ball fired at him with the heavy buffalo shield. Dreaming Wolf then tore a gap in the canvas cover and jumped the first of the men.

He was old, with long white hair that curled on both sides of a bald crown. Dreaming Wolf knocked his rifle aside and slapped his chest with a heavy hand.

"Yes, the old way," the *wihio* said, smiling faintly. He then pulled a knife. Dreaming Wolf drove his lance through the old man's ribs, and the *wihio* slumped across the nearby wheel, bleeding out his life.

Dreaming Wolf was gazing sadly at the dying

wihio when savage fingers tore at his back. The other *wihio* threw him down and drove a knee into his back. Pain surged up the Wolf's spine, momentarily paralyzing him.

"You red murderer!" the *wihio* shouted. Dreaming Wolf managed to turn his head in time to see a rifle lifted over his head. It never completed its killing descent.

"Wolf?" a startled Ike Williams gasped.

"Lone Hawk?" Dreaming Wolf asked in reply.

"Not you, too," Little Ike said, glancing around him at the smoke and flame and death.

"Come," Dreaming Wolf said, struggling to rise. "Stone Lance is near. We'll protect you."

"Wolf?" Ike managed to whisper as he turned slowly, revealing a pair of arrows protruding from his back.

"No!" Dreaming Wolf said as he suddenly saw Stone Lance's vision. There was the brother hawk, falling. He who couldn't kill was dying instead.

"Nah nih!" Stone Lance shouted as he climbed into the wagon. "Oh, no," he mumbled when he recognized his dying friend.

"He could have killed me," Dreaming Wolf mumbled. "He stopped."

"And died instead," Stone Lance said, trembling as he stared sorrowfully into Ike's eyes. Only now did Dreaming Wolf recognize the markings of the arrows protruding from Ike's back.

"You couldn't know, *See' was' sin mit,*" the

Wolf argued. "You didn't see his face."

"We've killed our brother," Stone Lance said, fighting to stem the blood. "Lone Hawk? Ike?"

"Not your fault, Lance," Ike whispered. "Can't stand in the middle forever and not get hurt."

The cousins carried Ike from the wagon and knelt beside him as he bled out his life. A group of pony boys, seeing the unmarked corpse, rushed over with knives to cut the hair away, but Dreaming Wolf, wild-eyed, halted them with his lance.

"No one will touch him!" the Wolf shouted, and the boys withdrew.

Dreaming Wolf and Stone Lance remained there, guarding the frail figure that had been a brother to them both. When the fighting finally ended, they carried Ike into the hills and placed him high in the fork of a cottonwood.

"Rest well, Little Ike," Stone Lance said, covering the body with a buffalo robe.

"Yes, rest well," Dreaming Wolf agreed as he hacked away at his hair. "There was never any darkness in your heart, little brother. You bought my life with your own. It was a poor trade."

Twenty-two

For three days, Dreaming Wolf and Stone Lance mourned their dead *wihio* brother. Then they returned to the burned wagon camp. Talking Stick was still celebrating his triumph. The Arrow-keeper had held a scalp dance, and many of the young men wore feathers tied in their hair. The dead and the wounded had received little attention, though, and the cousins hurried to offer what medicine cures they knew.

Talking Stick proclaimed the battle a great victory. Others saw it differently. Now that the bloodletting was over, and the flames had finished with the wagons, the *Tsis tsis tas* realized it was but a small camp. They counted only ten bluecoats among the dead. With them were two older men whose soft bodies marked them as strangers to the plains. Besides Lone Hawk Ike Williams, a pair of beaver men well known to the Eaters were killed.

"Here's your great victory, Stick!" Whirlwind

cried as he laid the body of his son, Grass Snake, on a travois. A bullet hole marked the boy's bare chest, and blood had washed the white horn paint away.

"Where was the bulletproofing?" Otter Foot asked as he helped Raven's Wing mount a pony. The Wing was hobbled by a bullet wound in the thigh.

Even the Crazy Dogs were shaken. Besides the five suicide soldiers, three others had been killed. In all, the raiders mourned twelve killed, and as many more were badly hurt.

"Victories like this will empty our camps," Dancing Lance observed.

"We also rubbed out many *wihio* along Shell River," Talking Stick boasted.

"Women," Whirlwind grumbled. "Children. A man can shoot camp dogs and claim the true aim, but what has he gained? If there are other bluecoats on Shell River, they will come to punish us. Who will fight then? Pony boys?"

"We'll drive them all from our country!" Talking Stick insisted. His eyes were glazed as he inhaled the smell of fire and death.

Dreaming Wolf turned away in disgust. The sight of an Arrow-keeper bright with blood lust was more than he could tolerate.

"Where are you going, Wolf?" young Bull Heart called.

"There are other *wihio* to kill!" Talking Stick added.

"I can follow your bad heart path no longer!" Dreaming Wolf shouted.

"He's mourning the *wihio*," Talking Stick said, laughing. "He's walked with them so long his blood's grown white!"

"Ayyyy!" Dreaming Wolf screamed, drawing his knife and cutting a shallow gash across his chest. Bright red blood flowed down across his belly, and the others gazed at him, stunned.

"Well?" Stone Lance asked. "Look at it!"

"What color do you see?" Dreaming Wolf demanded. "It should be familiar. You've painted the country with it! And what harm have you done the *wihio?* Look and see. A few wagons? A family here and another there? A hunting party or a band in search of a trail? You're like a flea on the back of a bear, Talking Stick! Of no consequence!"

The words rolled through the camp like thunder. Chiefs gazed at the Arrow-keeper scornfully. Famous fighters hung their heads. Even pony boys stared at Talking Stick with questioning eyes.

"A flea?" the Stick cried. "Look at the death I've brought!"

"I'm looking!" Whirlwind screamed as he stared at his dead son. "Ayyyy! What misfortune turned the bullets from your heart, prophet? You promise us honor and show us only death!"

There was a growing murmur of dissatisfaction. Men grouped in bands and spoke of riding home. Others set out singly or in pairs. Dreaming Wolf and Stone Lance chose to accompany Whirlwind and Grass Snake back to the *Hev a tan iu* camp.

"We have work yet to do!" Talking Stick called as the warriors scattered. Those who might have heeded his call were dead, though. The living had seen and heard enough.

Dreaming Wolf and Stone Lance joined in the mourning at the *Hev a tan iu* camp. Afterward, they bundled their possessions and prepared to leave.

"Stay," Otter Foot urged. "We Foxes grow fewer, and the People will need your devotion when winter arrives."

"There's hunting to do," Dancing Lance added. "Stay. You're welcome in my lodge."

"There's no harmony here," Dreaming Wolf explained. "Our hearts are heavy, and there's no medicine here to restore our balance. We must seek it elsewhere."

"Winter's coming," Dancing Lance warned. "Two men alone . . . with the *wihio* wary of us. You must rejoin the sacred hoop of the People. There you'll find the harmony you've lost."

"We'll return," Dreaming Wolf promised.

"After we have made peace with ourselves," Stone Lance added. "Uncle, we're grateful for your help, but this is no place for us. For anyone. Not so long as a dark heart keeps the Arrows."

"That may soon change," Dancing Lance insisted. "Talking Stick has few supporters in the council."

"When was it otherwise?" Dreaming Wolf asked. "After Shell River? He will have a new dream, and the old men will let him talk. Boys eager to prove themselves will paint their faces and ride to their deaths. And we'll have others to mourn."

Dancing Lance stood for a time, digesting the words. He started to argue, but Dreaming Wolf had already mounted a pony. The cousins left the camp quietly, glancing back at old friends and fighting off the memories that drew them back.

"We're *Hev a tan iu* no longer," Stone Lance whispered as they turned south.

"I know," Dreaming Wolf agreed. "We must find a new, better road to walk."

"Will we?" Stone Lance asked.

"We'll climb into the hills and pray for a vision, *See' was' sin mit. Heammawihio* won't abandon us."

"Perhaps our dreams will show us a road all the People can walk."

"That will be our prayer," Dreaming Wolf said, swallowing a growing sadness. He took up the words of an old warrior song then.

"Ayyyy! We of the *Tsis tsis tas,*
the original People,
brave up for the hard fight
we are facing.

"Ayyy! We few warriors
will stand on this ground,
protecting the helpless
and trusting in our medicine."

"It's an appropriate song," Stone Lance observed. "We are few. But is there medicine we can trust?"

"We must make it, *See' was' sin mit.*"

"Yes, we're Foxes. It's for us to do the difficult things."

Again and again, Dreaming Wolf sang the song. Once it had driven away his doubts. Now he heard only the haunting echoes of his own thoughts. *Where will we go? What will we be?*

The wind carried no answer to his questions, and it was the only sound to be heard. The world had grown silent. *It's fitting,* Dreaming Wolf told himself. *Even earth and sky should mourn what has happened to this country.*

They rode for a time, then made a camp in the low hills north of Shell River. Next morning they would make the dawn prayers, swim in the river, and ride on. It was a journey of the lost. It had no purpose, no destination.

They might have wandered aimlessly until first snow had the hawk not flown overhead.

"Look!" Stone Lance called, pointing to the bird.

Dreaming Wolf gazed up and smiled as a graceful red-tailed hawk turned slow circles in the sky. He might have been hunting rabbits or perhaps waiting for a slow-flying pigeon, but if so, he made no attempt to dive at it. Instead, he soared as if flying for the unreserved joy of it.

"He's watching us," Stone Lance said, brightening. "Our brother, Lone Hawk, is with us once again."

Dreaming Wolf thought to remark it was only a hawk, but the bird touched his soul. And when it turned eastward, the Wolf nudged his pony in that direction.

"Yes, he knows the way," Stone Lance urged. "Follow our brother."

All afternoon they followed Shell River eastward, carefully skirting the dust clouds raised by wagon bands or prowling Pawnees. Only toward dusk did they finally lose sight of the hawk.

"There's a good place to camp nearby," Dreaming Wolf noted.

"Yes," Stone Lance agreed. "Once we swam here with our *wihio* cousins. It was the time we gave Lone Hawk his name."

"We spoke then of better days," Dreaming Wolf said, remembering. "And of the peril of being caught between two enemies."

"We were never enemies, Lone Hawk and I, but I killed him," Stone Lance lamented. "Ayyyy! I've cut my hair and bled in mourning, but still his ghost haunts me."

"He didn't blame you," Dreaming Wolf told his cousin, hoping the reassurance would salve the Lance's wounded heart. "It was only circumstance."

"We hurried him up Hanging Road."

"Yes, and we took him to our hearts when he had no one else. Look at how he came to us when we were lost and showed us a path to walk."

"Yes, there's that," Stone Lance agreed.

When they came to the old camping spot at Shell River, they heard the sounds of laughter upriver. Cautiously, they hid their ponies and wove their way through the faint light to the river. There, barely visible in the fading light of dusk, were six boys, splashing in the river, laughing and shouting as boys were prone to do. Whether brown or white, who could tell?

"It doesn't matter, *Nah nih,*" Stone Lance whispered as if reading his cousin's thoughts. "That's why Lone Hawk brought us here. To say it doesn't matter."

"It does, though," Dreaming Wolf argued as they turned back toward their horses. "*Tsis tsis tas* or Pawnee, *wihio* or Crow, enemy or friend. Life or death."

291

"Even that's our own choice, though," the Lance argued. "Cut our hair short and steal the pigment from our skin. What would you have that was different from our *wihio* cousins?"

"Physically, yes, we would be alike," Dreaming Wolf agreed. "But we carry deep within us the knowledge of the old ones. To us it's only important to walk the sacred path. In this way, we complete the medicine wheel that is life. *Wihio* must build things. They mark the land and call it their own. They use all that a place has to offer them and leave it barren."

"It doesn't have to be that way."

"No, but it is easier to swallow a bear than to change a *wihio* heart."

"It's not so hard, swallowing a bear," Stone Lance said, grinning. "You cook a little at a time and eat only what you can."

"Maybe we should feed the *wihio* the same way," Dreaming Wolf said, laughing at the notion.

"If we could only do it, there might be peace here again," Stone Lance said, sighing.

They reached the horses, then, mounted, and rode off northward, away from the river.

When the hawk found them that next morning, neither cousin was surprised. Again the bird flew east, and Dreaming Wolf sensed he knew where. Three days they wandered north and east across the rough hills, trusting in the hawk's power. It was dreamlike, that ride, for the night filled with the howls of wolves and the call of a mourning dove. Finally, they glimpsed the familiar outline of *Noahvose,* the sacred heart of the world.

"It's here Sweet Medicine went when he was lost," Stone Lance noted. "Ayyyy! Brother Hawk, you brought us back to our beginnings."

"To our fathers, too," Dreaming Wolf added. "Here our grandfather's father and his uncle, old Touches the Sky, found a peaceful conclusion to their troubled lives."

"Have we come here to die, then?" the Lance asked.

"No, *See' was' sin mit,*" the Wolf answered. "I think we've come to dream."

It was Dreaming Wolf's first journey to *Noahvose* without his father, and recollections of Stone Wolf seemed to flood his mind.

"You've guided us well, Lone Hawk," Stone Lance declared as he took charge of the ponies. *"Nah nih,* we can make camp here, below Sweet Medicine's cave, where we prayed and dreamed the last time."

"Yes, it's a good place," Dreaming Wolf agreed.

Together they gazed overhead as the hawk completed a final circle around the summit of the sacred mountain. Then the bird flew off into the clouds, and the cousins were left to prepare for the dream.

Many times, the two young men had helped

293

Stone Wolf invite a vision, and they knew what to do. First it was necessary to build a fire. Then, after sharing a scant meal of dried buffalo meat, they rolled buffalo hides out beside the fire.

"It's for you to seek the dream," Stone Lance suggested. *"Nah nih,* I will keep the fire and watch for enemies."

"It's necessary," Dreaming Wolf said, knowing his young cousin would have preferred to seek the vision himself.

"I told you before," the Lance said as he arranged the medicine pouches. "I will walk at your side, aiding you when I can."

"The dream will come to me, but it will nevertheless be ours, *See' was' sin mit,"* the Wolf replied. "It must bring power to lead the People from peril."

"It will, *Nah nih."*

Dreaming Wolf nodded. After performing the pipe ritual, he shed his clothes and stood naked before the fire.

"Heammawihio, hear my prayer!" the Wolf began. "Fill my dreams with wisdom. Show the People what path to walk. Ayyyy! We rely on you to guide us!"

Stone Lance handed his cousin a knife, and Dreaming Wolf cut long lines in the flesh of his chest. As blood colored the wounds and ran down his belly and across his thighs, Dreaming Wolf sang the ancient medicine songs he'd learned from his father. He invoked the spirits of earth and sky, invited Bull Buffalo and White Buffalo Cow, and even called upon the ghosts of the old ones to impart their wisdom.

"Hear me, *Heammawihio,*" he prayed again and again. "Send me a dream."

Two days and two nights, Dreaming Wolf sang and prayed. He cut the flesh of his chest again and slashed his arms. Forsaking food, he felt himself growing weak and feverish. Finally, on the third day, he collapsed. Stone Lance covered him with a buffalo hide, and for a time Dreaming Wolf lay there, shivering. Then his body grew quiet, and the dream came.

At first there was only the deep blue of the autumn sky. Then Lone Hawk flew into the vision, screaming in a ghostly voice.

"All that's come before is past," he sang. "Now you must make your beginning."

As Lone Hawk departed, a great black thundercloud formed. The sky grew dark, and lightning slashed across the world. From amid the cloud roared Bull Buffalo.

"Where are the men who once walked the sacred path?" he bellowed. "Are they dead, or have they only forgotten to ask my help?"

"Yes," a milder voice said. White Buffalo Cow now entered the dream, followed by a herd of her children. "When you spoke to me of your need, I always provided," she said sorrowfully. "My children gave their skins to clothe you. Their sinew provided bowstrings to guide your stone points into their brothers' hearts. When you were hungry, you ate their flesh and were strong. All these things I gave you because you walked the earth reverently, with respect for what had come before. You took only what was needed, and you asked before you took.

"Now people come to this country with guns and slaughter us. Ayyyy! They ask nothing. They take everything. They spoil the country. They cut Mother Earth and foul our sisters, the rivers. They plant no seeds. They grow nothing. No, they know only the killing of things, hunting not to satisfy need but to appease their lust!"

"This must end," Bull Buffalo commanded, "or we will walk only ghost roads on the other side. First it will be the buffalo, elk, and deer. Then the People. Turn back to the sacred path! Leave the road of hate and ignorance."

"Hear them, *Nah nih*," Lone Hawk spoke as he settled on a cloud. The face of young Isaiah Williams emerged from the hawk, and the boy's sad eyes tore into Dreaming Wolf's soul. "Go and bridge the canyon that separates our peoples. Restore the lost harmony. Protect the helpless ones."

Dreaming Wolf had no voice to answer the phantoms. It wasn't required. They were there only to advise, to suggest. It was for him to act.

He awoke to the cool touch of a damp cloth. Stone Lance was chasing the fever from his brow.

"You dreamed?" the Lance asked.

"I saw it all," Dreaming Wolf answered. "There's much for us to do."

"First you must rest and eat. You've bled too much, and the fever's high. You're weak."

"Yes, it's necessary to regain my strength," the Wolf agreed. "But it can't wait long. I smell winter on the wind."

"Yes," Stone Lance agreed. "We won't pass it here, then?"

"We must find the People and make prayers. Then we must hunt Bull Buffalo so that the helpless ones won't starve."

"The hunt's begun already, *Nah nih.*"

"Perhaps, but did they make the proper preparations? If not, there won't be enough food to meet the winter need. People will starve!"

"We'll insure that won't happen, *Nah nih.* We'll make the medicine prayers, and we'll hunt."

"Yes, *See' was' sin mit.* All that and more."

Twenty-three

When the fever had passed, and Dreaming
Wolf had recovered his strength, the cousins left
Noahvose and rode westward. No hawk guided
them now. Instead, Dreaming Wolf crossed the
familiar streams and rode past hills where he'd
enjoyed better days. The dream seemed to draw
him, and he never doubted he would find the
People before the snows came.

As the sun hung high overhead, Dreaming
Wolf sang:

"Ayyyy! We of the *Tsis tsis tas,*
the original People,
brave up for the hard fight
we are facing.

"Ayyyy! We few warriors
will stand on this ground,
protecting the helpless
and trusting in our medicine."

Soon Stone Lance joined the song, and they journeyed northward with lighter hearts. Even the ponies seemed to run with a brisker gait.

For two days, they crossed the windswept plain, seeing no one. It might as well have been the valleys of the moon! They saw no sign of game, and if they hadn't plucked trout from a stream, they would have been hungry.

"Where's Bull Buffalo?" Stone Lance asked. "He's always walked this country when winter's near."

"We must make the prayers first," Dreaming Wolf insisted. "Then he'll come."

Dreaming Wolf's confidence set aside Stone Lance's initial doubts, but when they saw no buffalo the third day and the fourth, it was hard not to grow discouraged. Nightfall was approaching when Stone Lance spied the hunting party.

"There," he called, motioning to five horsemen silhouetted against the western sky.

"Be careful," Dreaming Wolf urged. "It's hard to tell who they are in the shadow light. Crows, too, ride here."

"They aren't Crows, though," the Lance declared as he held his bow up over his head. The approaching riders answered the salute, and soon the smallest of them charged ahead.

Dreaming Wolf's wrinkled brow faded when he identified Stalker. Close behind rode Panther Claw and Rock Turtle. Last came Goes Ahead.

"Nah nih, I'm glad to see you!" Dreaming Wolf said, greeting his brother.

"We thought you surely scalped," Goes Ahead said, clasping the Wolf's hands before turning to greet his cousin, Stone Lance, in like manner. The boys were as eager to see their friends, and for a moment all seven sang excitedly.

"You've come in time to join the hunt!" Stalker exclaimed. "Ayyyy! We'll find Bull Buffalo now!"

"We must," Goes Ahead said, dropping his gaze toward the earth. "Already hunger haunts our camp, and winter's yet to come."

"Where have you come from?" Rock Turtle asked, studying the eyes of his newly arrived comrades. "What's happened? Word came of the *wihio* fight. You didn't return with the others."

"No," Dreaming Wolf told them. "Our path led us to *Noahvose.*"

"Ah," Goes Ahead said, nodding somberly. "Did *Ne' hyo* speak to you, then?"

"He was near," Dreaming Wolf explained, "but it was Bull Buffalo that sent us to you."

"Did you see a herd, then?" Stalker asked excitedly.

"No," Stone Lance replied, "but we will. Bull Buffalo promised *Nah nih* a successful hunt."

"The others will cheer to hear it," Goes Ahead observed. "We have found nothing these many days, and even the brave hearts despair."

"Were the ceremonies performed?" Dreaming

Wolf asked. "Did the hunters join in the buffalo dance?"

"No," Goes Ahead admitted. "We were camped near the *Hev a tan iu,* and Talking Stick directed the hunt. We thought it good, for he brought out the Buffalo Arrows. His medicine prayers and charms gained us nothing, though. We left him behind."

"He was a long time returning from the fighting," Stalker explained. "He said there was no time to perform the old rites, and so he made only simple prayers."

"Can it be he's forgotten the ceremonies?" Dreaming Wolf wondered aloud. "Can any man be so foolish as to ignore the sacred ways of the People?"

"He has lost his way," Panther Claw declared. "His eyes are full of hatred for the *wihio,* and he's blind to the hunger in our camps."

"Some of us can't be," Dreaming Wolf said, frowning. "I would hold a council, *Nah nih,* and make the proper preparations. I don't keep the Arrows, but I know what should be done."

"I can't speak for all the bands," Goes Ahead said, "but Two Moons and Iron Wolf will agree to it. There's been enough starving in the Windpipe lodges."

"We'll go, my brother and I, to collect the others," Panther Claw volunteered.

"We can stay and begin the preparations," Stone Lance suggested.

"It's a good plan," Goes Ahead declared. "Let's do it."

So, while Panther Claw and Rock Turtle rode off to assemble the scattered hunting parties, Goes Ahead, Dreaming Wolf, and Stone Lance erected a sweat lodge. Little Stalker collected wood and stone for the ritual. Later they joined in a sweat.

"It's a heavy burden you carry," Stalker told Dreaming Wolf afterward. "I know only the obligation of the hunt. You must safeguard all the People."

"Sometimes I feel its weight," the Wolf confessed. "But no man picks the path he walks."

"It's for *Heammawihio* to do," the boy agreed. "You'll ride with us when it's time to strike Bull Buffalo, though?"

"Even a medicine man enjoys the hunt," Dreaming Wolf said, grinning. "It's part of the sacred hoop of life, and so long as the rituals are observed, and the killing is done of need, with respect, Bull Buffalo will give himself up to us."

"Many have forgotten that," Stalker noted.

"That, and more besides," Dreaming Wolf said bitterly. "We must draw the People back to the sacred path before it's too late."

Panther Claw and Rock Turtle were three days reaching all the hunters. Windpipes soon arrived, as did other northern bands hungry for success. Dancing Lance and Whirlwind brought a party of *Hev a tan iu,* but most of the Rope Men remained with their Arrow-keeper, well to the south.

"They'll find only death there," Iron Wolf declared as he greeted his youngest brother.

"We'll mourn them later," Dreaming Wolf replied.

"Yes," Stone Lance added as he clasped Iron Wolf's hands. "Now we must make medicine."

First, Dreaming Wolf drew the chiefs to a tall council fire. There they smoked and made plans for scouting the buffalo herds. Afterward, Dreaming Wolf invoked the spirits by speaking ancient hunting prayers. They made medicine and vowed renewed devotion to the helpless. Finally, Dreaming Wolf and Stone Lance readied the sweat lodge, and each hunter, man and boy alike, purified himself for the approaching ceremony.

Dreaming Wolf warmed to see so many discouraged *Tsis tsis tas* regain hope. The steam of the sweat lodge seemed to burn away the darkness in their hearts, and afterward, as they danced in mock combat around the towering council fire, the singing renewed even the darkest hearts.

"Ayyyy!" Two Moons shouted. "It's good we've come here to hunt!"

"Yes," Iron Wolf agreed. "The young ones

303

have brought us back to the sacred path."

As for the bony-shouldered boys who had known more starving and sickness than hunting, they gazed upon Dreaming Wolf and Stone Lance with something akin to reverence. Their admiring eyes stared in wonder at the Buffalo Shields.

"This will be a hunt long remembered," Panther Claw boasted.

"We'll feed the hungry ones!" Rock Turtle added. "Ayyyy! I will provide what's needed."

"Devote yourselves to the helpless!" Dancing Lance urged when the scouts prepared to set out. "Carry a prayer on your lips, asking Bull Buffalo to give himself up to your arrows."

"Ride with respect for the old ways," Whirlwind added. "Let the bad time of the People come to an end."

The hunters howled their agreement. Then the young scouts headed out in their small parties to seek out Bull Buffalo.

Dreaming Wolf and Stone Lance followed Goes Ahead eastward for a time before turning north. Behind them Panther Claw, Rock Turtle, and Stalker rode. As they fanned out across the broken ground, scouring ravine and hillside for buffalo sign, they sang the old songs and invited Bull Buffalo's generosity.

Toward dusk, they ceased searching and made camp on a low ridge where a good spring provided water. Stalker shot two rabbits, and the six scouts divided the meat among them. It was afterward, when only the faintest trace of sunlight remained, that Dreaming Wolf walked out alone to gaze at the grassland below. That was when he saw White Buffalo Cow.

At first, the Wolf thought it was an apparition. Weariness was making itself felt. He blinked his eyes and wiped his forehead, but White Buffalo Cow remained.

"Mother of all buffalo," Dreaming Wolf called, "we are a people lost. Our needs are many, and we lack the power to meet them. The young and the weak grow hungry. Our medicine chief leads us into peril. Save us, White Buffalo Cow, from our foolish ways. Bring us back within the sacred hoop of life."

The white creature turned and glanced up at the ridge with its pinkish eyes. It seemed to Dreaming Wolf that White Buffalo Cow had heard, but who could be certain? He sat for a long time, watching the darkness swallow the sacred animal. He remained there until Stone Lance called him back to the camp.

"We'll find Bull Buffalo tomorrow," the Wolf told his companions.

"You found sign?" Stalker asked.

"No, but I saw one," Dreaming Wolf explained. "It will be as in my dream. Bull Buffalo will give himself up to us, and the helpless ones will know no hunger."

"How do you know?" Goes Ahead asked.

"White Buffalo Cow appeared," the Wolf explained. "I remember the promise she spoke in my dream. We have done what she asked, and now she will give up her children to us."

Dreaming Wolf gazed skyward with glazed eyes, and the others grew unsettled. There was an odd feel to the wind, and the trees trembled so that leaves sprinkled down like snowflakes.

"It's time you rested, *Nah nih*," Stone Lance said, helping his cousin to the place they'd made for him beside the fire. The Lance covered Dreaming Wolf with an elk robe and sat silently until he closed his eyes.

"He'll dream tonight," Goes Ahead whispered. "Tomorrow he'll lead us to Bull Buffalo."

Dreaming Wolf awoke with the sun. He wasn't conscious of dreaming, but the image of a buffalo herd was fixed in his mind. As he made the dawn prayers, he thanked White Buffalo Cow for her sacrifice.

"It's time we struck the herd," he announced as he emptied the ashes of his pipe and rose from the fire. "Ayyyy! Bull Buffalo awaits us."

The scouts wasted no time readying their horses. No sooner had they mounted than Stone Lance was waving his bow toward the valley below. Overnight, it had filled with two hundred buffalo, and the scouts howled at the sight.

"Go and bring the others," Goes Ahead said

306

to the younger scouts. Panther Claw turned away, followed by Stalker and Rock Turtle. By late afternoon, the boys had returned, bringing word that others were on the way. Dreaming Wolf marked out a camp, and final prayers were spoken under the dying Plum moon. Next day, the hunting commenced.

Goes Ahead, as was his habit, led the first band to strike the herd, but he allowed Panther Claw to make the first kill. The young Windpipe counted coup on a young bull with a lance, then fired two arrows deep into its heart. Afterward, the bands hunted down and slew the lead bulls until the leaderless herd halted and accepted the inevitable.

Dreaming Wolf and Stone Lance chased a small breakaway band. The Wolf notched an arrow but fired it reluctantly, speaking the old prayer even as the arrow's deadly point pierced the bull's heart.

"Brother Buffalo,
give up your life
to make us strong."

Stone Lance, too, sang as he killed a second bull. The other animals were young, and so they were left to complete their escape.

"Ayyyy!" Dreaming Wolf shouted after them. "Grow strong to test us another year!"

The hunting continued for eight long days.

Other bands arrived, and new faces celebrated kills. The slower-moving camps of women and children came, too, and the butchering and smoking were turned over to their practiced hands.

Each night, the hunters feasted on thick hump roasts and smoked ribs. Boys who had never known a day free of hunger grew warm and satisfied. For once there was enough.

Dreaming Wolf carried one thick slice of shoulder meat to the nearby ridge and set it on a jagged outcropping.

"For you, Lone Hawk," he whispered.

He didn't remain to wait for the hawk's appearance, nor did he know for certain who devoured the meat. It was gone three days later when he returned, though, and several boys spoke of how a single red-tailed hawk had circled over them while they were swimming in the river beside which Iron Wolf and Two Moons had located the Windpipe camp.

"Our brother has remembered," Stone Lance said, smiling sadly. "I wish he was here to share the hunt. We spoke of doing so often."

"He's here," Dreaming Wolf said confidently. "Now, seeing us provided for and the People returned to the sacred path, perhaps he can find rest."

"And peace," Stone Lance added, nodding hopefully.

Once the hunting was over, the bands separated and continued the smoking. Grandmothers gathered together to work hides into new lodge covers, for many young men carved flutes and led girls upon the river walk. Boys were presented by their fathers and uncles to the People as men. As names were given, presents were meted out to honor the young brave hearts. In this way, families in need of horses or good robes were prepared for the coming snows.

Dreaming Wolf watched it all and was glad.

"Once our camps were always filled with such gladness," Stone Lance observed. "You have brought the People a rare gift, *Nah nih.* Peace."

"I only wish we had the power to make it last," the Wolf whispered. "That's for others to do, though."

Later, when Dreaming Wolf sat with the other young men, sharing tales of the hunt and recounting coups, he was reminded of other days passed with his age-mates. Where were they now? Was Raven's Wing still lame? Had Bent Arrow recovered the strength of his maimed arm? River Fork had taken a Lakota wife, someone had said. As to Otter Foot, his anger troubled the Wolf most of all.

"Winter's coming," Stalker observed as he added logs to the fire. "Soon snow will choke the land."

"At least there will be enough to eat," Rock Turtle noted. "That's your doing, Wolf. This will be no winter filled with dying."

"Not for the Windpipes," Stalker said, staring off out the narrow door of the young men's lodge. "Others may not be so fortunate."

"No one can save those who won't see the truth," Stone Lance argued. "There are always some who follow the dark hearts."

"It's said the chiefs are certain to choose a new man to keep the Arrows," Panther Claw said. "Then maybe the useless dying can end."

"Perhaps," Dreaming Wolf agreed.

"Wolf, you've done much for the helpless ones," Stalker said, "but you still appear sad."

"We lost a brother in the *wihio* fight," Stone Lance explained.

"Ah, yes, that's a deep wound slow to heal," Rock Turtle said. "But you shouldn't remain sad."

"A woman would cure him," Panther Claw suggested.

"Yes, and I know which one," Rock Turtle said, grinning. "Singing Doe."

"Nah nih, you haven't spoken to her since we've returned," Stone Lance observed. "I've seen her waiting outside her father's lodge. Others ask her to walk the river path, but she ignores them."

"She's waiting for you, Wolf," Panther Claw declared. "I wouldn't keep such a pretty one waiting too long. Many young men are rich in horses."

"Go and walk with her tomorrow," the young

ones urged.

"I'm young to take a wife," Dreaming Wolf argued.

"She's younger, but many her age are mothers," Panther Claw noted. "I know her father. He's poor in horses and rich with too many girls. Already two of them have wed your brothers. Surely he would welcome you."

Dreaming Wolf tried to conceal the grin surfacing on his face, but the others noticed. Soon he was mercilessly set upon by his jesting companions.

"If you act fast, you could have a small one before next summer's gone," Stone Lance whispered.

Dreaming Wolf kicked an ember from the fire. It landed beside Stone Lance, singeing the hair on the young man's leg. Even Stone Lance's yelps didn't quiet the others, though.

"She is pretty," the Lance said when he recovered his breath.

"Yes, she is," Dreaming Wolf admitted. "Perhaps I'll visit her father's lodge tomorrow."

"Good," Stalker said. "There'll be more meat for the rest of us to eat. You won't be here to share it."

And so, the following evening, Dreaming Wolf sat with Singing Doe beside her father's fire, listening to her recount the tale of her parents' courtship. She spoke of other things as well. When she turned to the future, she gazed deeply into his eyes.

"You're a man of many burdens," she whispered. "I could help shoulder them."

"I'm young to take a wife," he insisted.

"These dark times hurry us all," she observed. "You made the hunting prayers. Surely that's a task for an older man, too."

"I understand the medicine trail, Doe," he told her. "I know nothing of being a husband. I have vowed to protect all the helpless. Could I do so and not neglect a family?"

"A wife can help, Wolf," she argued.

He held her for a moment, and the need within them both threatened to overwhelm them. Finally, Dreaming Wolf drew back.

"You will talk to my father?" she asked.

"I'll smoke and ponder it," he answered. "If the signs are strong for it, I'll bring him ponies."

"At least four," she said, grinning. "Running Horse pledged three, and I was younger then."

"Four, then," he said, laughing. "Tell him I'll come."

"He expects you, I think, Wolf," she told him. "Everyone does."

Dreaming Wolf took a pipe into the hills and smoked on the matter. In his dreams, he saw a painted lodge bathed in happiness, with many little ones running around their adoring mother.

Yes, Singing Doe would make a good wife. As to Dreaming Wolf, hadn't he earned a taste of contentment?

Iron Wolf and Goes Ahead provided the horses, and they escorted their younger brother to old Gray Eyes, their father-in-law. The old man greeted his sons-in-law warmly, then turned to Dreaming Wolf.

"I've expected you," Gray Eyes said, gazing sternly into Dreaming Wolf's eyes. "You're a shield carrier, and your many brave deeds are well known among the Windpipes."

"You honor me," Dreaming Wolf replied.

"My daughter is very young, though, and you yourself have walked the world only seventeen summers. Winter's a hard time, and you have no lodge. Your brothers provide the horses you offer me. I recognize the power and energy of your spirit, Wolf, but you should wait. Let your shoulders broaden and your voice deepen. Winter's no time to begin a difficult task."

"No, sir," Dreaming Wolf said, dropping his gaze.

"I would enjoy another visit after New Life Lodge is made, and the summer hunting is concluded."

"Yes, that's a good time to talk," Dreaming Wolf agreed.

"Don't despair, Nephew," Gray Eyes added. "Man's road is often long, and disappointment hardens a man."

"I know the long hard roads a man can walk," Dreaming Wolf replied. "I understand disappointment. You will tell Singing Doe I came?"

"I'll tell her," the old man agreed. "She'll be honored to know you brought four good ponies. She'll stand high among her age-mates when it's known."

"She's always stood high," Dreaming Wolf noted. "Perhaps too high for a modest man to reach."

Twenty-four

Winter came early that year, and it was remembered afterward as the time of the deep snows. On three occasions, the Windpipes had to dig their lodges out of deep drifts and move to other ground. In spite of the meat smoked against winter's need, there was hunger in many lodges.

Dreaming Wolf and Stone Lance passed those hard days with Iron Wolf. Running Doe was carrying a child, and many times her young visitors suspected she had grown tired of her guests. She nevertheless remained cheerful, and they deemed her a true sister and a generous woman.

"You will always be welcome here," she remarked on a particularly bitter night. "You brought the smiles back to my people. When my son is born, you will help him walk man's road, learning the old ways his grandfather would have showed him."

Running Doe's cooking had a great effect on Dreaming Wolf. For the first time, there was more than flesh stretched over his ribs. Stone Lance was growing taller, and the softness of childhood was turning into iron.

"It's Doe's doing," Dreaming Wolf told Iron Wolf. "We've been too long away from a woman's touch."

"Her sister, too, cooks good corn cakes," Iron Wolf noted. "And Gray Eyes will soon welcome your ponies. An old man values his daughters more when approaching winter. He needs fewer horses, too."

When the snows finally lost their grip on the world, and the trees budded at last, the Windpipe camp returned to life. Parties of young men set out to hunt deer and elk. Old men made arrows and wove new bowstrings. As for Dreaming Wolf, he devoted himself to making medicine. Boys came, carrying elk teeth.

"Give them power, Wolf," they pleaded. "Make charms to keep us from peril."

Stone Lance made most of the charms while Dreaming Wolf worked to produce the first of many Fox Shields.

"I'm making them in the old fashion, as *Ne' hyo* showed," he explained to Iron Wolf. "You must decide who has earned the right to carry them."

"They will be given out to brave hearts, even as the Fox lances are presented," Iron Wolf promised.

It wasn't long after the shields were finished that a gaunt *Hev a tan iu* Crazy Dog named Yellow Tail appeared, carrying a pipe.

"I come to invite my brothers, the Windpipes, to a council," the Tail called.

"It's chiefs that are summoned to a council," Two Moons barked at the young intruder.

"I am a chief," Yellow Tail boasted.

Many laughed. Although a man of twenty-six summers, Yellow Tail was no taller than many boys half his age. Even clothed in heavy buffalo robes, he appeared fearfully thin. He wore many feathers in his hair, but Dreaming Wolf could think of no great deeds performed by this Dog chief.

"A man who carries a pipe should approach the head men of a camp," Iron Wolf instructed. "It's for chiefs to decide what direction a people will take."

"We all know how the Windpipe chiefs turn away when a call is made for fighters," Yellow Tail complained. "Chiefs are content to grow fat and leave others to endure hardship."

"Be careful," Two Moons warned angrily.

"It's well known a chief's responsibility is to protect the helpless," Iron Wolf explained. "Look around you! There are no starving children here. You come from a camp where men of power ignore their duty and ride to war."

"It's necessary," Yellow Tail insisted. "*Mahuts* warns of great danger, and . . ."

"He comes from Talking Stick," Panther Claw said, laughing.

"Yes," the Tail admitted. "He's had a great vision. Soon we'll strike a hard blow against the *wihio*."

"We?" Iron Wolf asked warily.

"Many raid the Shell River road already," Yellow Tail boasted. "Look!"

The Crazy Dog chief lifted a short stick with three scalps attached. Dreaming Wolf sensed the odious smell of death and looked away. Many of the younger Windpipes howled their approval, though. The hair was light, like winter grass.

"We'll meet and consider your words," Two Moons said, motioning for Yellow Tail to lower the scalp stick. "You can stay with the young men and have something to eat. We'll decide tonight."

Dreaming Wolf wasn't invited to the council until late. The fire had burned to embers, and yet hot words continued to fly across the council.

"It's the obligation of a warrior to defend this country from the *wihio*," Yellow Tail argued. "When did the Windpipes ever ignore a call from their brothers? The *Hev a tan iu* are too weak to fight alone. Eaters are coming. Why do you hold back?"

"We've known enough death," Iron Wolf grumbled. "Once, when the Arrows were kept by an honorable man, we would have listened well. Now, each time Talking Stick leads us to war, our young men die."

"He sees with far-seeing eyes!" Yellow Tail insisted.

"He sees nothing," Two Moons growled. "He only talks."

Yellow Tail rode back alone, but he returned shortly with another Crazy Dog chief, Spider,

318

and Talking Stick himself. The Arrow-keeper rode a tall American horse, white as snow, and he held his shield high so that the morning sun caught its paint and created a blinding glare.

"You've fared well," the Stick observed as he studied the camp. "In the south, the People starve. The *wihio* spoils the hunting, and his sickness murders our children. Ayyyy! We must punish him."

"Already we've killed twenty," Spider boasted. "Young Rope Men carry scalps. How does a Windpipe mark his manhood?"

"Manhood?" Yellow Tail asked, laughing. "There are only women here!"

"Is it the *wihio* you want to test, or your brothers?" Two Moons asked, brandishing a stone-headed lance. "We aren't impressed by empty promises and loud talkers here. You wear eagle feathers, but what enemy have you faced hand to hand? You shoot little white girls and take their hair. When a man appears, you leave the young brave hearts to face him and be killed."

"We haven't forgotten Shell River," Iron Wolf declared. "Panther Claw and Rock Turtle told of how you lost *Mahuts* and abandoned the wounded. You don't stand high in our eyes, prophet!"

"Go away!" an old woman shouted. "My son found his death following you!"

"This is your doing," Talking Stick said, turning to Dreaming Wolf. "This boy, who thought himself worthy to keep *Mahuts,* slanders me. He rode to retrieve *Mahuts* when the Arrows were torn from my lance. He speaks of brave deeds, but when did he charge the enemy and strike him down? In the *wihio* wagon camp, he carried a dead enemy into the hills to mourn. I've spoken before of the *wihio* blood in his veins. His heart, too, is white!"

"Be careful," Iron Wolf warned. "He's my brother, and you wouldn't find me an easy enemy."

"We don't come to make war among ourselves!" Spider cried. "What would that accomplish? No, we only ask that you hear Talking Stick's good words and decide for yourself their merit."

"It's not so much to ask," Yellow Tail argued.

"Perhaps not," Two Moons admitted. "I'll hear no more slander, though. Dreaming Wolf has made strong medicine here. While Bull Buffalo turned away from you, he gave himself to our arrows with a glad heart."

"We made the proper prayers," Dreaming Wolf explained.

"That or *wihio* magic," Yellow Tail grumbled.

"*Wihio* magic?" Stone Lance cried. "We hunt in the old manner, with the stone-pointed arrows of our grandfathers. Who walks the *wihio* path? Who carries his iron rifles and shoots lead balls?"

Yellow Tail shrank from the hot gaze of the Windpipes. The People shouted down Spider before he could speak. They grew quiet only when Talking Stick drew out *Mahuts* and raised the sacred medicine bundle.

"Hear me, brothers," the Arrow-keeper began. "All my life, I've watched the *wihio* spoil our good country with his crazy habits. My wife and my children climbed Hanging Road when the *wihio* brought his ghost sickness among us. Ayyyy! He's killed my brother. I have no family left.

"How many of our brave young men have died at his hands? Soon Bull Buffalo will no longer graze near Shell River, for the grass is eaten and the land is barren. And so I fight these *wihio!* I kill when I can. I burn all he brings with him. I will do so until there is no more of him."

"Or no more of us," Goes Ahead complained.

"If that's to be, then at least it will be said Talking Stick died holding a lance. Talking Stick didn't cut away his manhood and hide among the women!"

The insult stung, and Two Moons stood angrily. He towered over the Crazy Dog chiefs, and Talking Stick shrank from his glare.

"I'll hear no more of this!" Two Moons shouted.

"Who will come and follow us?" Spider called.

"Follow Talking Stick?" Goes Ahead called. "Who is he to lead us? He knows only the road toward death."

"When our grandchildren sing of the brave hearts, we'll be long remembered," Yellow Tail said. "No one will remember the Windpipes."

Those words carried more weight than all of the others, and the younger men turned to their chiefs, urging action.

"I won't lead you to your death," Two Moons told them. Iron Wolf, too, declined, so the Stick and his two companions returned alone to the *Hev a tan iu* camp.

It should have been the end of the matter. It wasn't. First, Dreaming Wolf envisioned the Arrows in peril. Second, a band of young Windpipes set off during the night to uphold the honor of their band.

"Panther Claw is among them," Rock Turtle said as he readied his pony. "I must follow my brother."

"And I my friend," Stalker explained.

Dreaming Wolf frowned. There was no one to protect boys in the fight that was coming. He turned to Stone Lance, confused.

"I'll collect horses, *Nah nih,*" the Lance said. "Make what prayers you know and take down our shields. They'll be needed."

By the time Stone Lance had cut the ponies from the herd, others had learned of the medicine cousins' decision.

"You must stay," Iron Wolf insisted. *"See' was' sin mit,* too many will follow your path, and there is only death there."

"Long ago, when *Ne' hyo* still walked the earth, I knew I would one day be called to save *Mahuts* from the enemy," Dreaming Wolf explained.

"You did," Iron Wolf argued. "At Shell River."

"It's not a deed performed once and forgotten," Dreaming Wolf said, frowning. "I will always bear the obligation."

322

"My son will need his uncles," Iron Wolf insisted.

"I hope to return in time to welcome him into the light," Dreaming Wolf answered. "But who can say what will happen? Only *Heammawihio* knows."

Dreaming Wolf rode south with great haste, hoping to catch Panther Claw and turn him back. But the boys had good horses and were already painting their faces when the Wolf arrived at the *Hev a tan iu* camp near Shell River. He'd seen much those past winters to chill his soul, but he wasn't prepared for what he now witnessed. The Rope Men were only a shadow of the proud band that had once ridden Shell River. Whirlwind and Dancing Lance had led some forty lodges farther south, but among the hundreds who had erected their winter camp around Arrow Lodge, only fifty or so famished horrors remained.

"What's happened?" Stone Lance cried in disbelief.

"We've starved," Bent Arrow said, gazing up at his old friends with empty eyes. "My sisters are all dead. *Ne' hyo. Nah' koa.* Cousins. Uncles."

"Otter Foot?" Dreaming Wolf asked. "Raven's Wing?"

"Ah, they had the far-seeing eyes, Wolf. They rode with the Fox chiefs south. Perhaps they're still alive."

It was a nightmare scene, and the survivors

glared hatefully at Talking Stick.

"False prophet, you should have set your lodge among the *wihio*," Bent Arrow growled. "You should have offered the enemy your medicine. Then they would be dead, and the *Hev a tan iu* would still walk the earth."

Others, too, hurled insults at the Stick, and had he not retained the loyalty of the Crazy Dogs, the People would have driven him from Arrow Lodge. Instead, reinforced by a large band of Eaters led by Bull Heart, the Stick built up a fire and sat with his war party to make plans.

When Dreaming Wolf dismounted and followed Panther Claw toward the council, Bent Arrow called to him in disbelief.

"Have you forgotten everything?" the Arrow called.

"I forget nothing," Dreaming Wolf answered. "But I am called to protect *Mahuts*."

"Poor fool," Bent Arrow lamented. But later, after the medicine prayers had been spoken and Talking Stick had dispatched his scouts, Bent Arrow brought his old friend a spare quiver of good arrows and an extra pony.

"I'll return the pony later," Dreaming Wolf vowed. "The quiver, too. The arrows will be harder to recover."

"Use them well," Bent Arrow urged. "If I could hold a bow in this useless arm, I would follow you myself. Ayyyy!" he shouted. "Here's a brave heart!"

Dreaming Wolf nodded. He then mounted his horse and led the spare pony along to where

324

Stone Lance was waiting. Panther Claw was there, too, as were Stalker and Rock Turtle.

"I, too, would follow you, Wolf," a smaller boy declared.

"I, too," another and another vowed.

Dreaming Wolf nodded to each in turn. With a heavy heart he led them south toward Shell River. Talking Stick, as he had so often, pointed the way to battle. *And to death,* the Wolf thought.

By the time Talking Stick reached Shell River, the scouts had located the enemy. A line of *wihio* wagons rolled along the rutted trail, unmindful of the danger at hand.

"These are the enemy?" Panther Claw asked as he studied the *wihio* band. Yellow-haired boys chased their sisters alongside the rumbling wagons. The men lashed their weary oxen along. No one held a rifle or seemed concerned about what lay ahead.

"Bull Heart, cut off the lead wagons!" Talking Stick instructed. "Spider, strike the rear. Yellow Tail, you have the honor of the first charge!"

"Ayyyy!" the Crazy Dogs shouted as they whipped their ponies into a run. It appeared so easy that Dreaming Wolf and his small party held back, scornful of fighting so pitiful an enemy. But often the world was not as it seemed, and hardly had Bull Heart turned the lead wagon when a volley of rifle fire cut him down. From the far, hidden side of the wagons, twenty well-armed *wihio* raced out to form a line. Shooting rifles and rapid-firing pistols, they decimated Yellow Tail's Crazy Dogs. Only Spider found any success at all. His band managed to encircle a small party of children. When *wihio* men rushed to rescue them, three were cut to pieces. The helpless ones, likewise, were killed.

"Again you've led us to our deaths!" Bull Heart's younger brother, Bear Claw, shouted after retrieving his brother's corpse. "Eaters, we're finished with this dark heart."

"Foxes!" Talking Stick called. "You can enjoy the honor of the next charge."

"Enough are already dead," Dreaming Wolf told the Arrow-keeper. "You have no vision, Stick! We'll recover the wounded, but I have no heart for seeing more brave hearts killed!"

"Trust in my medicine!" Talking Stick screamed. His eyes were wild, and he tied *Mahuts* to the old, painted lance. "Follow me!" he cried a final time. "The Arrows will blind the enemy!"

"They've blinded you, fool!" Bear Claw shouted.

Talking Stick was past hearing, though. He saw only the hated enemy. Rearing his white horse high and waving the Arrow lance at the *wihio* riflemen, he charged.

It was hopeless. They all saw it. There was no courage in it—only desperate defiance. Talking Stick galloped toward the *wihio*. Seeing only one man, the wagon people held their fire and waited for the others. Talking Stick rode before them, waving the lance, taunting them to fire. Only when he dismounted and drove his lance in the ground did the wagon men take interest. Talking Stick drew a rifle from his horse and aimed it.

Before he could fire, the *wihio* wagon chief fired a shot that tore the rifle from the Arrow-keeper's hands. Other shots followed. In an instant, Talking Stick was blown apart. He fell backward into the short grass, silent at last.

Dreaming Wolf made his charge even before the echo of the final shot had died. Stone Lance was at his side, and the two raised their shields in hopes of deflecting the expected shot. The Wolf reached *Mahuts* first and plucked the Arrows from the painted lance. Stone Lance followed, shielding his cousin's back as they rejoined their companions.

"Ayyyy!" the Foxes shouted. "The Arrows are safe."

Dreaming Wolf gazed down mournfully at *Mahuts*. The old stone points he had fashioned with such care were again spattered with blood. The People were in danger!

"What of the Stick?" Panther Claw called. "We should claim his body!"

"Leave him!" Bear Claw urged. "The *wihio* are ready now. Talking Stick brought enough brave hearts to their deaths. We have wounded men to tend and better men than him to carry home."

"He's right," Yellow Tail said, cradling a shattered left arm. "His power's broken. Leave his bones to mark this place of death."

Twenty-five

Dreaming Wolf led his young comrades back to the Windpipe camp with a heavy heart. He had returned the unused quiver of arrows to Bent Arrow. The Arrow had refused to accept the pony.

"I know you, old friend," Bent Arrow had said. "You give away all you have and will be poor forever. Take him."

Loud cries of mourning had risen from the Eaters, for many of their best young men were dead. Roaring Bear would have a son to grieve. Already, men were cutting their hair and tearing their clothes.

Among the *Hev a tan iu,* there had been a stunned silence.

"Talking Stick is dead?" many had asked.

"How was his power broken?" others cried.

"He should have been long dead," Bent Arrow had grumbled.

"He was just unlucky," Spider argued. "His plan might have worked another day."

Dreaming Wolf closed his ears to it all. He had

ridden with the Stick enough to know better. Too many had died. All the People, it seemed, had suffered. Now the Arrows were tainted, and it would require long days of ritual and much suffering to renew their power.

The custody of *Mahuts* had been debated hotly. Yellow Tail and Spider had attempted to claim them, for they were the only members of the council of forty-four present.

"What do you know of *Mahuts?*" Dreaming Wolf had demanded. "I won't place them at risk again!"

He would have broken down Arrow Lodge and dragged it along as well, but the Crazy Dog chiefs wouldn't allow it. So the Wolf bore the Arrows northward without their lodge.

"It's best," Stone Lance agreed as he pulled his horse alongside his cousin. "They are safe in your care, *Nah nih.*"

"It's for us to perform the renewal," Dreaming Wolf said. "No one else knows the required prayers."

"It will be good to return to *Noahvose* and pray in that sacred place. Perhaps Lone Hawk will visit us again."

"He showed us the way when we were lost, *See' was' sin mit.* We're confused no longer. Our path is clear."

It was not, in fact, clear at all, though. No sooner did the young Windpipes return than a pipe carrier arrived bringing word of a gathering of the chiefs.

"It's too early," Dreaming Wolf had observed.

"There's much yet to do. The Arrow renewal must wait for midsummer."

"Young Crazy Dog pups!" Two Moons complained. "They will have summoned the southern people before the grass is good for fattening their horses. Theirs will be a difficult journey, and what good will it be? Long days of waiting are certain."

Nevertheless, the bands broke camp and moved toward *Noahvose*. There, in the shadow of the sacred butte, the forty-four head men met and decided what was best. Never had there been more confusion. Dancing Lance and Whirlwind arrived late, and Roaring Bear was still gripped by grief for his slain son. Other chiefs had died, and replacements hadn't been chosen.

"Too many of the best men are gone," Goes Ahead lamented. "Our father and Younger Wolf. Old Wood Snake and Otter Skin. For his faults, Thunder Coat was a brave man. Now there is only discord, and no one can bring order to it."

Northerners like Morning Star and Two Moons soon joined with Southerners Black Kettle and White Antelope, though. Peace blossomed from chaos, even as plums grow on thorny plants. New chiefs were chosen to replace the dead, and many old quarrels were settled.

Dreaming Wolf was summoned the third day of the council.

"We've all seen *Mahuts*," Two Moons noted. "It's necessary the Arrows be renewed. Talking Stick is dead, and he's left no son behind to pass on the Arrow knowledge. Iron Wolf says

330

you can restore the sacred power, though."

"I know what's to be done," Dreaming Wolf answered.

"Your cousin, young Stone Lance, can help you," Two Moons said, gazing at the assembled chiefs. "If not for your knowledge, our greatest power might have been lost. We all owe you much."

"It's an old obligation," Dreaming Wolf told them.

"Yes," Two Moons agreed. "Even so, it's thought . . . feared by many . . . that the Arrow knowledge should not rest with a single man. Two Humps and Little Wound will watch and learn."

Dreaming Wolf eyed the chiefs suspiciously. Why had those old men been suggested? It would seem wiser to give the knowledge to younger men.

Nevertheless, Dreaming Wolf accepted the decision. And when it was time to begin the renewal, Two Humps and Little Wound brought Arrow Lodge with them to *Noahvose.* Dreaming Wolf brought the sacred bundle, and he demonstrated the removal and burial of the old points and withered fletchings. Together they sang the required prayers, and each fashioned a new stone head for one of the sacred Arrows. Later, when it was time for the ten bands to join in the larger ritual, Dreaming Wolf guided the two old men through each step.

"It seems strange, *Nah nih,* that we should instruct these grandfathers," Stone Lance observed.

"Yes, but odder things have happened," the Wolf said, shaking his head in dismay.

"Have you received a vision?"

"No, my dreams tell me nothing. I can only wait until the direction our feet must take is revealed."

Dreaming Wolf was alarmed to hear Two Humps speak of the uses a man might make of the Arrow medicine, and Little Wound was known to be making charms he claimed bore the power of *Mahuts*.

"Some say he kept the old head from his arrow and chipped pieces of it to make the charms," Stone Lance muttered. "Talking Stick is not dead after all. He's reborn in these old men."

It was only when the ceremonies were concluded and the hunting prayers began that Dreaming Wolf was called back to the council.

"You've done well, Nephew," Two Moons told him. "The day will come when the People will look back on your devotion as the saving of the People."

"Devotion is good," Roaring Bear said, "but we've all seen how a young man may recklessly endanger the People through reckless acts. An Arrow-keeper should be old and wise."

"It would be good to have it so," Dreaming Wolf agreed, "but it's vital he know and respect the old traditions. That he understand the ceremonies."

"That's why Two Humps climbed *Noahvose*," Roaring Bear explained. "He will keep *Mahuts* in the old, sacred manner, devoting himself to the

332

ceremonies and making medicine that will aid all the People."

"He only knows the renewal," Dreaming Wolf argued. "There's more."

"*Mahuts* will give him the power to understand the rest," Black Kettle declared. "Too long, *Mahuts* has been among the northern bands. The Arrows should return south."

"North, south, are we two peoples now?" Iron Wolf asked.

"The *wihio* wagon road makes it so," Two Moons observed. "It's a hard thing, parting from our good friends, but it's not for us to set the moon in the sky or say what will be."

"*See' was' sin mit,* you've done well," Iron Wolf said, plucking a feather from his hair and giving it to his brother. "It rests heavy on your heart, this choice, but you've carried too many burdens. For a time, your walk will be easier. It's good. You've earned a rest."

"Ayyyy!" the chiefs howled. "Here's a brave heart, a man of the People."

But as Dreaming Wolf departed, he couldn't avoid the notion that somehow he had been robbed of his destiny. Fortunately, it was time to hunt Bull Buffalo, and there would be long days of riding to work the sting from his soul.

Dreaming Wolf and Stone Lance again followed Goes Ahead north in search of Bull Buffalo, but they failed to repeat their autumn success. They were far east when the herd was sighted by a party of Eaters, and when they found the main hunters' camp, most of the mature bulls and older cows had been killed.

"There's meat enough for summer," Two Horns declared. "This herd should be left to recover its numbers."

The decision worked a hardship on those men who hadn't made a kill, for their families would now rely on the kindness of relatives or the generosity of the chiefs. Young men like Panther Claw were deprived of a chance to stand high in the eyes of their age-mates.

"It's wise we not kill too many," Dreaming Wolf said as he sat with his young friends around a small fire, chewing rib meat. "Perhaps we can shoot elk in the Big Horn country."

"It's far to go," Stalker grumbled.

"We might find Bull Buffalo south, on Shell River," Rock Turtle suggested.

"The *wihio* wagon bands are thick this year," Stone Lance reminded his young friend. "There are Pawnees there, too. You didn't enjoy your last visit to their camp."

"You enjoyed yours," Stalker said, grinning.

"My medicine was strong then," Dreaming Wolf said, frowning. "Now I have lost the far-seeing eyes. Bull Buffalo evaded me, and I've done nothing to provide for the helpless ones."

"You've done enough, *Nah nih,*" Stone Lance argued.

"Nothing at all," Dreaming Wolf insisted. "Nothing at all."

"You'll do better," Panther Claw said, grinning.

334

"On Shell River."

And so it was decided. Dreaming Wolf and Stone Lance, accompanied by Panther Claw, Rock Turtle, and Stalker, rode south to hunt. They had ridden out before to safeguard *Mahuts,* knowing danger lurked nearby. Even so, their hearts had been light, and their confidence abundant. Now they rode slowly, cautiously. It was like a man climbing a mountain with unsure feet.

As they approached Shell River, they grew ever more wary. The flicker of *wihio* campfires painted a road of yellow light across the world. There was no end to the wagon people, and stories of *Tsis tsis tas* raiding brought the sharp crack of rifles whenever any of the young riders drew close.

"Bull Buffalo won't graze here," Panther Claw said, gazing at the short stubble of grass that was left behind a wagon band.

"No, we should return north," Dreaming Wolf agreed.

They found no buffalo herd there, either. Instead, they crossed a hill and found themselves confronted by twenty prowling Pawnees.

"Ayyyy!" Stalker screamed without thinking. He kicked his pony into a gallop and charged the closest Pawnee. The startled enemy, not quite believing the foolhardy charge of this single boy, tried to string his bow. Stalker raced on, though, and with a cry of triumph clubbed the Pawnee senseless with a lance and stole his horse.

"Ayyyy!" Rock Turtle shouted. "We'll run them!"

Now he and Panther Claw charged. The Pawnees tried to form a line of sorts and string their bows. Two carrying rifles fired wildly at the onrushing *Tsis tsis tas,* but in the end the whole party turned and fled. Stalker chased down his dismounted victim, clubbed him a second time, and stripped the unfortunate Pawnee naked. Laughing wildly, he tossed the breechclout to the wind and waved the moccasins overhead.

"Come, they won't remain confused forever," Dreaming Wolf called. "There are too many of them, and they have rifles."

"Should I take his scalp?" Stalker asked. "Or an ear, maybe?"

The Pawnee, understanding enough to shudder, clasped a hand over each ear and curled into a ball to protect his vitals.

"You've taken enough," Dreaming Wolf said, pointing to the captured pony. "And what good would a Pawnee be? You can't eat him, and his skin's too thin for a robe."

Waving his lance defiantly, Stalker rejoined his companions, and the five raced off westward.

They didn't go far, though. The Pawnees were part of a large band, and Dreaming Wolf counted two hundred horses in their pony herd.

"Too many to drive home by ourselves," Panther Claw noted.

"And too many to guard, too," Dreaming Wolf said, grinning. "This horse I'm riding was raised by the Pawnees, and it's been a good mount. I think I'd like another."

"A man needs good horses to get a pretty

wife," Rock Turtle said. "Four wasn't enough. Perhaps five."

"Seven even," Panther Claw added.

"Why not a hundred?" Stone Lance asked.

"We'll run them all north," Dreaming Wolf suggested. "Those we can control will come along. The others will provide our Pawnee friends with some amusement."

"Friends?" Rock Turtle cried. "I have no friends among the Pawnee. What they intended to do to Stalker and me would keep children from sleeping."

"Maybe we should have let Stalker cut that one's ears then," Dreaming Wolf suggested. "If you like, you could always go into the camp and find that old woman. She was fat enough she could lose some flesh and never miss the weight."

The others laughed at the thought—all except Rock Turtle and Stalker, who remembered their captivity all too well.

"There's risk to this venture," Dreaming Wolf told them. "It's not so hard for a pony boy to notice approaching riders. The whole camp might fall on us."

"A hundred or twenty," Stalker said, laughing. "We'll run them!"

Dreaming Wolf smiled at Stalker's confidence. It was contagious. The Wolf set aside his own doubts and mounted his pony. Slowly, as quietly as was possible, the raiders descended the ridge and approached the Pawnee ponies.

They were almost among the grazing animals when a pony boy cried out in alarm. Stone Lance charged the young Pawnee and lifted him off his feet. For a time, the Lance rode on, carrying the Pawnee across his thigh, before releasing him in a heap near a dying fire. The boy rolled across the coals and yelped in pain.

Meanwhile, Dreaming Wolf started the horses in motion by waving a buffalo hide at them. Panther Claw had a wolf's pelt, and its scent started an immediate stampede. Soon two hundred horses thundered through the Pawnee camp, upsetting smoking racks, trampling kettles, and even breaking down lodges.

"Ayyyy!" the young raiders howled as they drove the ponies past sleepy-eyed Pawnees. It was as good a trick as Dreaming Wolf had ever played on an enemy. Young Pawnees flew like startled prairie chickens from the snorting ponies. Some hadn't bothered to dress, and the sight of them running bare-bottomed drew hoots of pleasure from their tormentors.

Dreaming Wolf would have liked to stay and watch as the Pawnee chiefs raged at their camp guards, but the horses were more important. He waved his companions on, and they kept the horses moving north toward the Windpipe camp.

They arrived with forty animals, and a cry of triumph met them. Small boys ran alongside, shouting brave heart songs. Goes Ahead and Iron Wolf rushed over to greet their renegade brother and found him laughing as Stalker told of his coup on the naked Pawnee. The tale of the horse stealing was saved for the Fox council.

For Dreaming Wolf, a brother's praise or an

eagle feather presented in a warrior council mattered little. He had a single purpose. Next morning, after making the dawn prayers, he appeared outside Gray Eyes's lodge leading his eight captured Pawnee ponies.

"These you took yourself?" Gray Eyes asked with raised eyebrows. "It's a rich gift you offer me."

"I ask only equal value in return," Dreaming Wolf said, catching a glimpse of Singing Doe through the door of the lodge.

"Yes, your gift's appropriate, Nephew," Gray Eyes admitted, "but perhaps it would be better to speak of this later."

"Tonight?" the Wolf asked.

"When you're taller," Gray Eyes suggested. "Older."

"I don't come from a family of tall men," Dreaming Wolf explained. "I already stand as tall as my brother, Goes Ahead. It may be that I'll grow no more. Is height the measure of a man?"

"That's not my meaning," Gray Eyes said, frowning.

"When we spoke before, you said I should wait until winter had passed. Is there ever a time when I will prove acceptable?"

"You're young, Dreaming Wolf. Be patient."

Patient? Dreaming Wolf silently asked. It was not something young men manage to be. He turned and led the ponies through the camp, giving each in turn to some young man in need of a good mount.

"You should have kept the horses, *Nah nih,*"

Stone Lance argued when they sat together in the young men's lodge that night. "He's certain to change his mind."

"Yes, when I'm taller," Dreaming Wolf muttered. "I will never be tall enough for him. Haven't you seen the way he looks at me when I walk with Singing Doe beside the river? He doesn't deem me fit to be my father's son. Nor even my brothers' kin."

"It's not true," Stone Lance objected. "You stand foremost of all the young men in the Windpipe camp!"

"I don't even belong here," the Wolf grumbled. "I'm lost again, *See' was' sin mit,* and there's no Lone Hawk to guide me. Where will I go? What will I do?"

"Hunt," Stone Lance said, clasping his cousin's hand. "Raid ponies. Protect the helpless and fight the enemy. You will walk the sacred path as you've always done."

"It's not enough, *See' was' sin mit,*" Dreaming Wolf declared. "I need to belong."

"You do, *Nah nih.* Here for now. Later with Singing Doe and an army of little ones. Look at the glow in Iron Wolf's eyes. His son put it there. You, too, will know that warmth."

"And if not, I can rest well knowing I will always have someone to ride beside me."

Stone Lance grinned and whispered, "Always, *Nah nih.*"

Twenty-six

Talking Stick was dead, but that didn't end the conflicts with the *wihio* wagon people. More and more of them traveled the Shell River road, and confrontations were inevitable. It proved to be another bloody summer, and even winter snowdrifts failed to bring peace. No, that would wait for the following autumn.

Earlier, Corn Hair Louis Freneau had brought word that the chief of the *wihio* bluecoats had agreed that bad feelings should be put aside. A famous beaver man, Tom Fitzpatrick, had been asked to speak for the American government, and chiefs of the plains tribes were called to old Fort John to consider his words. Broken Hand, as the *Tsis tsis tas* called him, had led wagons west himself. Now he was a trader, like the Freneaus. He knew the peoples of the plains well and spoke many tongues.

"There's no fighting this," Fitzpatrick had told the chiefs. "The wagons will come. What you must do is mark off places where the *wihio* will be forbidden to come."

"Where?" Two Moons was said to have asked.

Broken Hand then displayed a paper with many lines drawn upon it. It told where the People would live and hunt. The sacred hills north of Shell River were given over to the Lakotas. Crows, Pawnees, Arapahoes, and Rees all had their own territories. The *Tsis tsis tas* bands were given the prairie country south of Shell River and north of Swift Fox River. The Pawnees, who hunted buffalo there, were to camp farther east.

The southern bands welcomed the agreement, but the northern peoples objected.

"Are we to lose *Noahvose?*" Iron Wolf cried. "The sacred heart of the world? Where will we make New Life Lodge? Can we turn away from the bones of our fathers?"

There were Arapahoes who were also unhappy about their assigned lands, but the Lakotas, who were to occupy the northern territories, solved the matter.

"Our brothers are welcome there," Conquering Bear declared. "We've always hunted with our *Tsis tsis tas* cousins, and that shouldn't change."

The *wihio* chiefs agreed, and it was decided all the People should come to Horse Creek, near Fort John, and receive presents.

"It will be a giveaway to remember," Louis told his Windpipe cousins. "My brother John, the black-robe priest, is bringing in many of the northern people. Peter, who is a soldier, will be

342

there, too. Charlie is bringing wagons of trade goods out from St. Louis. If only my sister Mary would come, all the Freneaus would be reunited in one place."

"It will be a remembered day," Dreaming Wolf observed. "All the People at Fort John!"

"Now the army's taken over," Louis explained. "They call it Fort Laramie."

"More *wihio* craziness," Stone Lance grumbled. "Give a place a good name, and some *wihio* will change it!"

"Yes, we have the habit of doing that, all right," Louis agreed. "No matter what the name for the place, this treaty paper will be a great thing. Perhaps it will even be the bridge old Stone Wolf dreamed of, the thing that would draw our peoples together."

"It would be a good thing to put the fighting behind us," Dreaming Wolf said, nodding. "A paper won't remake the bad hearts, though."

"There'll be presents," young White Elk Tom argued. "Cloth. Beads. Money to buy good rifles and powder."

"The *wihio* wouldn't give us so much without taking something in return," the Wolf noted. "They will use their road to move in soldiers. They'll make new roads through the heart of our hunting grounds, and they'll kill our game."

"No, the soldiers will keep the wagon people out," Tom argued.

"You'll be left alone," Louis insisted. "It's intended to end the hard feelings as well as the fighting."

343

"It's only a paper," Dreaming Wolf grumbled. "It's what men hold in their hearts that's most important."

"My people want peace," Louis declared.

"Then why do they send soldiers to touch the pen to this paper?" Stone Lance asked. "Once, a man's word was enough. I'm afraid this will only be another *wihio* trick."

Nevertheless, when the *Tsis tsis tas* bands moved west toward Horse Creek, the chosen site of the great council, Dreaming Wolf hoped his cousin was mistaken.

No one was even half-prepared for the treaty gathering. Word of the promised presents had spread across the country, and great numbers of *Tsis tsis tas,* Lakota, and Arapaho arrived. The black-robe priests brought in parties of Crow, Assiniboin, and Ree. Even some who claimed to be Mandans appeared! A hundred times a hundred people camped along Shell River.

"There's not food enough to feed so many!" Broken Hand Fitzpatrick exclaimed.

There were other problems, too. Young men raided the horse herds of old enemies, taking good ponies. There were too many animals to watch and far too many young men to oversee. Even among the friendly bands, men and boys challenged each other to wrestling matches and pony races.

"There are some good Crow ponies here," Iron Wolf told his brothers as they waited for the *wihio* chiefs to appear.

"That spotted mare is fast," Dreaming Wolf declared. "She wins many races."

"My black stallion can beat her," Iron Wolf argued. "If I had the right rider on him."

"Me?" Dreaming Wolf asked, realizing his brother was staring at him.

"Who else can turn a pony's feet to wings?" Goes Ahead asked. "Take the black and challenge that Crow."

"If you win," Iron Wolf added, "both ponies are yours."

"If I lose?" Dreaming Wolf asked.

"You won't," Iron Wolf assured him. "No *Tsis tsis tas* could permit such a terrible thing."

"The spotted mare's fast," Dreaming Wolf argued.

"Make your medicine strong then, *See' was' sin mit*," Iron Wolf advised. "It's well that our enemies see our strength."

Dreaming Wolf nodded although he was far from sure of winning.

Most of the races were simple affairs, but the pairing of two famous ponies drew great crowds of onlookers. The chiefs of the two tribes marked out a course, and even before they had finished, young Crows were hurling taunts at their old enemies.

"Enough!" Standing Elk, the Crow chief, commanded. "We chiefs have given our word there will be no fighting here!"

"Ayyyy!" a dozen Fox Warriors howled. "Yes, we'll fight you later!"

"Are horses running this race, or shall we let

the tongues do it?" Iron Wolf asked. When the crowd calmed, he motioned to the handlers to bring forward ponies and riders.

Dreaming Wolf hugged the neck of the big black. Its lines were sleek, and it had the heart to run all day. The Crow chief's son, Elk Tooth, rode the spotted mare. He was a little younger than the Wolf, but his intense eyes and quiet concentration marked him as a worthy adversary.

"Remember, you ride for all the People!" Stone Lance called to his cousin as the riders readied their mounts.

"Ayyyy!" the Foxes shouted. "Ride well, Wolf!"

Dreaming Wolf stole a final glance at his Crow opponent and gritted his teeth. It wasn't a long way to ride, but there were many turns. He wondered if the Crow mare behaved better than the big black. The race would be won turning those corners.

For a brief moment, doubt flooded Dreaming Wolf's mind, but when Standing Elk threw a red rag in the air, the Wolf urged his stallion on. The Crow pulled briefly out in front, but the big black made the first turn well, and Dreaming Wolf pulled ahead. Afterward, the two horses alternated leading the way. One would manage a slim lead, and then the other would catch up. Going into the final turn, the Crow had the advantage. Dreaming Wolf slowed a bit early, then made an abrupt move that cut inside the mare and left the big black surging ahead. At the finish, Iron Wolf began to smile. On and on the stallion thundered, finishing three lengths ahead of the spotted mare.

"Ayyyy!" all the *Tsis tsis tas* yelled in one voice. "Here's our brave heart! Here's Dreaming Wolf."

Stunned, Elk Tooth climbed down from his pony and reluctantly surrendered the animal.

"She's a good horse," Dreaming Wolf said, smiling. "Maybe we'll race again sometime."

"Only when I raid your herd and steal her back," Elk Tooth said, grinning.

There were less friendly encounters, too, for too many hunters competed for the scant game to be found near the fort. A pair of Arapahoes fought some bluecoats over a woman's honor, too. There was too much gambling, and it was hard to forget old quarrels. Considering the great numbers, though, relatively few problems arose, and those rarely led to bloodshed.

When the *wihio* chiefs came to sign the treaty paper, bands of young men performed tricks on horseback. Others demonstrated their marksmanship. There was considerable trading, and most of the giveaway money was eagerly spent at the *wihio* stores.

The *wihio* chiefs themselves wore fine clothes and spoke good words. They made many promises, and when they offered their hands to the tribes in friendship, they swore the agreement would last so long as the rivers ran.

"Can the *wihio* change even the rivers?" Stone Lance whispered.

Dreaming Wolf wondered. Looking deep into the eyes of the *wihio* speakers, he saw dark hearts. If sickness and hunger didn't sweep the People away, then they had bluecoat bullets that would.

"Sometimes," Dreaming Wolf told his brothers afterward, "I think *Ne' hyo* and *Nah' koa* were the fortunate ones. They have found their peace. Maybe they were the fortunate ones."

"You're wrong, *See' was' sin mit*," Goes Ahead insisted. "These are exciting days. Ayyyy! There are buffalo to hunt, and many good horses to ride."

"Sons to raise," Iron Wolf added. "Good women to share the cold winters."

"For you, maybe," Dreaming Wolf said, frowning. "My walk will be a lonely one."

"You'll soon have a wife," Goes Ahead told him. "Stone Lance, too."

"When I'm taller," Stone Lance said, shrinking from the notion.

"I won't be taller," Dreaming Wolf told his brothers. "There's only one woman I would welcome into my lodge, and her father has no use for my ponies."

"The world turns," Iron Wolf declared. "Things change."

It was after the feasting held to celebrate the treaty signing that Dreaming Wolf walked off alone to guard the pony herd. While others sang brave heart songs and fattened themselves on *wihio* food, the Wolf sat between the black stallion and the Crow mare, frowning.

"They would be a good pair to mate," a familiar voice suggested.

Dreaming Wolf rose with a start. He expected to see Crow raiders, or perhaps the Freneaus. Instead, Gray Eyes stood there, watching.

"Have you come to see if I'm still a small boy?" Dreaming Wolf asked. "I'm not tall, but I've walked man's road many summers."

"Some would judge you tall enough," Gray Eyes answered.

"I'm as tall as I will ever be."

"You rode well, Nephew. This mare's a good one, and the stallion's better. You didn't have him when we talked before."

"Has that changed anything?" the Wolf asked. "It wasn't my ponies you refused."

"It's said you gave them away, all eight."

"I no longer needed them."

"You're an unusual man, Wolf."

"I didn't know I was a man at all in your eyes."

"You are," Gray Eyes insisted. "I've grown old, and I have only one daughter left to tend my lodge. Her mother's gone. I would miss her."

"A daughter's bound to walk her own road," Dreaming Wolf argued.

"She's reminded me of that," Gray Eyes said, running his hand along the sleek flanks of the mare. "Singing Doe is worth eight horses, of course."

"Worth all I own, Uncle."

"This is a fine mare, though. Crows know horses! Clearly the match of any I've seen. Worth any eight ponies the Pawnees ever had. More even."

"Yes?" Dreaming Wolf asked, studying the stone-faced Gray Eyes.

"A strong-willed stallion and a good mare might produce many colts," the old man argued. "We should mate these two."

"We?"

"Perhaps if you brought the mare to my lodge. I would welcome the visit. As would my daughter."

"I would only come to ask her to share my life."

"It's all a father can ask of any man," Gray Eyes said, turning away from the ponies and setting his weathered hands on Dreaming Wolf's shoulders. "I know her road won't be an easy one, but I also know she won't know any peril that can be kept away by a brave heart."

"I vow it!" Dreaming Wolf shouted.

"Bring the mare and make Singing Doe happy."

"It's all I ever wished," Dreaming Wolf insisted.